WE ARE LUCIFER

AMY McLEAN

Published in Great Britain
by GJB Publishing

www.GJBpublishing.co.uk
@GJBpublishing

For Virginia Woolf

Other books by the author

Walk On

Celestial Land and Sea

Robin Mutt: The Haunted Clown (13 Tales of Death)

Hallow series

Hallow Be Thy Name

Death of the English Rose

A thick fog descended across London without warning, the autumnal night plummeting down a bitter chill to smother the moist air. For many dwellers of the hasty city life, the imminence of shorter days was a yearly curse, without which they were adamant they would all be happier. For Amber though, the darkness was a blessing.

The hours had crawled by while she'd waited, tapping her foot against the laminate floorboards, anxious for the sickly winter sun to disappear. It would have been impossible for her leave earlier, to go out while it was still light. She couldn't risk being seen.

For a brief moment she had toyed with the idea of downing a small glass of wine to calm her nerves, but after much deliberation and pacing around the kitchen she'd decided against it. All it would take was one incidental encounter with a breathalyser, and her plan would be scuppered. She couldn't be stopped on the road. Not tonight. Nobody must know where she was.

Despite her earlier impatience, she was ultimately glad

she had waited until later in the evening to leave the house. She had passed so few other cars on the journey through the city that her anxiety was able to subside a little. Once she reached the outskirts of inner London, she took the long route from south of the river up to Hampstead, partly to avoid manoeuvring through the heart of the city and partly because she needed that time to calm her remaining nerves.

It wasn't that she anticipated any of this going wrong. No, this was the easy part of her plan. But one slipup, one tiny error, and it would all crumble to the ground right before she'd had the chance to make any progress at all.

Of course, she was well aware that she was at risk of backing out of her own intentions without warning. It wouldn't have been the first time she'd been dead set on an idea, only to stall or, worse, give up on it entirely. There was always a chance that she would come to her senses, realise that this was not her punishment to deliver. She could easily run away from the situation. Yet she was too tired to run. This was the first thing in months that had made any sense to her, finally allowing her to feel like she had a purpose again; giving up would take more strength than she had to give.

Determined to power ahead without any opportunity for faltering, as soon as the bitter night had arrived she grabbed everything she needed, bundled it into the boot of her car, and sped off through the darkness, not allowing herself any time to look back.

To drown out the imposing silence as she drove, she flicked on the radio to whichever station she reached first. An obnoxiously upbeat pop hit from the Eighties blasted throughout car; it was like the audial equivalent of something one would drink to banish nausea. No, that would never do. She changed the station. And then changed it again. And again.

Finally, after sifting through countless grotesque and invasive modern music programmes, she settled on a news show. For the most part, she was able to ignore the voice of the newsreader, employing it only as background noise to drown out her own thoughts as she fixed her attention on the empty road in front of her. Every so often, however, the odd word would stab its way into her thoughts, reminding her of the hatred that damaged the world each day: murder, death, disaster.

That was hardly the distraction she had been seeking.

She jabbed at the button to kill the voice, surrendering to the company of her own mind. As she tapped her fingers irritably against the side of the steering wheel, her eyes flittered around her as she tried to distract herself.

She furthered away from the main roads, the trees growing around her as their remaining leaves danced in the darkness, threatening to detach from their final threads of

3

security. They would be mostly shades of brown now, Amber thought as she neared her destination, but it was too late in the day to see their colours properly; the dull moon had smothered everything in a pale and lifeless grey as she snaked along narrowing roads towards Hampstead Heath.

The clicking of the indicator penetrated the silence as Amber turned onto the private lane. She headed straight up the narrow way, the trees closing in on her until she emerged onto a small driveway.

The car tyres crunched against the gravel as she pulled up outside the house. The large nineteenth-century building was not as imposing at night as she could remember it in daylight, with its vast size largely shadowed and hidden behind the shrubbery that surrounded it. Amber, having only created memories of the home during the warmer, brighter months of the school holidays, could have easily convinced herself she had arrived at the wrong address, were it not for the fact that it was the only house nearby.

No, even in the dark she had managed to navigate her way successfully: this was definitely her grandfather's home.

Well, *her* house now, she corrected herself. Not that she had been particularly moved by the bequest. She had visited her grandparents only a small handful of times in her childhood, and rarely in her adult life. But, as her late grandfather's only grandchild, Amber had been his favoured, if only, choice when it came to leaving behind his property. What she was supposed to do with it though, she had no idea. At least, that had been the case until recently. Now she knew exactly what she was supposed to use it for.

Not wanting to hang around for any longer than was necessary, she clambered out of the car, leaving the door to close behind her as she shifted around to the boot. The wind billowed around her, forcing her to pull the belt of her coat more tightly around her waist. She was dressed entirely in black, and her dark hair was pinned up out of the way. Even if anybody had been watching her in that moment, she would have been entirely unidentifiable as she blended into the night.

The tool bag was heavier than she remembered as she dragged it out of the boot. She let her forearm take most of the weight as she trundled towards the front door, then dropped it down onto the step with a thud as she fished in her pocket for the key to the front door.

After she dug deep into the front of her trousers to unhook the key from where it had become entwined with a loose thread, she at last fitted the key into the old lock. She turned it, and the door unlocked with a sharp click. She returned the key to her pocket, then pushed the door open with a creak.

As she flicked the switch that was on the wall just inside

the entrance, she was relieved to discover that the light in the hallway still functioned. The bulb emitted a disconcerting faint hum above her as she treaded heavy footsteps across the wooden floorboards, but the light, though dim, was enough at least to guide her in the unfamiliar feel of the space.

Dragging the tool bag across the floor, she steadied herself with a hand on the wall, pulling both her own weight and that of the bag deeper into the house. With a final heave, she let the bag drop down, the end onto which she had been holding thumping down onto the floor with a soft thud.

Straightening up, and taking a moment to crack her spine as she placed both her hands at the base of her back, she could feel the throbbing pain that had persistently soared through her body all week. She had struggled with sleep, and, even when she did manage to drift off for a short while, she awoke to find herself lying in some awkward and twisted position into which she had no idea how she had manoeuvred.

Hopefully that would all be over soon though: her plan would work, and her normal life could be restored.

She thought about that word. Perhaps her life had never truly been *normal* before. Certainly it couldn't be considered normal for the average person to be subjected to such immense suffering as she had been, she thought; that wouldn't be right at all. If that were the case, society would have crumbled long ago.

Not wasting any more time than was necessary, she glanced briefly at the bag, satisfied that it was secure where it was, then returned the house to darkness and headed back outside. She made sure the front door was firmly locked behind her, before rushing back to her car to escape the growing bitterness of the tormenting wind.

As she set the car in motion and pulled away from the driveway, Amber fought against her thoughts of jealousy. It wasn't targeted towards anybody in particular, no specific group of people, just humanity in its entirety. No-one else could possibly know how it felt to be torn apart like she had been. The memories alone were gut-wrenching, haunting; an entire world full of people, and she was suffering entirely on her own.

But that wouldn't be the case for much longer.

Chapter One

There was nothing unusual about the weather that morning. The sky was overcast, the earth was sodden, and a subtle breeze transcended intermittently into irritating bursts of gale. It was exactly the climate that could have been expected for the funeral.

Not that too many mourners were affected by the prickling chill of autumn. The turnout was so poor that Amber barely needed both hands to count the number of people standing around the hole in the ground into which her grandfather was being lowered.

She wasn't particularly surprised though; her family had always been limited in number, and her estranged father had been distant with *his* father, Amber's grandfather, since she herself was a little girl. This meant that there was seldom the opportunity for family visits, resulting in only one recognisable face at the procession. Even then she couldn't be sure if her Great Aunt Muriel was an actual blood relative or just somebody her grandfather had known for a very long time. Either way, she hadn't seen either of them in years.

As the coffin continued to make its way deeper into the earth, she bowed her head and took the chance to cast her eyes around her. Nobody looked particularly saddened by the occasion; she had expected at least a few tears for the dearly departed. Mostly though they just seemed bored, as if having to say goodbye to a loved one was more of a chore than a sorrowful final farewell in a celebration of the life of the deceased.

Amber's own expression remained vacant as the vicar muttered a few words about the quality of life and the significance of one's passing. She wasn't really paying as much attention as she probably should have been, didn't really want to be there anyway. She had never cared for funerals. In her thirty-four years she had only been to a small handful, but that was still more than enough for her.

She had overheard some of the elderly mourners before the service began, as she was eavesdropping on their conversations for something to occupy her bored mind, that, for some of them, this was their third or fourth funeral that month. How dire it must be to grow old, becoming increasingly lonelier as everybody around you dropped like flies.

Amber tried to hide her sudden smirk as the expression leapt from her mind. It had been a phrase her mother often

9

used, and she herself had picked it up along the way. It was an odd phrase, she thought.

Her mother's funeral had been the last one she'd attended, a little over two years ago now, and it had been a disappointing affair. She had hoped, maybe even assumed, that her father would have had the decency to turn up to say a final goodbye to the woman he had once loved. But there had been no sight of him.

And since her relationship with her father had not been granted the opportunity for rekindling on that bitter day, as it now occurred to her as her eyes followed the sprinkling of earth as it scattered down on top of the coffin, her last remaining relative was dead.

Her paternal grandfather had passed on to greener pastures, and in doing so had left Amber stranded on earth as the last of the Quigley bloodline. Worst of all, she'd been bequeathed a house in which she would no doubt be expected to live, all alone, floating around the family home with neither offspring nor loved ones by her side.

Chapter Two

Streaks of sunshine yellow glided across the canvas as the brush stroked from right to left, tickling its bristles against the clean white surface. The powerful smell of acrylic paint filled the studio as Victoria hummed a nameless tune to herself. She paused, the tip of the wooden paintbrush poised on her lower lip as she studied her current project.

'Needs more orange,' she muttered to herself before reaching for the steaming cup of freshly brewed coffee that she'd placed on the coaster to her right. After a near miss with a cup of dirty paint water a few months back, she had made sure to place any consumable drink as far away from her art tools as possible. Still, even if she *had* ended up swallowing a mouthful of the murky liquid, it wouldn't have been enough to dampen her spirits. She had never felt so elated, so on top of the world, as she had done in recent weeks.

As she returned the cup to its coaster and reached for a different brush to stipple some orange texture into her design, she couldn't hide the smile that had spread once more across her lips. Jason had just left to pick up their ritual weekend takeaway, and soon they would be lounging together on the sofa while devouring noodles and binge-watching whatever sitcoms were on TV that evening. She was pleased with the way her latest project was developing, and only yesterday had she received several emails from new clients requesting quotes for work they'd like to commission. Being a freelance artist was much better than she had expected, almost easier too. Her creativity was more productive than she had ever known it to be, and on top of all that she was soon to be moving in with the man with whom she was so madly in love.

As she deposited the paint brush on the easel and cradled her cup of coffee, absorbing its warmth as she contemplated the next stage in the painting, she basked in her own good fortune. Not once did the thought ever cross her mind that nothing perfect could last forever.

Why did authors always feel compelled to write about characters who wrote books for a living?

It was only a fleeting question in Amber's mind, but it caused enough of a distraction to plunge her deeper into her own pit of procrastination.

No, she wasn't procrastinating, was she? That wasn't her problem. She was simply useless creating anything of any worth. Her mind was blank. She had no ideas. She should be ashamed to call herself a writer.

The lamp in her office – and by office, this referenced only the old desk she'd fixed at the bottom of her bed to make the best of the space with which her dingy flat provided her – had been dimly lit. The softened glow had been intended to help her mind to relax, but she just seemed to be increasingly winding herself up. Three years had passed since her debut novel had been published, and, although it hadn't even come close to making it onto any of the bestseller lists, enough copies had been sold to make her feel like her efforts had been fruitful. But she'd failed to produce anything since then, and now her publisher was laying on the pressure for her to pick up her pen again.

But what did she have to write about? 'Write about what you know,' her publisher had suggested. Sebastian Browning of Browning & Carrington was a charming man; he'd been in the publishing industry for longer than he would dare to admit, and she trusted his advice. But she didn't know anything that was worth writing about. At least, everything she'd known over the past few years had been foul and painful and certainly nothing she wished to commit to paper. She had fought with herself to lock those demons away, and the last thing she wanted to do was to unleash them just to satisfy the needs of her publisher.

It was no use. She slammed down the lid of her laptop, before cursing at her own heavy handedness, and pushed her chair away from the desk. She knew it would be pointless trying to force the words out when they were refusing to cooperate; she'd only write poorly, and then that would mean she'd only have to redo it all again anyway. Instead of wasting her time, it would be much better for her if she just escaped from her bedroom for a bit. Sleeping each night in the same room where she worked – or *tried* to work – proved to be an impractical nightmare as her mind never seemed to rest.

And yet, in all those hours she spent wide awake, tossing and turning as she tried to find what it was she was meant to be doing, her brain always failed to come up with anything useful.

Why couldn't she be like all those other writers, she thought to herself as she shuffled aimlessly through to the sitting room, who managed to churn out story after story, endless bestsellers and admirable tomes, and all without ever losing their spark? They made it look so easy.

Still, she wasn't asking for quite that much out of life.

Right now, Amber would have been thankful if she could come up with something that could at least be sold at all, forget topping the charts. Any words on the page would have been progress. Instead, she found herself crouched down in front of the bookshelf beside her sofa, fingering the spines of the small display of tattered paperbacks she'd rescued from charity shops over the years.

She lifted a few out in turn, flicking through the stained pages of *Orlando* and *Northanger Abbey* and *Finnegans Wake* (she'd never actually read that last one, and still didn't know what she had been thinking when she'd bought it). In her fervour to find something, anything, inside of those pages that would provide her with the inspiration she needed to coax her into a more fruitful excuse of an afternoon, her elbow collided with a glass she'd left on the coffee table the night before.

'Shit!'

She jumped, and tried to catch it before it was too late, but the remnants of red wine spluttered across the carpet and over the worn copy of *Les Misérables* onto which she'd been clutching.

Amber emitted a low Gruffalo-like groan as she pulled herself up off the floor. She shuffled her way through to the kitchen; there had been no need to hurry, since a carpet stain wasn't exactly going to make her dank flat look any worse.

Her landlord would probably think otherwise, of course, but right now she had more important things to worry about.

But *was* she actually worried? It occurred to her, as she swiped a dish cloth from the kitchen table and slumped her way back to soak up the spill, that she couldn't really care less if she couldn't write anything. It didn't actually matter if she never told another story again.

So what if she had nothing to say? If she let her publisher down, then so be it. It wouldn't be the first time somebody was disappointed with her.

'Oh, woe is me!' she exclaimed to herself as she returned the sodden dish cloth to the kitchen. It was now covered in faint, vinegary patches of pale red. Like remnants of blood after a cut, she thought to herself.

Cuckoo! Cuckoo! Cuckoo!

'Oh, shut up!'

The little bird inside the cuckoo clock obeyed Amber's mumbled order as she flopped down into a chair, dropping her torso against the cold, hard surface of the wooden table.

'Urgh!'

The sound was muffled as she groaned into her sleeved arm. She was fed up, bored, and tired of trying.

Before Amber had a chance to pull herself together and return to her bedroom-come-office to continue her pointless struggle to put words on the page, a sickeningly merry jingle

16

burst out of her mobile phone.

She lifted her head up, her fringe ruffled and hanging down in front of her eyes, and stared bemused at the phone. She had discarded it on the table the previous night; there was no need for her to keep it on her person at all times, as she rarely received any phone calls. And the calls she *did* receive were dull, or tedious, or difficult.

She made a feeble attempt to stretch out her arm and grab onto the phone. She glanced at the number. It wasn't her publisher. It wasn't even her job-seeking advisor demanding that she submitted more complicated forms and supporting documents despite the fact she'd done so a thousand times already.

No, to her surprise, it wasn't anybody she loathed talking to.

It was Claire.

When Amber had still been teaching, Claire Boyd, a flamboyant art teacher ten years her junior and bubbling over with enough energy for them both, had always been there to keep her sane. It turned out that teaching English to children at a comprehensive school wasn't quite what she had imagined: it wasn't simply a case of enjoying long holidays and inspiring pupils to stand on tables in her name. Oh, it wasn't that she didn't like teaching. She loved discussing literature with her classes, and, for the most part, it had been

17

a pleasant job. She had been devastated when she left her position. But when the opportunity for a voluntary redundancy – and the pay packet that came with it – presented itself, she decided it was the perfect time to put aside a little money, see the light in her career break, and start a family.

There was only one problem with that plan, however. Almost immediately after leaving her job, Amber also lost her boyfriend, and with that the family home they shared together. She had been cast aside, stranded in the gutter with no income, no love, and a distinct lack of happiness.

Several months and an ongoing routine course of antidepressants later, Amber was now able to stand on her own two feet again, but only just. Her life was so empty now that something as previously commonplace as a phone call from Claire was now all that was required to give her that little ray of hope that she wasn't entirely alone in the world. She hit the button on the phone to answer the call.

'Hi, Claire,'

'Amber! You alright?'

'Yeah, good,' she lied. She slid herself out from the table and crossed over to the cupboard above the sink. 'Aren't you supposed to be teaching just now?'

'Oh, I have a free period. God, I envy you for not having to work on a Friday! Want to trade?'

Amber almost spluttered a laugh as she reached for a packet of biscuits. 'You've no idea how much I wish that were possible!'

She would have given anything, in a heartbeat, to be back in her classroom, piles of classic novels and plays and poetry books precariously balanced by her side as she waited for her next class to scuttle to their seats. It would certainly beat spending the afternoon alone in her draughty flat while she prodded her finger at a stale digestive.

'Anyway, I was just wondering what you were up to this weekend!'

Amber shrugged fruitlessly before cramming half of a biscuit into her mouth. 'Same old. Nothing much. Why?' she said as she failed to catch the crumbs spraying from her lips.

'Well, the thing is, I was waiting for the Year Eights to finish sculpting their pots – you should have seen the state of some of them, and I swear they managed to get clay down the back of my dress, only I can't see it properly – and, anyway, I was bored, and my mind was wandering, as it does, and I thought it would be a fantastic idea if you and me hit the town this weekend! Grab a few drinks, dance a few moves, that sort of thing, you know? It's about time we had a good catch up!'

'I hardly think I'm the clubbing sort!' Amber retorted, before cramming the rest of the mushy digestive into her mouth.

'Oh, come on! Say yes! Please!'

As Claire continued to whine down the line, Amber could envision those wide puppy-dog eyes and raised eyebrows that she'd seen so many times before. And yet she'd not seen them for months now, had she? God, she missed Claire.

'What's the worst that can happen? Besides, you might actually enjoy yourself. Treat *yourself! Let your hair down!'*

'Well...'

Amber sighed, unsure of where she was going with her protest. She slumped her weight against the sink, admitting defeat.

'Oh, alright. Fine. Okay, you win.'

'Yes! Fantastic! Look, I should probably go now as the bell's about to ring, but I'll give you a call tonight to work out the deets, okay?'

'Deets?'

'The details, *silly!'*

Claire definitely knew how to make a woman feel old. Past her prime, even. Decaying, slowly rotting away from the inside as time unkindly passed her by. Amber could hear her biological clock ticking as she rubbed at her forehead with the palm of her hand. She swallowed down her discontentment with a sip from her milky coffee.

The reverberating tinny ring of the school bell intruded their conversation, causing a small knot in Amber's stomach to lurch. It had been so long since she had heard that sound. What had once been so irritating, a hinder to the freedom of free periods and lunch hours, now brought bitter-sweet nostalgia to her watering eyes.

'Oh, shit. I better go. Speak later, and make sure you look out your shortest dress!'

The call ended, and Amber dropped her phone into her pocket. In the time it took her to nibble at the second half of another stale biscuit she'd been working on, she realised she already regretted her decision. She was weary, her mind as aching as her aging bones; there was no way she would be good company for the younger, more sprightly Claire.

Still, she had spent so long on her own that it would be nice to have somebody around her, if only for a few hours. She had been starved of any meaningful conversations; if anybody could cheer her up, it was Claire.

Besides, Claire was probably right. One little night out wouldn't do her any harm, would it?

Chapter Three

Nights were always the worst.

There was a distinct lack of spring in Amber's step when the following morning arrived. During the weekdays, she could maintain some level of hope, if only enough to see her through the day, as she dreamed of a change in prosperity. But as soon as the evenings dawned, there was no longer any scope for a job offer, and no chance of receiving any life-enhancing phone calls. Weekends were just as bad. She knew she'd hit rock bottom when she caught herself willing the return of Mondays.

It would take too much of her already-sparse effort to pretend that today would be any different from every other Saturday; nothing was going to change for Amber.

Having awoken bleary eyed and yawning, she'd dragged herself out of the security of her bed to face the day. Just like she did every morning, she slipped her bare feet into a pair of ill-fitting slippers, and slumped her way into the bathroom.

She squinted at her reflection in the mirror through heavy eyelids, and sighed.

After confirming to herself that she looked just as pale and exhausted as she did every other day, and that she would have been a fool to expect anything else, she reached for her toothbrush from the cup by the sink, and squeezed out a minty-fresh dollop of white paste. This was just as routine as the rest of her existence: brush the top teeth, brush the bottom teeth, spit; repeat; gargle mouthwash; spit; rinse.

Something as consistently monotonous as brushing her teeth required little to no thought, her actions mechanical with the familiarity of thirty-four years of personal hygiene. Her morning pattern may have changed dramatically in recent months, but there was a peculiar comfort to her daily performance. And it was just that: she was performing to herself, her only audience, putting on a façade as she pretended that she could do this. She went about her day as if nothing was the matter, putting on a brave face for the sunken eyes that stared back at her whenever she glanced at her own image. It was all pretence though. She never could deny to herself that, below the numbed surface, she was screaming. It echoed throughout her thoughts, travelling deep into her heart; day and night, her own agony soaked through her, prevented her from hearing anything else. It was at the front line of her battle, and she knew she couldn't fight it on her own.

Her therapist, with whom she had an appointment later that day – Amber grimaced as she remembered her only, and dreaded, plan for that morning, which had become ritualistic over the last few weekends – had tried to convince her that she *wasn't* doing this alone. There were lots of people there to help her. Unfortunately, none of those people had as of yet been willing to present themselves. Not that Amber blamed them; she too would always avoid the problems of others, given the choice.

She couldn't avoid her own problems though, but at least she could suppress them with the addictive effects of Western medicine. She reached into the cabinet that was hidden away behind the bathroom mirror, and pulled out the little plastic bottle of tiny white pills.

Where she would be without her antidepressants, she wasn't sure; they were her lifeline. The only thing she was certain about though was that she genuinely believed she wouldn't be *here*. In her bathroom. In her flat. On this earth. Of course, she had to thank her therapist for that one, as she had been the one to refer her to a specialist practitioner to have them prescribed after just one therapy session. It had only taken her therapist that one hour to see just how messed up Amber truly was. She was good at her job, Amber had to give her credit where it was due.

Which was just as well, considering she was costing her a small fortune. Following her first major breakdown after finding herself abandoned and in her own isolation, with nobody to turn to and nowhere to run, finding a private therapist was the only feasible plan that had crossed Amber's mind. She had nobody else to talk to; at least this stranger, who would be paid to listen to her problems, was bound to straighten her out.

Seven invasive sessions and a massive deduction in her bank balance later, and Amber still felt screwed. Still, she'd booked a block of sessions in advance, draining the majority of her redundancy pay, so she had convinced herself that, regardless of whether or not she found the sessions to be of any help to her, she might as well continue with them.

Ignoring all thoughts of her next imminent session with the therapist, she instead observed her hands in the reflection of the mirror as she pushed down then twisted the cap of the medicine bottle. It popped off, and she tipped two little round pills into her palm. They looked so clean and pure, not offering any indication of what mysterious ingredients were really locked inside of them. Amber didn't really understand how they worked, but neither did she care. They were her friends now, and she trusted them to prevent her from doing anything she'd regret.

With another sigh, she threw the pills into her mouth, gulped them down with a mouthful of water, and slammed the medicine cabinet shut. As she wiped at her mouth with the back of her hand, her own judgmental reflection scoffed at her scraggly hair, her baggy pyjamas, her sallow cheeks and bloodshot eyes.

For now, the antidepressants were strong enough to keep her stable throughout most of the day. But what about the distant future, or even just around the next corner? Would they still be there for her then? Just how much of a mess did a person have to become before they were beyond help?

'I'm not going to lie to you, Amber. You look like shit.'

To anybody loitering outside the room at that moment, Jo's comment would have sounded harsh. To Amber, however, the blunt remark was nothing other than the honesty that she had come to expect from her therapist. Jo Robins-Fry was, as therapists went, full of insights and knowledge of practicable theories to help her patients. When it came down to human interaction though, she was less than efficiently equipped. She was good at her job, typically spot on with her analyses, but never in her forty-eight years could she have been considered a people person.

Jo, with her cropped blonde hair and crisp white blouse, was a stark contrast to Amber's dark apparel as she sat behind her desk, idly twisting in her chair from side to side while repeatedly clicking the end of her pen. She sighed, leaned forward, and shuffled through a small pile of papers before pulling out Amber's file.

'So how have things been since our last appointment?'

Amber shrugged. 'Alright, I suppose.'

She was leaning against the arm of the sofa, with her coat draped over her legs. Her posture was rigid as she tried to hide the fact that she'd not exactly been successful with making the progress that Jo had explicitly outlined for her during their previous encounter. She hadn't even come close to it. If Jo considered for one second that Amber hadn't been making the effort, she'd no doubt force her to schedule more sessions during the week, and Amber simply didn't have the energy for that.

'Well that sounds like fantastic progress,' Jo retorted, not bothering to mask the sarcasm in her tone. She cast an eye down at the notes in front of her, before peering up at Amber over the rim of her glasses. 'Are you still taking your medication?'

'Yes.'

The answer seemed to be satisfactory enough for her.

27

She returned her attention to the paperwork and continued to read, leaving Amber to tap her foot absentmindedly against the wooden leg of the coffee table, while the room remained in otherwise near silence for a long minute. Finally, Jo looked up, and pulled her glasses away from her face.

'Yes, of course, I'd almost forgotten. We didn't meet last weekend, did we? I'm sorry I couldn't make our appointment. Family stuff, you know how it is—'

She didn't.

'—but I see I noted down here that you were due to sign the documents for your grandfather's house last Tuesday. Well, *your* house now, I suppose. How did that go? Everything run smoothly?'

'It's just a house, isn't it? I hardly knew the man. My grandfather. I hadn't seen him in years, and even when I did it was never anything particularly interesting. My memories of that house are sparse; it doesn't mean anything to me.'

'This could be a chance for you to turn over a new leaf, see this as an opportunity for a new start. Have you thought that this might actually be a good thing for you? You could move out of the flat you're renting just now and set up a new life for yourself in the house, couldn't you? Maybe turn it into something more than just bricks and mortar.'

'What would be the point? I hardly need a house that size. I haven't got any family, do I? No husband. No kids.'

28

A brief silence passed between them as Amber's lip curled upwards. Then she snarled:

'*He* made sure of that.'

Jo sighed again – her fourth time in the last ten minutes, if Amber had counted correctly – and dropped her clasped hands down onto the desk in front of her as she leaned in closer towards Amber.

'Amber, we've been over this, haven't we? You can't let what Jason did to you affect the quality of your life. He shouldn't be able to set you back. You mustn't let him.'

Amber threw her eyes in a sideways glance towards the carpet. 'I don't see why he gets to be happy all the time,' she muttered. She turned her head back to face Jo, her eyes wide and her voice raised as the suppressed pain fought its way to the surface. '*He*'s the one who had the affair. *I*'m the one who's suffering here! Some silly little house isn't going to change that!'

'I thought you said it was a big house?'

The sarcasm was met only with rolled eyes, which was followed by a deflated harrumph. Attempting to diffuse the angst that was rising within her, Amber closed her eyes and slowly released an exhale. If her brain didn't uncloud soon, she was in for another restless night.

'Yeah, well,' she finally replied, breaking the silence, 'it doesn't matter what size it is. It's still a family home, and I

29

still don't have a family.'

'Have you thought about getting a dog?'

When Jo was met with the silent response she'd predicted, she scribbled something down in her notebook, the scratchy pen nib leaving a trail of illegible sprawl across the paper. She looked up at Amber, and paused as if considering asking her the question that was resting on the tip of her tongue.

She had never been one for holding back though. Any other person may have decided to word their query a little more delicately, but not Jo. No, she chose to go straight to the heart of the problem.

'Why do you feel you need a child to complete you?'

Amber fidgeted, shifting her bottom along the sofa cushion. Her guard was always up to protect her against the unexpected whenever she was around Jo, fully aware that her approaches were not always exactly considered to be orthodox, so the question hadn't really throw her as much as it could have done. She was more uncomfortable with the fact that she, who had once been so headstrong and confident in her own thoughts, didn't have a solid answer.

'I dunno,' she finally said. 'I just…I guess I've just always had this vision of rocking my child to sleep, his little button nose turned up to mine, his tiny clammy fist wrapped tightly around my thumb. I've always wanted to be a mother, ever since I was a little girl. My baby dolls, they were real to me. As real as any living baby. And over the years, I just...I don't know, my child would depend on me, wouldn't it?'

Lowering her voice into a level of whisper that Jo would have described as being indicative of Amber's vulnerability, she added: 'He would *need* me.'

It was fortunate that Amber's attention had then returned to a miscellaneous patch on the carpet, as it meant that she had been unable to see Jo twisting her face. The thought of a squirming, screaming, tiny pinky-coloured human depending on her was almost too much to bear. It was absurd to Jo that anybody would ever desire the responsibility of raising anything that could send such shivers up the spine.

Still, she thought, if this lonely woman felt like she needed a baby to fill the void in her life then that's the situation with which she was going to have to work. It seemed like a reasonable direction in which to take the session, and if nothing else it beat the usual drivel about broken hearts or squabbling partners that she had to put up with every day.

Jo leaned into her desk again, her movement drawing Amber's attention back to her. 'I want you to answer me this question honestly. If you'd been able to carry your baby to full term, do you think – and I mean *truly* think – that you'd

31

be in a better frame of mind right at this very moment?'

'Yes.'

She hadn't missed a beat, and Amber's stern response and sharp expression were enough to cause Jo's eyebrow to arch. The therapist decided that it wasn't worth pushing the matter any further that day. Instead, she turned her attention back to her notes, and addressed Amber while she sifted idly through the pages.

'What about Jason? Have you seen him since our last meeting?'

She didn't reply, but shifted uncomfortably as she fiddled with the hem of her coat.

Dissatisfied with being ignored, Jo pressed, '*Amber*, have you seen Jason since our last meeting?'

It would be easy for her to lie to Jo. Tell her what she wanted to hear. It wouldn't be a crime.

But then she was paying for these sessions, wasn't she? Paying quite a lot for them too. She might as well be upfront and as honest as possible. Who knew, maybe Jo would actually end up being able to help her.

And pigs might fly.

'I might have done,' she muttered at last.

Jo raised an eyebrow, but, before she had a chance to launch into full lecture mode, Amber jumped to her own defense.

'I can't help it if he still goes to the same café, can I? I still need to walk down that street, and if I happen to see him then it's hardly my fault.'

'And you're certain there's no other route you can take that would allow you to avoid that road?'

'No. There isn't.'

Jo stood up from behind her desk and headed to the water cooler on the other side of the room. She kept her attention on Amber while she filled her glass. 'Really, it's not a good idea to keep upsetting yourself like this. I know I usually advise people not to distance themselves from their problems, but in your case that's exactly what you should be doing.'

She paused to glug from the glass, before crossing the room and dropping back down in her chair. 'You don't need to constantly remind yourself of the very heartache that brought you to my office in the first place.'

'But I have every right to walk that way! Surely I shouldn't let him dictate where I can and cannot go!'

Jo angled her head towards her desk as she muttered, 'Now you're just being awkward.'

'What?'

A brisk exhale escaped from Jo's lips as she shifted forward, her eyes locked on Amber's. 'Look, Amber, I know you're going through a tough time at the moment. That's why

33

you're here. But I also know that my sessions are expensive. I know how much you're paying for the high quality of support that I provide for you. And you *have* been making some good progress, and I'm very happy about that, but if you want to start feeling more like yourself again and avoid spending the rest of your life handing over your money to me, then I strongly suggest that you at least try and meet me halfway. Does that sound reasonable?'

Like a child who'd just been given into trouble, Amber averted her gaze as they both allowed the silence to brew. Yes, she was paying for these sessions. But she was paying for them to hear what she wanted to – that she wasn't at fault, that she wasn't doing anything wrong – not to be told that she wasn't cooperating or making an effort. Over the last few months her mind had developed a tendency to cloud over whenever she was confronted with a situation that she wasn't comfortable with. She would become vacant, unresponsive; if she didn't pull herself out of such an impending mood right now before it was too late, she was risking sliding down that slope right in front of Jo.

And there was no way Jo would respond well to that.

Once the words had sunk in and Amber realised that there was nothing she could do but admit that Jo was right, she turned to her therapist, her face scrunched up as she pretending like she had not been affected by the brutal truth.

'Yes, boss.'

The smile that managed to crack across Jo's otherwise disinterested expression came as a surprise to both women. She had said the right thing. That *had* to be progress.

Of course, just as quickly as that smile arrived, it disappeared into a controlled blankness as the therapist bowed her head and began flicking through the notes she'd made during their previous session. It would have been too much for her to look in Amber's direction while she was awash with the peculiar sense of satisfaction that was usually so elusive to her. She kept her eyes buried within the paperwork as she spoke:

'Good. Now, I want you to promise me that you'll at least consider the suggestions I'm giving you today. And that includes the possibility of accepting your grandfather's house as a sign that you're allowed a fresh start. Life is to be *lived*. You write books, don't you? How can you possibly call yourself a writer if you don't experience what the world has to offer? There's no point in punishing yourself; do something that'll make you happy. This is a great opportunity for you to do something new, so go grab that freedom with both hands!'

Surprised by the fervour the situation had elicited in herself, Jo finally stopped fruitlessly rummaging through the notes. She looked up at Amber, who unawares to Jo had been watching her the entire time she'd been talking. Amber hadn't known where else to look, having unexpectedly shed the hardened exterior with which she'd earlier sloped into the room. Perhaps considering the option of heeding Jo's rants wasn't *entirely* out of the question.

'You need to help yourself, Amber. I'm here for you, you know that, but if you don't start doing things for yourself then you won't see any further improvement. I can promise you that much. You'll feel so much better if you at least try to bring yourself out of this temporary depression. And it will be only temporary, I'm sure of that. You just need to take a step in the right direction. I've every faith—'

Jo paused to take another sip from her glass. She tilted her head slightly upwards, pre-swallow, as she tried not to let the pool of water that was balancing precariously under her tongue spill out.

She gargled, swallowed, and concluded:

'—that you'll do the right thing.'

Chapter Four

The dull throb of pounding music spilled out of the nightclub and bounced down the street as a herd of scantily clad tipsy clubbers huddled behind the red rope. A cluster of cackling blondes in matching pink-sequinned cocktail dresses staggered forward, their heels clacking against the pavement, as Claire and Amber sidled up behind them to join the queue.

'I'm so glad you agreed to this. It's been ages since I had a proper night out!'

Amber wasn't entirely sure if she'd ever actually had a 'proper night out', having been unbearably studious at university, and then falling straight into a steady job after graduating. Sure, she'd done the odd pub crawl in her youth, but that was more like the equivalent of pre-drinks to the unyielding youngsters of today. Before Amber had a chance to voice such an embarrassing confession to Claire, their arrival at the back of the line had attracted the attention of the somewhat disappointing excuse for testosterone in front of them. One of the men in the group glanced Claire up and down, before clicking his tongue.

'Alright, sweet cheeks?'

His eyes were wide with superficial lust as he studied the top of Claire's thighs, which were displayed with pride below the tiny hem of her skirt.

'Oh, give it a rest, Bradley!' one of the blondes barked as she prodded at his chest with an immaculately painted hot-pink acrylic nail. 'Sorry,' she said to Claire as she flicked her razor-straight, heat-damaged hair over one shoulder. 'He's been at it all evening. You must be the twentieth girl he's hit on in the last hour!'

'I bet that makes you feel special,' Amber muttered in Claire's ear as the blonde returned her attention to her posse.

They shuffled a little further up the queue as a batch of teenagers was carted inside the building. Claire must have been freezing, Amber thought as she wrapped her arms around her own chest. She had played it safe with a black dress with three-quarter-length sleeves. She would have preferred to have brought her coat out with her, but Claire had insisted that it was out of the question. Still, at least she was wearing tights, which was more than she could say for her bare-skinned colleague.

Former colleague, she corrected herself. Of course, the

memories, the bitter reminders of her current state of worthlessness, were bound to have surfaced right when she was finally trying to let her hair down for an hour or two. She should never have expected anything else; hope was always so misleading.

It wasn't as if she *wanted* to be out though. She would much rather have stayed at home, tucked up in bed, sleeping away the remainder of another meaningless day. But in her unguarded moment of indecision she had ended up agreeing to this. She was here now, and all she could try to do was make sure that the depression didn't push its way to the surface, if only for one evening. Tonight, she *had* to control it. If nothing else, she couldn't allow herself to ruin Claire's night.

'How many?'

The bouncer gruffed at them as they approached the front of the rope, and Claire stuck two fingers in the air. He lifted the rope to let them slip inside.

Claire wasted no time as she grabbed onto Amber's hand and dragged her down the dark stairway, away from the safety of the fresh air, and plunging them deep into the illuminated pulsing chaos of drunken fun.

The pulsating throb of techno rippled across the dancefloor. Peep-toe stilettos and rubber soles thumped against the sticky surface as the throng of clubbers bounced to the rhythm in one giant, sweaty mass.

They had only been there for an hour and a half or so, but Amber and Claire were now fully immersed in the atmosphere. For Claire, this was always to be expected; she had slipped with ease straight into the vibrations of the room, absorbed in the vibrant strobe lights that washed back and forth over the milky-white flesh of her bare arms.

She danced wildly in the centre of the club, her hands thrown into the air as her cocktail sloshed around with uncertainty. Bodies were pressed together all around her as she danced, her thrusting movements angular and sharp.

At the beginning of the night, Amber had been cautious of Claire's flailing arms as she crammed herself into the small space between the other dancers. She had kept her attention firmly on her friend, not wanting to consider the other people around her for fear of inducing any sense of claustrophobia. The air was hot and stuffy, and the music was so loud that she struggled to hear herself think.

But then she soon realised that this was, in fact, a good thing. With the deafening volume drowning out her own thoughts, she no longer had to contend with the constant intrusion of her own morbid daymares. It may have only been a temporary relief, but she vowed in that moment to enjoy it while she could.

Several drinks later, Amber was finally able to ignore her earlier preconceptions; it didn't look like the evening was going to drag after all. In fact, she was even willing to admit that, ever since she had actually started to relax and embrace the fun, time had flown by. If only she could pause the night and remain lost in its escape forever.

'Are you having a good time?!' Claire screeched over the noise surrounding them.

Amber nodded, a little too enthused, and at the same time two men sidled up to the women. They were smartly dressed, one a little older than the other; Amber guessed their ages were sandwiching somewhere between hers and Claire's. Perhaps they were friends, or maybe brothers, lads on the town looking for a good time. There wasn't anything wrong with that.

As the older of the two placed a hand on Amber's arm, a small flutter of goosebumps protruded onto her skin. It was the first time she had been touched, however unexpected it had been, in longer than she would like to remember. To her surprise, it felt good.

The song segued to the next track, and the sudden increase in tempo rocketed Claire's youthful energy. 'Wooo!'

A small giggle escaped Amber's lips as she found herself amused by Claire's relentless delirium. She did have the right attitude though. This *was* fun, and there was no reason why

41

Amber shouldn't be able to enjoy herself too.

As Claire turned around to gyrate with the younger man, Amber cast her eyes over towards the other man beside her. He was warm, tipsy, and willing to dance with just a breath of space between them. It was a closeness that Amber had missed.

It was also, she believed, a closeness that she deserved. After the incalculable pain from which she'd suffered over the last few months, she should at least be able to allow herself this much.

She swigged the dregs of her drink, allowing the thick vodka to trickle down her throat, then sidled closer to her stranger. Whatever happened from here, she was going to make sure she had a night that was worth remembering.

The music grew fainter as Amber and her stranger stumbled into the corridor, the door to the dancefloor swinging shut behind them and cutting them off from the main hub of the club.

They narrowly avoided colliding with a fire extinguisher that was hanging on the wall as they staggered towards the toilets, their intoxicated state rendering them oblivious to the comatose and inebriated clubbers that were slumped against the sticky walls and slouched on the stained carpet around them.

They brushed past a drunk brunette as they stumbled into the ladies' toilets. The stranger wasted no time in forcing his lips upon Amber's, pushing his weight against her torso as they skirted along the flaky painted wall. They tumbled into a cubicle, and the stranger pressed Amber against the back of the graffitied door.

The stifling heat inside the cramped space rose as the stranger fumbled for the hem of Amber's dress, his fingers grasping with haste at her thighs. His hand wandered until he found the elastic of her knickers.

He tugged, then slid his fingers inside of her, stirring Amber's desires as she fiddled with the clasp of his belt. She floundered, her actions uncooperative and smothered beneath the influence of vodka, before finally releasing the stranger's throbbing urgency from its confinement.

They staggered, the stranger groping at Amber's breasts with one hand while repositioning himself with the other. Their lips remained suctioned as the stranger at last managed to enter Amber, not too intoxicated to perform as he began thrusting upwards.

Amber fought for something onto which to hold as she lost herself in the stained and sticky toilet cubicle. Specks of green paint from the back of the door flaked and tumbled down into her hair as her hips gyrated, her body sliding up and down the back of the wooden panel. As the pressure

43

mounted between her legs, the euphoria grew from deep within her, and all the repressed tension that had built up in the agony of the preceding months escaped from her lips in a single desperate and uncontrollable moan.

Chapter Five

The only sound that could be heard in the otherwise-silent bedroom was the soft release of air as Amber exhaled. She breathed gently through her nose as she slept; she would soon waken to realise that it had been many months since she had slept quite as soundly as she did that night. If only for a few hours, she had been granted an undisturbed slumber, remaining blissfully unaware of the troubles that routinely hindered her rest.

Eventually she stirred, and rolled over onto her side, absent-mindedly dragging the duvet over with her so that it wrapped her up in a hug. With her head poking out through the top of the covers, her face landed directly in the path of a sickly yellow sunbeam that had poked its way uninvited into the bedroom through the narrow gap in the curtains.

Her left eye twitched as the ray of light tickled against the thin veiny skin of her eyelid. Her lashes fluttered in protest, pulling her out of a dreamless sleep, before forcing her to give in to the awakening. She narrowly opened one eye as she squinted through the harsh midday light.

'Oh God.'

The room seemed to spin as she pulled herself upright and leant against her headboard. She rested her head in her hands as she sat there, her knees tucked up to her chest and her back pressed against the bunched-up pillow, naked save for her underwear.

She pulled the duvet more tightly around her as she shivered. It had been a long time since she'd felt this hungover; she couldn't be certain, but it was definitely likely that she had been mixing drinks the previous night.

She couldn't actually remember arriving home. Claire had probably bundled her into a taxi. She must have been fairly efficient through her intoxication though, as she had managed at least to remember to fill a glass with water and leave it beside her bed before she no doubt crashed in a snoring state of comatose.

She reached for the drink now and gulped greedily as the cool liquid washed over her tongue and down her throat. She swallowed, and rasped at her front teeth. Her tongue felt fuzzy, and tasted repulsive. She should probably get up and give her teeth a brush, but the thought of putting anything in her mouth right now was enough to turn her stomach and make her gag.

She closed her eyes again as the dull ache intensified around her forehead. She pushed her hair out of the way, and groaned as she massaged at her temples.

Her grumbling was responded by the merry chime of her phone, indicating the arrival of a text message.

'Kill me now,' she muttered as the chirpy alert penetrated her delicate ears. Her brain felt thick with fog as she shifted to retrieve her phone from the floor by the bed where she must have dropped it in the early hours of the morning.

Amber grunted as she screwed up her eyes at the bright screen, displeased that the intrusive noise had alerted her only of a short message from Claire. It was something that could have waited until she was feeling a little rosier, with Claire only explaining that she had had great fun and that they should definitely do it again some time.

'Not a chance,' Amber murmured. She was getting too old for this. The mornings after her pub visits as a student were bad enough; this was something else entirely. No matter how much fun she may or may not have had – she couldn't quite recall the precise details right now – it just wasn't worth it.

She was about to drop her phone back down onto the carpet and force herself back to sleep when she noticed a second text message. It must have come through earlier that morning when she had been content and undisturbed in her deep sleep. After dimming down the brightness of the screen, she scrolled through to read the message.

She didn't recognise the number displayed at the top. It wasn't the part that bothered her most though. When she read the message, her brow scrunched up.

'Hey, it's Greig. From the club. I just thought I'd drop you a text to say cheers for your number. I had a really good time last night. I hope you did too. Give me a call if you want to grab a coffee or something. You've got my number! Greig x'

'Greig?'

She mouthed the name to herself. It didn't ring any bells. Too exhausted to overthink it, she shrugged it off. It had probably been meant for somebody else. The number hadn't been saved in her phone book, after all. No doubt they had just mistyped the digits. It was easily done.

Dismissing any further thoughts, Amber rolled onto her side and pulled the duvet over her head to block out the light. She'd forgotten to check what the time was, but she didn't really care. All she wanted to do right now was close her eyes and go back to sleep. And, since nobody needed her to get out of bed and get on with her life, that's exactly what she was going to do.

For some thirty seconds or so she managed to remain

blissfully ignorant of any memories from the night before. But then, just as she was about to drift away from consciousness, the penny dropped, and it did so with a deafening and reverberative *clank*.

She bolted upright with absolutely no regard for her throbbing headache. Suddenly her bloodshot eyes were wide and alert. Clearing her mind to help induce the return of her dreamless sleep, the antics of the previous night had all come flooding back to her. Despite her desire to remain contently unaware, she remembered it all: the vodka, the cocktails, the music, the dancing.

And she realised then, as her nostrils filled with the memory of the pungent fragrance of public bathroom fornication, that she did, in fact, know who Greig was.

'Shit!'

It was a very British thing, wasn't it? Reaching for a cup of tea whenever life threw down another problem. Of course, in Amber's case, it was her remedy of choice only second to the now-empty carton of orange juice that had failed to relieve her hangover. She plopped several heaped teaspoons of sugar into her mug, stirred, and carried it over to the kitchen table.

'I don't see what the problem is!'

Claire's muffled voice drifted from the phone that had been wedged between Amber's ear and her shoulder. She

49

placed the mug down, tucked her legs beneath the chair, and retrieved the phone. Her neck felt stiff as she rubbed at it with her free hand. She had managed to wash her face, and had snatched a pair of reasonably clean slack jeans and an oversized t-shirt from the top of the washing basket, but despite her best efforts she still felt like death.

'I don't know,' she replied to Claire before blowing on the surface of her tea. 'It's just…it's not me, you know? I was so disgustingly placid in my youth. I've never done anything like that before.'

'Well, maybe this is just a new you that you didn't know about until now. Honestly, honey, it's not really that strange these days to hook up with a guy the same night you meet him – even if it is just in the toilets of the nightclub!'

Amber felt a sudden rush of rouge to her cheeks as she tried but failed to stop herself from blushing. The faint memory of the mixed aromas of vodka and urine curdled the milky tea as she forced it down her throat, before she replied, 'Really?'

'Really! I mean, okay, so it's a little less common for the catch of the night to message you the next day, but it's not entirely unheard of. If this Greig guy is genuinely interested then maybe you should just make the leap. Who knows, even without your beer goggles he may still be your Prince Charming! So you're going to call him?'

Amber, who didn't know how else to respond to the

question, took that moment to lose herself in a sweet sip of her cooling drink. She closed her eyes, oblivious to her surroundings in a brief escape from reality, until the chirpy voice penetrated the silence.

'Hello? Earth to Amber! You're going to call him, yes?'

Amber swallowed. Claire's shrill tones were amplified in her ear as they sliced right through her hangover. She winced, then mustered a reply: 'I don't know. I really don't. I've no idea what I'm supposed to do anymore.'

'You're supposed to call him! Oh, you must! Think of it this way: at the end of the day, what do you have to lose? Really?'

'My dignity? My sanity? My life?'

Not that it was much of a life, but it was her life nonetheless. It was one of the very few things over which she still had control, and she wasn't about to relinquish that in a hurry.

'Well, besides all those. I think you should give him a call right now.'

Amber allowed Claire to rabbit on as she jammed the phone underneath her ear again and fumbled for her packet of cigarettes. She found them in her front trouser pocket where she'd stuffed them alongside her lighter, and proceeded to light one.

'If you don't make the move soon, he'll move on, and then it'll be too late. Bye-bye, Prince Charming. I promise you'll regret it if you don't!

In fact, I'm going to hang up now, and you can call him straight away. I expect to hear from you within the next half an hour with news of your arranged date. I'm not taking no for an answer, and neither should he. Okay?'

Amber could fight it, or she could strive for an easier life and just agree with her. She drew on her cigarette, curled her lower lip up to exhale smoke, and let out a low groan. She couldn't be bothered to argue with Claire.

'Okay,' was all she could summon the strength to say.

A brief pause hovered down the line, before Claire queried the response. *'Really?'* She hadn't expected her to cooperate so early into their conversation.

'Yeah, well, doesn't look like I have any other choice, does it?'

'That's the spirit! Right, I'll let you give your new man a ring, and I meant what I said about you calling me back straight away with all the deets! Ciao for now, bella!'

The line went dead, leaving Amber staring blankly out in front of her, the phone still pressed against her ear and her cigarette poised between her fingers. Her mind blank, she could think of no way out of this.

She sat like that for another minute, not sure of what she was supposed to be thinking. It was not a situation in which she had ever found herself before. But then, just as her therapist had stressed, she was in a position in life where she was free to latch onto new opportunities with zeal. If she didn't call Greig, would she feel any different? It was almost guaranteed that she would still be spending every day moping around her flat, unneeded and unloved, with no career, no companion, and no passion. Maybe it wouldn't hurt to seize the day for once.

Snapping her brain back into action, she stubbed out the cigarette with vehemence into the ashtray, and proceeded to scroll through her phone. She found the text message from Greig, and locked her eyes on the screen without really reading his words. It was now or never. All she had to do was make the call and open her mouth.

She sighed, her finger poised over the little call symbol beside his number, then relented. She tapped the button to connect the call.

After five or six rings, a voice sounded down the line.

'Hello?'

'Hi, Greig?'

'Yep?'

'Hi, it's Amber. From last night.'

'Amber, hi! How are you?'

She paused. Such a question, more of a greeting than it was an enquiry, did not need an honest response. But perhaps, she thought as a thin smile spread across her lips, there was no need for her to sugar-coat the truth at all. If

Jason could enjoy his new life with his precious girlfriend, then maybe it was about time Amber listened to the advice she had been given and allow herself to explore a little adventure of her own.

She leaned forward, resting her elbows on the surface of the table, and reached for her mug to cradle it for its lukewarmth. Her sudden enthusiasm, sincere as it was, had taken her so much by surprise that she struggled to mask the smile in her voice.

'You know, I'm good, thanks. Really good! I just thought I'd call and say that I got your message.'

She was certain about this, wasn't she? If she didn't start making the effort to do something with her life while it was still hers to live, then there was probably no point in being alive.

Carpe diem, Amber! She stressed in thought as a palm went up to her forehead, a gesture of what she could only have described as self-disbelief. S*eize the day!*

'And I was just thinking that, if it's still on the table, I'd very much like to take you up on your offer. Coffee sounds like a really good idea!'

Chapter Six

It was possible that eternal happiness was highly overrated. To be constantly smiling, permanently content with life across each and every one of the twenty-four hours of every single day, was surely counterproductive; there would never be any genuine appreciation for that unexpected delight that could occasionally rear its oft scarpering head.

Oh, she knew there would be a rapid decline soon enough. She'd reached the peak, and couldn't remain there forever. However, the sudden arrival of prosperity in her mood was so refreshing that she had made a conscious decision to lap up every second of it that she could. It would be over quickly enough, so she might as well make the most of it while it was still hers to enjoy.

She was treading on eggshells though, and she was all too aware of that. One slip and it would all tumble away from her. The last time she had felt this elated had been when she was babysitting the puppy next door while the neighbours were on holiday. Rover, the tiny beagle, was a soft bundle of adorable soppiness, and had smothered her with wet licking kisses; it was the affection she had needed so soon after she had been abandoned by the man she had been so sure she would spend the rest of his life with, and his tiny whimpering and delicate nuzzles left a smile on her face. But then the neighbours returned, Rover had to go back home, and suddenly the void in Amber's life seemed only to expand. She remained comatose for several days after that, and had only managed to pull herself some way out of the darkness when she made the concrete decision to seek help. That was the point in her struggle when Jo came in, and whether or not forcing herself into therapy was the right thing to do, Amber had to conclude that it was better than doing nothing at all.

Ignoring the inevitable downfall, she could think of no better way to bask in this brief contentment than with a large glass of wine as she lounged on the sofa. It was almost nine o'clock in the evening, little under twelve hours since she'd returned Greig's message, and so unaccustomed as she was to being out of her bed at this time of night that she took great delight in sitting back and listening to classical music on the radio while doing nothing and thinking nothing.

At the very least, living in that moment alone allowed her to focus less on her failed relationship and her redundancy and her lack of human interaction and prospects, and more on the fruity, vinegary aroma of her glass of red.

She gulped down another mouthful and swirled the liquid around in its deep bowl, then leaned her head backwards to rest it on the back of the sofa. She shivered as she did so, her midriff exposing itself as her pyjama top rode up. The nights were becoming increasingly impossible to handle as the frosty chill filtered its way into the building through every crack and opening that it could find.

For a moment, Amber considered turning on the radiator – which was inconveniently situated directly behind her; a poor location, she realised, since all of the heat would be trapped against the back of the sofa – but she was a pauper now, wasn't she? She couldn't afford to waste money on gas for something as luxurious as central heating. A hot water bottle and a thick fleecy blanket would have to do instead.

Bracing herself for the upheaval, she swigged down the dregs of her wine, deposited the glass on the table in front of her, then hauled her weary weight upright. She staggered, not from the alcohol but as a result of the anxiety-induced brain fog that seemed to be ever present, and reached for the cardigan she'd left hanging on the handle of the living room door.

She'd just about managed to wedge her arm into the

second sleeve and pull the material around her chest when the solid noise of pounding on wood punched through her brain.

'What the...?'

When she didn't move, it sounded again. She found her bearings, located the direction in which the noise was coming from, and realised then that there was somebody at the door. It was such a rarity nowadays for her to have any visitors that she had quite forgotten what that sounded like.

'Oh, go away,' she muttered to herself as she reached for the stereo remote to shunt Ethel Smyth's soothing *Serenade in D* into an abrupt silence. She shuffled, not expeditiously, towards the front door, flicking on the hall light as she went.

She squinted as the brightness intruded her natural vision. It was probably best if she didn't direct her attention towards the mirror that hung in the doorway; nobody looked good beneath garish lighting, least of all when their hair was tousled in a disarray and their baggy pyjamas hung off their awkward, angular frame. Just head straight for the door, she told herself, and find out who it was who had chosen so brashly to interrupt her peaceful evening.

She turned the key, pushed down the handle, and pulled back the door.

It took Amber all her concentration to make sure her jaw did not slack as her eyes widened in disbelief. Had she felt

58

any inclination about whom her visitor may have been, her guess would have been way off.

Way, way off.

'Jason?' The name escaped from her lips as little more than a whisper.

Jason smiled awkwardly as he rocked back on his heels, his hands stuffed firmly in the front pockets of his jeans.

'Hi, Amber,' he replied as he reached up a hand to scratch at the back of his head. Was he nervous? Any onlookers would never have suspected that they had once been an item, so happily in love and carefree in each other's company. In that moment, they may as well have been two complete strangers meeting for the first time.

With Amber too frozen to utter anything further, Jason sucked in air through his teeth and forced a smile upon his lips. 'Mind if I come in?'

If, during his journey to her flat, Jason had predicted that Amber would welcome him into her home with open arms, he would have been severely mistaken.

She had granted him permission enough to step over the threshold into the hallway, where they stood together now, both forced together beneath the spotlight of the unshielded bulb of the ceiling light. Amber's arms were folded firmly across her chest, her face a mask to the genuine agony that now coursed through. She had been unprepared for this encounter; there had been no time to build a barrier against the barrage of emotions that had been induced without warning by Jason's visit. For so many months now she had been desperate to see him, longing to hear his voice again, yearning for his touch, but there was something about this sudden appearance that just didn't feel right. She didn't feel the way she imagined she would have done, though she had no idea why.

'What are you doing here?' she managed at last. The words came out more forcefully than she had intended, but she was in shock, and not thinking straight. Perhaps not able to even think at all. Nothing Jason could say to her in that moment could possibly comprehend.

'Look, Amber,' Jason replied as he rubbed at an ache in his shoulder, 'can we go into the living room and sit down or something?' He shifted uncomfortably on the spot.

Amber hesitated, genuinely considering his request for a moment, but then realised that she didn't actually wish to bring Jason any deeper into her own personal space. No, she couldn't have him contaminating the place after she'd spent so many gruelling days and nights trying to disinfect it of the memories they had once shared.

'No. No, I don't think that would be a good idea,' she said, shaking her head without once meeting his eyes.

'Whatever you have to say to me can be said out here.'

A heavy sigh fell from Jason's parted mouth. He dropped his hand from his shoulder and let it swing down by his side again, admitting defeat. There was no point in pushing Amber to cooperate with him. This was going to be hard enough as it was, without actively seeking to make it worse.

He needed to stand his ground though and hoped she couldn't detect how uncomfortable he felt. He would have to be as blunt as possible with her, show her she couldn't affect him. He didn't want to be there any more than she undoubtedly wanted him standing in front of her, but it had to be done. It was best to do this quickly and painlessly, like ripping off a sticky plaster.

Yes, like ripping off a plaster to expose an infected, seeping wound that had for so long been starved of oxygen beneath the itchy fabric, itching and prickling as it repeatedly tried and failed to fully heal.

'Right. Well, I guess there's no easy way to say this, so I'll just come out with it. The thing is, Victoria and I are having a baby.'

The news sliced through Amber like a serrated butcher's knife through a slab of melting butter. The seamless incision that cut straight through her heart was enough to force her into a stagger as she threw a hand out to the side in a feeble attempt to regain her balance. She stepped backwards as she pressed her palm weakly against the wall, and brought her other hand to her chest, where she could feel her heartbeat pounding against her thin skin.

'I—I don't understand,' she murmured. It was all she could manage to say as her eyes swam around inside of her head.

Jason puffed out his cheeks as his own gaze wandered about the hallway, glancing in any direction that wasn't towards Amber. He exhaled, almost not quite believing his own words. 'Victoria's pregnant. About three months now.'

Deep breaths, Amber. She couldn't let Jason think he could affect her this way. It was just shock, that was all this was. Nothing to worry about. It would pass quickly enough. It had to.

She straightened herself up, smoothed down her pyjama top. 'What does that have to do with me?' she asked as she angled her head towards the carpet in a bid to feign nonchalance. She was sure she could successfully look disinterested – after all, it was the truth that she really couldn't care less about that stupid bitch Victoria – but if Jason noticed her watering eyes then he was bound to get the wrong impression. The fool that he was. 'Do you think I give a fuck if that stupid little tart has got herself knocked up?'

'Amber, please don't speak about Vick like that. You

know that none of this was her fault—'

'Oh, don't give me that bullshit!' Amber retorted, suddenly too angered to remember that she was supposed to be displaying a lack of concern about any cheap and sleazy affair that now existed in her *former* partner's life.

Jason, who was becoming more agitated by the minute, took a moment to inhale, focusing his attention inwards. This shouldn't be this complicated. It was late, he was tired, and he just wanted to get what he came for then get the hell away from there.

'Look, I don't want another argument. I just came here to ask you for something, and then I'll be on my way.'

An unsettling pause hung in the air as neither Jason, who was too scared to spit it straight out for fear of causing a further argument, nor Amber, who was too nervous to discover what he was there for, was able to speak.

In the end, it was Amber who eventually took the leap.

'What do you want?'

It was a simple question, usually harmless, but occasionally it was enough to tear apart an entire life.

'Do you remember that cardigan my mother knitted when you were…well, the one she knitted a while back. Yeah, I'd like that back. Please. For the baby.'

The tension that smothered the hallway the moment the words had left Jason's mouth was so thick that Amber could almost taste the bitterness in the back of her throat. She curled her upper lip in disgust, no longer worried about what Jason had to say to her. No, she wasn't worried at all. She was just plain angry.

'No way! No fucking way! How *dare* you come here and ask me that?! That cardigan belonged to our baby!'

'You know that was never the case. Not really. And I was just as upset that we lost the baby as you were—'

'*Were*?!'

Jason held his hands out in front of him to try and calm Amber down, but there was no chilling the aggro as she snapped away from him.

'I'm *still* upset, you heartless bastard! There's not a night that I don't think about him!'

'I understand that, Amber, I really do. But I know my mother would like our baby – mine and Vick's baby – to wear the cardigan. It's her first grandchild. It would mean a lot to her.'

Knowing he was taking a risk, Jason stepped closer towards Amber and reached out, as would a wary stranger reaching to pet an unknown dog, to place a hand on her arm.

'Come on, now. It's no use to anybody if it's just sitting gathering dust in a box somewhere. Don't be unreasonable—'

Amber's entire body flinched backwards with such ferocity that Jason found himself startled.

'Excuse me?! *Unreasonable*?! I'm not the one being fucking unreasonable! That cardigan belonged to my son! *Our* son, you fucking...!' She paused, steadying her racing heart, before regaining momentum to yell, 'Get out! Go on! Get the fuck out of my house!'

She lunged forwards, thwacking her palms against his chest and forcing him to stumble towards the door. He crashed into the back of it as Amber fumbled for the handle. It didn't hurt him, not physically, but the bruise on his feelings that she had inflicted would linger for a while.

'Amber, come on, this isn't right,' he pleaded as she shoved him out of the way. She swung the front door open, letting it bash against the wall with no concern for what her neighbours might think of the unusual disorder of the late evening.

'Don't you dare talk to me about what's right, you lying, cheating, selfish arsehole!' Every word seethed out through gritted teeth. It was almost out of a fear for his own wellbeing that Jason backed out of the hallway and back over the threshold to the other side of the door, convinced that Amber would begin frothing at the mouth at any moment.

Amber's shouts grew louder as Jason shuffled away, not turning his back on her until he was forced to turn the corner onto the main path. Her eyes grimaced at she yelled after him, even after he had finally disappeared out of sight, rushing off into the night's darkness.

'I hope you and your precious slut of a girlfriend are happy together! Lord knows you don't deserve it though!'

The crescendo concluded with an almighty crash as she slammed the door shut, trapping the outside world on the other side as the rush of energy she'd felt only moments before now drained from her.

In an exhausted state of temporary delirium, she managed to summon up enough strength to slump her way through to the bedroom and pull open the wardrobe doors, before she felt her entire body give in and drop down onto the carpet beneath her.

There she remained for what would have been only a few minutes, but for Amber the passing of time was presently an unknown and irrelevant concept. Fat, heavy tears spilled down her cheeks as her heart pounded furiously in her chest. Her surroundings could not penetrate her thoughts as the dense fog of her depression absorbed her mind. She could see nothing but darkness, could feel nothing but pain.

It was only once a sliver of reality from a narrow recess in her brain managed to infiltrate through the chaos of her thoughts that her heartrate slowed and her breathing became less erratic. Any suggestion of the contentment she'd felt earlier that evening, however, was long since restorable.

As Amber scrabbled to rest her back against the side of

the bed, pulling her knees up around her as she wrapped her arms around her legs, only then was she able to collect her thoughts with the memory of why she had started for the bedroom in the first place.

The wardrobe still stood wide open in front of her. Its contents – the clothes, the shoes, the handbags and belts that had been scattered beneath the railing in a disarray – were displayed for full observation, but it was only the shelf lowest down that fixed Amber's attention.

She leaned forward and shifted her weight from her bottom as she rested her knees on the rough carpet. Almost without expression, she pulled back the thin summer blankets that lived for most of the year on the bottom shelf, revealing in their wake a small shoebox.

As she lifted the shoebox out and placed it in her lap, she had no thoughts for the Prada heels, all shiny and bright, that were once held inside of it. They were from a different time, a different life. Inside the box now was something so much more precious than anything money could buy.

The lid was removed with care and placed on the floor beside her, unleashing the memories from within. Amber couldn't bring herself to handle the contents immediately, but instead stared blankly down at them as she felt every emotion at once and yet somehow also remaining numb to feeling anything at all.

A small shiver raced through her, coaxing her to reach into the box. She knew what she was looking for.

Several months had passed since she had last handled the cardigan, but now, as she separated it from the other tiny articles she'd purchased for her baby and lifted it in her arms, it felt like it had never left her. It was the first garment her son had ever owned. Even though it was designed for a child of three to six months, they had planned to wrap him up in it when it was time to bring him home from the hospital. Back when they were a *they,* and not the single, lonely *I* her life had become.

But her baby had never made it into the world to wear his cardigan. Holding it in her arms was the closest she would ever come to cradling her dead child.

As the image of his tiny corpse forced its way uninvited to the front of her thoughts, it was too much for Amber, in her fragile state, to handle. She doubled over, a sharp pain soaring from the pit of her stomach, lurching straight through her heart, and lodging in her throat in the guise of an inaudible wail.

She rocked the cardigan back and forth as she clutched it to her chest, her own body creased in half as she rested her torso against her thighs. She couldn't pick herself up. Didn't care about calming herself down. She trembled as her entire existence seemed to shake through the internal, uncontrollable agony. With the garment firmly clasped in her hands, she could do nothing but sob with grief as she mourned the loss of her baby whose nose she would never kiss, whose laugh she would never hear, whose life would never be lived.

Chapter Seven

The one silver lining that came with an emotional breakdown was that, for Amber at least, a long and unbroken sleep would almost always follow in its wake to curb her body, if not her mind, of its exhaustion. Her dreamless rest had been undisturbed, and her mind didn't dare to wake her until she surfaced naturally in the early afternoon of the following day.

When she finally did crawl out from under the covers, the sky was overcast, but since the curtains remained closed the heavy clouds made little difference to her already darkened mood. If it wasn't for the fact that the tiny frosted window in the bathroom allowed in only a little light anyway, she wouldn't have bothered to turn on any of the house lights. As it happened though, she was too weary and bleary eyed to grapple around in the dark for her toothbrush, and so decided it would be best instead to risk flicking on the main light above her.

Even the weak strength of the cheap lightbulb was enough to force her to clamp her eyes shut in protest as it cast a sickly yellow wash over her already sallow skin. Not overly concerned about anything as trivial in her existence as the cleaning of teeth, she brushed and spat just the once, all the while keeping her attention firmly on the sink below. When she returned the toothbrush to its holder though, and made to reach for her daily dose of drugs from the medicine cabinet, she was forced to confront her own face in the ungainly reflection.

The taut skin of her cheeks was mottled with rash-like red blotches, one of the more flippant side effects that surfaced whenever Amber's stress had peaked. She ignored it, and prodded a finger at each of the puffy bags beneath her eyes. It would take more than a night of unbroken sleep to reduce the dark circles that made her eyes look sunken and lifeless. There was no spark in them anymore, and there hadn't been for a long time. Their dullness, which Jo had assured Amber would only be temporary, looked to be a permanent fixture of her vacant expression.

But that lack of emotion displayed in her features was only artificial, a pretence that took her no effort to uphold. On the surface she may have appeared to not feel anything at all, but inside her, locked away against the consumption of those around her, she was a river of pain and agony and

71

heartache. It was only her magic little pills that were able to numb them, and prevent them from surfacing in a reality in which they did not fit.

As she retrieved the bottle from the cabinet, she wondered whose benefit that was for. The doctor assured her that the pills would help her to block away the torments of her mind, and on a good day that seemed to be the case; if nothing else, they *did* keep them at bay, ensuring the emotions remained buried from sight. But surely feeling nothing at all was far worse than feeling something real, no matter how difficult it was to face?

She unscrewed the cap of the bottle, tipped her routine dose into her outstretched palm, and stared down at them. With each popped pill she felt increasingly dehumanised. Maybe it was all a ruse. This numbed existence was her punishment for her failures, and merely prevented her emotional outbursts from making others feel uncomfortable. People would enforce anything to assure their happy little minds that they didn't have to deal with the mentally unstable woman and her unfixable woes.

With the pills clasped in one hand, she turned on the tap with the other, and filled a cup with water. The liquid looked clear through the glass, but Amber couldn't help wondering what monstrosities lurked in there that remained naked to the human eye. Not that it mattered; filling her body with a few more toxins or invisible little insects wasn't going to do her any more damage than that that had already crippled her.

She drew the glass to her lips to take a sip of the soothing water before necking her pills, but paused with the rim of the glass pressed lightly against her mouth. She had been swallowing these tiny tablets day in, day out, for months now, and for what reason? Quite simply, she'd taken them because somebody had told her to. Her doctor, whom she had met only a handful of times and who was in reality a stranger to her, had prescribed the medication for her without really knowing anything about her. How could these little white pills, which she now studied closely in her flexed hand, claim to help so many people when their ailments varied so greatly?

It didn't seem right. She was being instructed to feel not like herself but like a machine, trudging through her pointless existence with neither purpose nor interest. Unless the power of her grief was strong enough to push through the medicinal barrier, as it had done so the previous night, it was no use. She was existing as a robot, and little more.

'Aargh!'

The cry escaped from Amber's lips with little effort as she groaned into her clasped fists. She doubled over to rest her arm on the sink, and dropped her forehead down onto her forearm. She was going round in circles: every day was a repeat of the previous, nothing changing, nothing ever getting any better.

She may have lost many things in recent months, but one thing Amber knew she was entitled to was her own ability to feel raw emotions. She may not have full control over them, but they were hers, as wild and unruly as they threatened to be. At least they had once been her own, but had since been stolen from her.

Not for any longer though. It was time for her to take them back.

She had made her decision. She couldn't go back on it now; she needed to prove to herself that she could stay true to her own thoughts. This was the right thing to do, she was certain of that much. Straightening her back, she loosened the grip of her fists. The pills clanked against the sink as they tumbled out of her hand and down the plughole. With a little shake of the bottle after she swooped for it from beside the sink, the remainder of her prescription spilled out, tumbling down and clattering against the porcelain. They swirled around in the water as it gushed from the tap, sending each tiny pill spiralling down the plughole, racing through the drain, and out of Amber's life forever.

Without further thought, she twisted off the tap, threw the empty bottle back into the medicine cabinet, slammed the door shut, and stormed out of the bathroom. What fresh pain the future had in store for her, she didn't know, but at least she would actually be able to feel again. Whatever she would be forced to face, she would do it with her own honest thoughts. Her emotions would once again be her own, and there was nothing anybody could say or do to encourage her to relinquish her unexpected rebirth; at last the numbing inside of her could subside, and in its wake there would finally be room for her true nature to surface.

Chapter Eight

The café that was once known to Amber as 'the café down the road' had quickly come to be known to her as 'that café near Jason's house that was now several miles away from where she slept each night following their separation'. Admittedly, she knew it didn't have the same ring to it. However, she refused to think of it as anything other than her local humble eatery; it still held fond memories for her, and for Jason too it seemed as he still frequented there most weekends.

He still popped in some evenings after work for a coffee while he caught up with his emails, but Amber didn't always have the energy to leave the house to find out if that was the case every day. Still, there was no reason why she shouldn't continue to go there when it pleased her to as well, and at the end of the day it was the perfect place for her to meet Greig for coffee.

The week preceding their first proper date, if she was prepared to call it such, had passed with little difference to any other in recent months. The days were still slow, perhaps even more than usual as her most recent breakdown had distorted her sense of time, damaging her body clock and ruining her ability to sleep for more than a few hours at a time.

In the first few days after the fateful encounter with her former lover, she had been able to think of nothing other than Jason's unborn child. Both her waking thoughts and broken nightmares alike were plagued with her resentment. By midweek though she had become too exhausted to think about very much at all. If she wasn't hibernating beneath a blanket, curled up in a ball in a bid to force her mind to switch off, she was knocking back oversized mugs of extra-strong coffee to prevent her eyelids from constantly drooping shut.

The prospect of proper coffee was one of the more dominant reasons she had been able to drag herself out of the house at all. She had considered cancelling the occasion, but in the end she couldn't bring herself to do it; disappointing Greig would only make her feel guilty, and she couldn't afford to increase her anxiety where it could be avoided.

She had managed to bundle some clothes into the washing machine the day before, and decided to pair some loose dark-blue jeans with a cream knitted jumper she'd had for more years than she cared to remember. There was a slight hint of makeup on her cheeks and about her eyes, just enough to make her resemble a little less akin to a lacklustre zombie.

It was a relief to her that Greig was in a chirpy mood when they finally met up. Her mother would have said he could have talked the hind legs off a donkey, whatever that meant, as he sat opposite her in the café, chattering on about the weather and his journey to the café and the quality of the hot chocolate he'd ordered.

The verdict on that last one, he'd concluded, was beyond satisfactory. Amber was admittedly enjoying her own cappuccino, bought by Greig at his own insistence, as a rare and luscious delight. So used to cheap supermarket own-brand granules as she was that it was a treat to enjoy a cup of steaming hot proper coffee. She inhaled the addictive aromas as she cradled the cup.

The ambient atmosphere in the café was as always unrivalled, but she was beginning to regret her decision to choose a table for them by the window that looked out onto the main street; a gush of wind blasted in their direction whenever the main door to the café opened to let in another stream of customers. Still, at least they were tucked away in the corner, cut off from the majority of the rest of the room.

She shivered as a pack of youths stumbled in to seek out their own caffeine hits, then took a sip of her own bittersweet drink. If only in those few seconds as the hot liquid raced down her throat, nothing seemed to matter. She was utterly immersed in the moment of temporary relief.

Greig wiped a smudge of whipped cream from his upper lip with the back of his hand, then leaned closer into the table. There was a nervousness amidst his jolly chattering that made Amber sense that there was something naturally quite vulnerable about him. Whereas she was just glad to finally have a reason to drag herself out of the house, this meeting – or date – clearly meant a lot to Greig.

Maybe it meant something to her too. She was just too drained to see anything that lay beyond her exhaustion.

'You know,' Greig finally said, breaking the silence that hovered awkwardly between them, 'I'm really glad you agreed to meet me.'

'Me too,' Amber replied. She'd made a mental note to routinely check that she was smiling at him, before glancing back down at the table to fiddle with a stray packet of sugar that had been discarded there by a previous diner.

'I must admit though, this isn't something I normally do. I mean, meeting random girls in clubs, and then…well, you don't need me to tell you what else happened! You were there!'

Greig's face beamed as he tucked the wooden chair a little closer into the table. As Amber glanced back up to meet his attention, attempting to pull her drifting mind back into the conversation, his eyes panicked as he rushed to finish his thought.

'Not that I think you're just some random girl or anything! I just mean that, you know…oh, I don't know! You know what I mean. Don't you?'

The genuine concern in his intonation went unnoticed as Amber remained distant, flicking the sugar packet back and forth with her fingers as her eyes were locked on the surface of the table.

Greig slumped. 'You don't know, do you? Have I put my foot in it? I have, haven't I?'

It was then, as the worry in Greig's voice couldn't have gone unnoticed, that Amber realised she hadn't been paying any attention to a word he'd said. She dropped the sugar packet, snapping her mind back to the company in front of her.

'No. No! You haven't, you haven't done that. Don't worry!'

A waitress, a petite faux redhead with a traditional black-and-white apron strapped around her waist, sidled up to the table, unwittingly causing a welcomed distraction. She deposited a plate in front of Greig, accepted his gratitude, then left the pair to dine in peace.

Greig lifted up his spoon and nodded his head in a gesture towards the hearty triangle of Victoria sponge. 'Looks lovely! Are you sure you don't want a bit of this?'

Amber shook her head. 'No, really. I'm okay. But thank you.'

Truthfully, she couldn't stomach the idea of eating anything that was richer or any denser than the occasional slice of dry toast she'd been nibbling on recently. It had taken her a little while to notice any side effects of stopping her medication cold turkey, but after a few days there surfaced a combination of nausea and a suppressed appetite. Along with the odd spell of dizziness that caught her unawares now and then, that was all she seemed to have experienced so far. That could all change very quickly though, so she had to count her blessings while she still could.

'Mmm, well, it's really good. You're missing out!' Greig mumbled through a mouthful of cake. Specks of glistening sugar tickled at the sides of his mouth, and Amber couldn't help finding it mildly amusing.

'So,' Greig continued once he swallowed, 'the ultimate cliché of a question! Have you, you know, been single for very long?'

Amber had to stifle a splutter. She felt like she'd been on her own for years, cast aside in her prime and abandoned to rot into old age. In reality, it hadn't been very long at all, but then was linear time ever really an accurate measure for heartache?

'Um…almost…a year,' she replied, pretending to calculate the length of time in her head, as if she wasn't aware that Jason had discarded her from his life exactly eight months, three weeks, and four days ago to the date.

Greig pressed his lips together and nodded slowly. 'Yep, pretty much the same here. A little over a year now for me. Was it serious, your last relationship?'

Amber opened her mouth to speak, but quickly snapped it shut. If she told him the truth, then it was very likely that he'd end up probing her for the details. But she wasn't prepared to discuss her relationship with Jason, at least not with anybody who wasn't her therapist, and certainly not with this man who was still little more than a stranger to her. She spent enough time opening up her wounds with Jo; it was probably best if she just let it lie, and sugar-coated things a little.

'No, not really. Yours?' she replied. It wasn't entirely a lie; after all, not *everybody* in the relationship had taken it seriously.

A squeak of nervous laughter fluttered from Greig's lips. He studied intently the surface of his hot chocolate, watching the drooping marshmallows melting into the hot liquid as if seeking in them the right answer to his own question.

'Well, we were married, me and Mindy, so I guess you could call that pretty serious! Not that there was much love between us towards the end. But I guess that when you've been with the same person for so long it does feel a little strange being back out in the dating game like this. I'm not usually one for picking up girls I've never met before. My cousin, the one I was with at the club, he's quite a bit younger than me. He thought it'd be fun to challenge me to a drinking competition, and, well…I was going to say I completely lost that challenge, but then…'

Greig furrowed his eyebrows, contemplating his next words, before finishing his thought, his eyes softer and his tone more gentle. 'Now I'm not so sure that's entirely the case.'

He rested his elbows on the surface of the table and clasped his hands together, admiring his undeserved prize in front of him. When he noticed Amber's flat, distant expression, however, he pushed himself back into his chair.

'You seem a little down. Are you okay?' he asked. Then, without allowing any time for a response, the paranoia kicked in. 'Oh! Is it me? Sorry, am I…Am I not what you remembered from the club?'

Amber's hand rushed up to her mouth as a splutter of cappuccino flew from her lips. She used the back of her hand to wipe away the lukewarm dribble from her chin, struggling to control her unexpected chuckling.

'Oh gosh! I'm so sorry! No, I didn't mean that at all! That was so rude of me. Sorry! It's just that, oh God, I can't remember anything from the club that night at all!'

She nibbled at her lower lip as she tried to ignore the prickling certainty that she was now blushing.

She composed herself, wiping away a watery tear of laughter from her eye. 'Honestly, I had a lot to drink that night, and quite a bit of it is still a little fuzzy. But I'm fine. I promise. Everything's fine.' And then reality came crashing back down, stamping away any lingering amusement. 'My mind's just a little elsewhere today,' she admitted.

'Anything I can help with?' Greig's hand twitched as if struggling to resist the temptation to reach out and grab onto Amber's own fingers as they rested on the surface of the table. She noticed this, and quickly picked up her mug as a deterrent.

She shook her head. 'Just family stuff. It'll sort itself out soon enough.'

The café door opened again as two elderly women waddled in, causing a brief welcomed distraction. They disappeared towards the counter, and Amber turned back to face Greig. She was about to divert the conversation down a different path, when he spoke before she had a chance to decide on a new, safe topic.

It was becoming quickly apparent that Greig wasn't too fussed about divulging his personal information on a first date. Either that, or he was usually much more reserved than this, and he simply found Amber to be easier to talk to than anybody else he'd ever dated. She didn't know which it was, and right now she didn't really care to find out either. Still, at least it meant that she didn't have to think of too much to say if all of their energies were concentrated on Greig's problems instead of hers.

'If it makes you feel any better, I know exactly what it's like!' Greig assured her, oddly doing so with a smile still stretched across his face. 'Mindy's constantly on my case if I haven't sent her the maintenance money on time. You'd think my daughter—'

Amber's stomach knotted. Her warm coffee threatened to clog up her throat as she gulped down another bittersweet mouthful.

'You have a daughter?'

'Yep, I do indeed. Her name's Emily. She'll be six next month. Here, I have a picture with me…'

Amber's eyes shifted as Greig fished into his back pocket for his wallet. He pulled it out, and opened it up for Amber to see inside.

Sure enough, the photo window beside the card slots

displayed the pearly-white smile and blonde plaits of a little girl. She looked so happy as she posed in front of the camera, one hand on her hip and the other clutching to the hem of her summer dress. She was a vision of childhood innocence.

'She's gorgeous,' Amber whispered. Her eyes remained transfixed on the photo until Greig folded the wallet back up.

'I certainly think so!' He stuffed the wallet back into his pocket, then returned his hands to his drink. He swallowed a mouthful, then continued: 'We were so thrilled when we found out Mindy was pregnant. Admittedly this isn't exactly what I had always imagined family life would be like, all this living apart from my own child and everything, but Emily's my world.'

'Yes, I…I can imagine.'

And, as Amber was all too aware, imagine was all she could do. Unlike Greig, she would never truly know the unconditional love of her own child.

As Greig scooped up cake crumbs with his fingertips and sucked on them contently, a heavy silence hung in the air that surrounded Amber. She didn't know what else to say. She didn't know how she was supposed to respond to the situation. Was it even a situation? Not really. Not for anybody other than Amber, who was realising that what was normal for everybody else would never be normal for her.

She longed to change the subject, to remove herself as

far away as possible from her own childless existence, and yet there was a part of her, a feeling that she hadn't expected, that craved this conversation. There was nobody else in her life with whom she could talk about babies and infants and children until her heart's content. As much as she needed to take flight, her mind was firmly rooted.

'I take it you don't have any children then?' Greig asked after washing down the crumbs with another hearty glug of hot chocolate.

With her head cocked to one side by way of physical response, it looked as though Amber was considering the words that were about to leave her mouth. It was nothing but a wish, a silent plea, that she could answer differently.

But then she'd be lying only to herself if she fabricated some fictitious truth.

'No. No, I don't, unfortunately.' *My child died before he could see the world*, she refrained from adding.

'Oh, they're great!' Greig chimed, understandably unaware of the sadness that lurked deep within Amber's heart. 'You mentioned that you were a teacher, didn't you? I suppose you probably have enough kids to deal with every day; having to run after other people's snivelling children would certainly be enough to put me off having any of my own! But they can be a lot of fun, can't they? Emily, she's a great kid. So full of this youthful innocence, you know? She's always full of these nonsensical stories, but so fun, so enlightening to be around.' Greig emitted a sound akin to something halfway between a chuckle and a sigh. 'Really, you should head down to the baby factory and get yourself one!'

It was a joke, and nothing more. A fleeting moment of humour intended to make her smile. But for Amber, it was the words she had unwittingly been waiting to hear.

Maybe there was no such thing as a baby factory, but that didn't mean that Amber was entirely out of options. She would soon be past her prime, was still single, at least until the verdict of this date was revealed, and if she wanted a child of her own then she was going to have to think about what actions she could feasibly take to ensure her own happiness. As a lightbulb lit up from somewhere in the back of her mind, a sliver of a smile reached across her lips. She lifted her drink towards her face, and met Greig's gaze with her own wide eyes as she stared across the rim of the mug.

'You know, maybe I should do just that,' she spoke softly before taking a sip.

Greig beamed back at her, elated in her company. He mirrored her actions as he lifted his mug to salvage the remaining melted marshmallows, blissfully oblivious to the darkness that had without warning begun to take hold of his companion.

Chapter Nine

The curtains were parted just enough for Amber to peer out onto the main street, coating the kitchen in an almost colourless hue. She refused to turn on the main light though. It came as no surprise to her when she had barely slept, but for once it wasn't insomnia that had taken hold, instead finding herself overcome with a burning desire to purge all of her thoughts for her new project.

She had been up most of the night scribbling down the specifics of her new plan as and when they came to her. Her eyes were bloodshot, and they stung every time she blinked; having little light in her life just now was precisely how she needed it to be.

Angling her torso so that she could no longer see out of the window, Amber let the curtain drop back down, closed her eyes tightly, and took a long drag on her cigarette. Her attention was fixed firmly internally as she exhaled towards the ceiling, sending a cloud of smoke into the room. She had lost herself in that moment, her mind as blind to her surroundings as were her closed eyes: she could pretend the sink wasn't full of dirty mugs and wine glasses; she didn't need to think about the unpaid bills that were piling up on the table by the door, their envelopes still unopened. Inside her mind there was nothing, nobody, and nowhere. Nobody to impress, nothing to believe. No battles to be fought and won. It was her own dark, solitary existence and only in there could she be truly content.

By the time she opened her eyes again, the smoke had faded entirely from around her, stealing with it any sense of Amber's internal escape. Everything around her became animated as she was forced once more to face the reality of her feeble existence.

She flicked ash from the end of her cigarette into the metal sink, where it mingled with the cremated remains of the pages of her notebook. She may have been an amateur, but she had seen enough crime dramas to know that she needed to destroy any evidence of her plotting if she didn't want to risk being found out. It had been surprisingly therapeutic, watching her former partner's name curling and burning into a worthless pile of ash and cindered flecks of paper.

The sentiment was short lived though, as, as soon as the remaining page of evidence had disappeared in front of her, she knew she now needed to prepare herself to set the next stage of her plan into action. She was keen to advance with it, of course she was, but she was also incredibly anxious.

At least she was feeling something akin to real emotion though, she thought as she stabbed the butt of her cigarette into the sink before washing it down the drain with the rest of the ash. If nothing else, she should be pleased about that. This is exactly what she'd wanted: to be able to feel real, human emotions again. And who didn't enjoy being enveloped in waves of bitterness, wrath, and resentment?

Besides, this was the card with which she had been dealt, and there was nothing she could do about it. Even if she ever did wish to start taking her antidepressants again, which, as she frequently needed to reassure herself, she definitely did not, it would have been no use. She wouldn't be in a position to get any more medication so soon. She'd thrown almost two months' worth of those little white pills into the basin and straight down the plughole; there was no way her doctor would prescribe her any more just now. It wouldn't have been for want of trying either. She recalled a panic-inducing morning two, maybe three, months ago when she hadn't been able to locate the prescription she'd just the day before picked up from the chemist. She'd rummaged in her handbag, almost tore the house apart as she struggled to find them. She'd admitted defeat and ended up pleading down the phone to the surgery in a fretful state, desperate for them to issue her with a fresh prescription. But they wouldn't. For all they knew, she could just be trying her luck, planning to do herself some lasting damage. Of course, they didn't phrase it like that, but the implication was crystal clear.

To Amber's relief, after several hours of frantic pacing and uncontrollable nervous fidgeting, she finally stumbled upon her prescription by chance in the washing basket. How it got there, she had no idea still to this day, but she was too relieved to think too much into it. But had she not been able to find the prescription, she would have been well and truly screwed.

That was all in the past though. She needed to think more progressively. As she brushed her fringe back from her forehead, she puffed out her cheeks, bored and frustrated with the unseasonable heat that seemed to be sticking to her skin, then reached for her phone from the table. She leaned back against the kitchen counter, resting her weight into it as she scrolled through her messages.

There was one there from Greig, attempting to arrange another date; they had both individually taken to calling it such, which had to be a good sign. She tapped out a quick reply to provide him with her availability – something in which wasn't exactly lacking – then continued until she reached the most recent message.

The text told her only that there was a voicemail waiting for her. Correction: a*nother* voicemail. She didn't have to listen to it to know whom it was from, or what it was about, and she wasn't particularly interested in anything he had to say. All the same, she activated the message, switched it onto loud speaker, then dropped her phone onto the table while she reached with her hands free to light another cigarette.

The tinny sound of Jason's voice drifted out of the phone as he delivered what was his seventh attempt that week at trying to persuade Amber to return his calls.

'Amber, please call me back. Look, I know I've said this already, but I need to say it again. I'm sorry if I upset you the other day. Really, I am. You know fine well that it wasn't my intention. It's just that, you know...'

He paused to release an exasperated sigh, inducing in Amber a smirk of triumph that she felt no need to suppress. She forced the cigarette smoke to plume in front of her as Jason continued: *'I know this is difficult for you, but it's hard for me too. You must try and understand that. I was hoping we could maybe just be a bit more civil about all this—'*

'Fuck that!' Amber retorted. She flicked ash into the sink then nestled back against the counter with her arms folded over. Staring in the general direction of the phone, she let Jason continue with his drivelling.

'—and if you do change your mind about the cardigan, which I really hope you do, give me a ring. You've got my number, of course. Please, Amber. It's not for me. I don't want you to think that any of this is for me. Please, only think of the baby.'

Jason's voice went silent. The monotone of the voicemail menu kicked in, and Amber stretched out with her free hand to hit the keypad. Message deleted.

She knew then, with the aftermath of Jason's curdling tones, which had once been able to induce such sweet happiness in her, that she couldn't wait any longer. If she wanted to act as she had planned, then she was going to have to take that leap now, while she still had her nerve.

With her cigarette still poised vicariously between her fingers, she swigged down the dregs of cold coffee and slammed the empty mug down onto the table. She swung her bag over her shoulder and headed straight for the front door; she had nothing to lose, no reason to look back.

As she shoved the key into the lock of the door, she drew on her cigarette and snarled her upper lip. How strange it was to be so devoted to one person, only to become so sickened by the very sound of their voice in such a short space of time. He had damaged her, hurt her, dragged her down to Hell. For weeks Jo had tried to convince her that it wasn't her fault; maybe she was finally starting to believe that.

Turing her back on her home and heading out towards her car, Jason's voice lingered in Amber's thoughts.

'Oh, I'll think about the baby, alright. Don't you worry, sunshine,' she muttered to herself, with her eyes kept low on the ground, her lips twitching into a grin. 'In fact, I promise

I'll think about nothing else.'

Chapter Ten

Dauntingly high shelves, unnecessarily wide aisles, and a draught so bitter it could chill the bones even if the sun were bold and beaming. Would a DIY store be anything without them?

Not that Amber tended to frequent such places very often. In fact, she couldn't remember the last time she'd been in one. It was possible that decades had passed since she had last whizzed down those wide aisles, staring with equally eager eyes at entire rainbows of paint colours, stroking her fingers across extravagant patterns on rolls of wallpaper, and aimlessly pretending to open up drawers and cupboards with their array of decorative display handles. The trip would always finish off with a visit to the adjoining garden centre, where she would sniff the pretty pinks and purples of petunia petals, and dance around the snaking water hose that always discarded haphazardly on the ground. Everything could be seen as one great adventure in those days. There was so much play to be had as a child.

But Amber wasn't playing anymore. She'd never been more deadly serious about anything in all her years.

As she turned a corner and started down the next aisle, a middle-aged man was loitering in the centre, his shopping trolley outstretched from one side to the other. He seemed to be feigning ignorance as Amber approached him, not bothering to look up from the packet of screws he was fingering or make any attempt to move for her.

'Excuse me,' Amber muttered as she stopped dead in front of him. Still the man didn't shift. On a good day Amber couldn't stand ignorance; on this day she was in no mood at all to find the patience to deal with this moron. He had left her no choice but to barge straight past him.

'Have it your way then,' she grumbled, before she forced the end of the man's trolley to the side, causing it to bump with a clatter against a shelf of screwdriver heads.

'Oi!' The man's attention was suddenly snapped in her direction as he jerked his head around to lock his eyes on hers. 'Watch it!'

Without wasting another word on her, the man shoved his trolley back into its previous position then returned to his screws.

Amber froze to the spot, considering saying something

further. If there was one thing that made her blood boil, it was ignorance. How dare this man talk to her like that after so rudely choosing not to notice her in the first place!

With Amber already on edge, she felt herself beginning to seethe. With her fists clenched by her side, her fingers squeezing in and out, and her nails digging into her palms, she was ready to explode into a stream of expletives. Tell this unkindly stranger exactly what she thought of him. But then…

No. She couldn't cause a scene. She needed to avoid drawing attention to herself. Not here, not now.

With a deep, cleansing inhale, she turned her back and walked away. It was done reluctantly, but then she figured that it was probably best to do the right thing in this situation, no matter how against her wishes that went, than it was to do the wrong thing as she desired and risk scuppering her plans entirely.

She continued down the next few aisles, gathering together everything she needed as she reeled through her mental list. She wouldn't be able to come back to the shop again after today; the risk of frequent visits would be too great, so it was imperative that she didn't forget anything. Once she was satisfied that she'd checked everything off from her hastily formed list, she headed for the till, keeping her head down and her eyes to the ground as she snaked in and out of the other shoppers.

There was already a queue of people waiting at the only available till; she found this inconvenient at best, and deeply agitating at worst. She couldn't hang around for too long. The more time she spent there, the greater the likelihood that she would be noticed. Noticed by whom, it didn't matter; she needed to remain as inconspicuous as possible.

While she waited for the hefty number of customers in front of her to decrease, she fiddled with a button on her coat, twisting it round and round. The mutterings and idle conversations of the other shoppers around her were lost to Amber's ears as she withdrew into her own thoughts. The less she acknowledged reality, the less likely it was that reality would notice *her*.

After an age of waiting, it was time for her to bundle her purchases onto the conveyor belt. She dropped down the rope, the duct tape, and the cordless electric drill, along with a few smaller miscellaneous items that she'd scooped together into a pile, and waited some more while the cashier began scanning each item in turn. She did this without once giving Amber so much as a glance, not because she was concentrating effectively on beeping in the purchases, but because, quite simply, she was fed up and lacking in any skills for human interaction.

However, while such poor customer service would

typically aggravate Amber, it worked out well for her on this occasion. Her eyes shifted around her, making sure nobody was looking her way. It was only when the final item had been scanned through the till that the cashier paid her a sliver of attention. She mumbled the total cost of the items in Amber's general direction, then angled her head slightly towards her.

'How are you paying?' she grunted.

From start to finish, this was the part of her trip that Amber had most rehearsed. There was only one answer to the question, only one way that would eliminate any chance of her purchase being traced back to her. She turned to the cashier, looked her dead set in the eyes, and replied without hesitation.

'Cash.'

The basement of the old house was cold and dusty, a vast and imposing space scattered with bits of abandoned furniture and anomalous boxes. Damp crept up the walls where they met at the corners of the room. There was a faint musky smell that clung to the air, the source of which presently remained unidentified. Mould, perhaps. Or a dead rat. Goodness knows how much time had passed since her grandfather had done any work on the place.

Aside from the few encounters she'd had with the

property over the last month or so, during which times she'd merely popped in to sign a bit of paperwork or drop something off that she'd need at a later date, Amber had not spent any time in that house since she was a child. Even then, her memories of visiting were sparse, what with her estranged father, and the few times she could recall didn't exactly fill her with any particularly strong sense of nostalgia.

The basement itself, which spanned the entire width of the house and almost all of its length, was cluttered with old furnishings and tattered cardboard boxes that had been sealed up years ago with what was now brittle disintegrating tape. The space was poorly lit by one single working lightbulb that swung unshielded from the ceiling, spilling out a watery yellow tint across the room. Coupled with the weak sunlight that trickled in through the frosted window at foot height with the ground outside, it was just enough for Amber to see what she was doing.

With a quick glance around her to assess how much floor space she had to work with, she shuffled forward towards the old chest of drawers she'd found discarded to one side of the basement. She pushed it towards the centre of the room, straining against the resistance of the heavy antique wood, not relenting until there was enough space behind it for her to squeeze into.

Despite its weight, she'd already removed the drawers

earlier, which had been a task in itself, as they were individually almost as bulky and heavy as the main chest, the produce of genuine craftsmanship. The mahogany design must have been sitting around for at least thirty years, if not even older than she was. If nothing else, it had certainly aged a lot better than she had. It was a beautiful, albeit somewhat dusty, carved furnishing; she almost felt guilty for what she was about to do to it.

Not wishing to waste any time, she dragged her tool bag across the ground so that it lay by her feet. Then, almost mechanically, she reached in for the hammer and chisel, and began hacking away at the top of the chest. Each strike against the butt of the chisel reverberated around the room, bouncing off the crumbling, flaking walls, and clanging against the naked pipes.

As she chipped into the wood, her eyes remained fixed on the splintering top of the chest. She moved her way around it, dislodging the top in small sections until, at last, it had separated enough from the main body to be fully prised away.

There was something oddly satisfying about the sound of the splitting wood as she pulled and tugged at the surface until it cracked away entirely. She stumbled backwards slightly as the top scraped forwards, before she wrestled it down onto the ground. It wasn't too heavy, but it was thick and awkward in shape. With the rough splintering sides, it was difficult to achieve a firm grip.

Once it was safely out of her arms, she wiped her brow with the back of her hand, then used her foot to push the board across the floor in the direction of the window. Then, as she affixed a series of long, chunky screws into the corners and across the edges of the board, she decided that it would be best practice for her to ignore the fact that this was supposed to be the *easy* part of her plan. Manual labour had never been her forte.

With the wooden board prepped and ready for the next step, she crossed over to the bag and whipped out her next tool. Opting for a cordless electric drill had definitely been the right decision, she thought to herself, as at least it was free from any irritating wires. It would have made it increasingly more difficult for her had she needed to contend with fiddly extension cords while also trying to balance the board precariously on one knee as she positioned it directly over the window.

The low, penetrating sound of the drill flooded the room as she blasted each screw in turn, sending them burrowing deep through the heart of the wooden board and straight into the wall around the edges of the window. The drill continued to whir and hum until the final screw was firmly embedded, securing the board to the wall to block out what little sunlight had previously managed to creep its way into the basement.

Only then, once she was satisfied that the board wasn't going to budge out of place, could Amber silence the drill and take a step back to admire her hard work. Her heartrate began to slow as she panted through the exertion. The first stage of her plan was complete, and she could now reward herself with a little deserved rest and a cigarette or two upstairs before she would need to commence with the next steps. She still had a few hours remaining undisturbed, but then the real work would begin.

She always did love a challenge though. She dropped the drill into the tool bag before heading for the stairs. The voice behind her creeping smile was concealed in the darkness of her mind as she flicked off the basement light and began her ascent.

Chapter Eleven

The journey back home a little after midnight, in the early hours of the following morning, had taken Amber down a series of deserted streets and empty back roads. Every now and then she'd drive by a cluster of swaggering drunks or the occasional lone dog walker, but for most of the drive she was able to pretend she was the only person remaining on this formidable earth. Still, she kept her guard up as she headed south, and it wasn't until she was finally back on the other side of the river that she was able to feel her heartrate dropping a little.

Of course, it couldn't have helped at all that she'd been pressing her foot against the peddle with a little more force than was necessary. She'd been in a constant battle with herself as she alternated between fleeing as quickly as possible from the house in Hampstead and trying to not draw attention to herself by pushing the boundaries of the speed limit.

After the physical strain of preparing the basement, she had been in need of a restful sleep that would not come in the old house. It had been an exhausting twenty-four hours, fuelled by little more than adrenaline and copious cups of rich coffee, and by the time she did finally arrive home her eyelids were so heavy that it was almost impossible for her to keep them open. She'd mapped out her time well though, and had, to her fortune, left herself with a little under twelve hours with which to play. That meant she still had a good ten hours or so until she needed to make an effort to leave the house again, enabling her to clamber under the bed covers as soon as she arrived home, still fully dressed, and sleep away the bleak interim.

When she finally did wake to the blaring ring of her alarm clock, the sun was hiding behind the clouds, casting a dull blanket across the sky. There was so little colour to be seen outside. Exactly the way Amber liked it.

It took her almost half an hour to drag herself out of bed, before she finally changed out of the previous day's clothes and replaced them with a pair of black jeans and a creased long-sleeved t-shirt, retrieved from the washing basket. With nothing else to do, there was no point in pottering around the house. After splashing a few handfuls of cold water across her face and glugging down a mug of coffee at double strength, she clambered back into her car, locked her eyes in front of her, threw her hands at ten and two, and drove.

She travelled mechanically, indicating when required and letting others drive past without care. Anybody who saw her would have assumed she was just like everybody else that bleak rush hour, trudging home from work, rushing to late meetings, or heading to one of too many crowded supermarkets. They were all routine, expected activities. And all so much more mundane than the real direction in which Amber was actually heading.

By the time she arrived at her destination, having previously diverted her route to take her through a different borough so that she could fill up her car with petrol as far away from the scene as possible, a gentle rain had begun to fall in specks from the blackening clouds.

It was a trivial thing though, not too much of a problem in the moment at least, as she remained safe and dry behind her steering wheel. Once she'd parked by the kerb, she'd unfastened her seatbelt so that she could stretch out her limbs, then pulled out a map from the glove compartment before stuffing her Sat Nav in its place, out of sight. The map was discarded on the passenger seat and her attention returned to the rear-view mirror.

There wasn't much to distract Amber's attention around

about her as she rarely used her car, and therefore didn't give it the opportunity to become cluttered with unnecessary bits of tat. Still though her fidgeting hands managed to find things to fiddle with, as she mindlessly clicked her seatbelt in and out of its clip, or twisted the knobs of the radio, or slid the controls on the air conditioning back and forth. Anything to distract the loud, droning scream that echoed throughout her impatient mind.

It wasn't until she heard the intense echoing of chunky low-heeled shoes clacking against the pavement that she managed to still her hands. She snapped her head in the direction of the mirror again, her breath lodging in her throat.

Her ears became deaf to the noise of the footsteps growing louder as they headed in her direction. Only her eyes were alert, as her frozen expression stared at the woman now approaching her car.

No, she wasn't actually approaching her car, Amber reminded herself. She was heading towards the house outside which she had been parked for the last half an hour. The one with the sash windows and the green door with the built-in cat flap that was never used.

Of course, it was never used because Victoria Atkins was allergic to cats.

Not that Amber knew this. It was a peculiar thing for Amber to be contemplating, wondering whether or not she and Jason had planned to add a pet to their brood.

Victoria drew nearer to her. She was about three metres away, maybe two and a half; if Amber didn't act now, she would end up missing her only chance.

Grabbing the opportunity while she still could, she leaned over towards the passenger seat and rolled down the window just as Victoria was approaching the rear of the car. A cold breeze whooshed into the vehicle, soothing her flushed face and filling her lungs with a refreshing intensity. It was timely as her cheeks began to redden in anticipation for the anxiousness she knew she would feel when she spoke her first words to the woman who had wrecked her life.

It was only then as she leaned slightly out of the window, having been too distracted with nerves to notice anything beyond her plan, that she realised it had started to rain. Quite heavily too. This would have been much easier if the weather had remained dry, as there was no way Victoria, or at least anybody in their right mind, was going to stand outside for too long in the rain to help a stranger. There was no point in complaining about something that was beyond her control though; she was just going to have to work with whatever conditions the heavens had cursed her with.

As Amber inhaled, holding her breath as she counted down from five, Victoria chose that moment to pause just in front of her garden path, and consequently just a step ahead of the passenger side of Amber's car, as she rummaged inside her coat pocket for her house keys. She was, almost too literally to believe, right where Amber wanted her.

'Excuse me?'

The words flew out of Amber's mouth independently from her control. They were delivered clearly and confidently; she couldn't overthink this or she'd lose her nerve.

Startled by the unexpected intrusion that had headed straight for her through the pattering rain, Victoria turned to see where the voice had come from. She was looking straight at Amber.

Now that Amber could see her face close up, rather than from the usual distance at which she typically observed her and her former lover, she was struggling to force down the sick that threatened to lodge in her throat. She detested the fact that this prissy bitch looked just like a character from one of her own books. Her only book, in fact. Oh, she didn't resemble anyone specific, but she possessed that elegant natural beauty that Amber loved to pour into her half-formed protagonists. She was tall and quite slender, with no visible signs of the child that was growing inside of her. There was no doubting that the stupid bitch would carry her baby weight well, and lose it just as quickly as the act of conception itself.

After a glance up to the sky, as if willing away the rain,

Victoria shuffled slightly towards the car. 'Hello?'

Urgh. Her voice sounded so soft. Even from that single word could Amber tell she was going to be a handful, with her proper, enunciated speech and a lack of any interesting accent.

'Sorry, I don't mean to bother you. It's just that I'm not familiar with the area, and I think I've made a wrong turning somewhere. I'm a bit lost! I'm trying to get to Belmont Street. Do you know it?'

Victoria shook her head. 'I'm afraid I don't, sorry.'

Of course you don't, you silly cow. I've just made it up.

Victoria turned, and was about to head towards her house, but was forced to retreat when Amber interjected her movement.

'Damn. I really need to get there. My daughter's been at a sleepover at a friend's house. The parents are expecting me, and I'm already really late for picking her up. She's…she's got anxiety, and she'll start to panic if I'm not there soon. Are you any good at reading maps? I really need to get to my daughter.'

As Amber gestured to the map that now lay open on the passenger seat, something struck a chord deep inside Victoria's heart. She didn't really feel comfortable standing outside in the wet, talking to this stranger. But then she was naturally maternal, and she had a good heart. If it had been

111

her in this woman's position, desperate to be by her daughter's side, she would have felt frenzied at the thought of not being able to reach her child.

Her fingers fluttered to her stomach as she clocked the woman's pleading eyes. There was nothing else for it: she was going to have to swallow her discomfort and try to help her. That would be the kind, motherly thing to do. This woman would no doubt help her too if she had been in the same situation.

'Okay, I'll try,' she finally replied. 'But I'm not too sure I'm any good at reading maps either!'

With a nervous laugh, she took another step closer to the passenger side of the car. Amber made a show of tilting her head up through the window.

'Gosh, that rain's starting to fall pretty hard, isn't it? Here, why don't you come in to get out of the rain? You'll catch your death otherwise!' Amber pushed open the passenger door and gestured for Victoria to join her in the vehicle. 'I don't mind you getting the seat wet, honest! I'm sure it'll only take a minute.'

Victoria was a big girl now. Even without the tempting allure of offered sweets, she knew she shouldn't get into this strange woman's car. Her shifting eyes displayed that much. But she looked so helpless and really did sound like she was desperate to get to her little girl. It was a perfectly plausible situation. And if Victoria didn't at least try to help her out, her conscience would torment her for eternity. She was sure of it.

Relenting against her better judgment, as one who was always seeking to do the right thing, Victoria climbed into the car. The door shut naturally behind her as she reached for the map.

She was too busy studying the pages that were laid out on her knees, too focused on trying to locate the grid where they were at that moment, to notice Amber's eyes shifting back and forth to the passenger door lock.

'Ah, here we are!' Victoria exclaimed as she pointed to their current location on the map. 'Did you say it was Belmont Street you were looking for?'

'Yep.' Amber couldn't look at Victoria as she replied.

'Any idea roughly how far away it is from here?'

'Not far, I don't think.'

'Hmm.' Victoria rubbed at her chin. 'I can't immediately see it. I could always check the map on my mobile. It'll only take a minute to load it up, and maybe it'll be—'

There was no time for Victoria to finish her sentence. Just as she was about to reach into her pocket for her phone, Amber jumped into action. In quick succession she locked the car doors, rolled the windows halfway up, changed into the correct gear, and launched the car forward. Not once from then on did she look directly at Victoria.

'Stop! *Stop!* What are you doing?!'

As the car sped down the street, Amber didn't need to look at Victoria to know that she had successfully instilled in her in those few seconds the uncontrollable panic that now quivered in her voice and coursed throughout her entire body.

The map slid down from Victoria's knees and landed by her feet onto the floor as she tugged pointlessly at the handle of the passenger door. 'Stop the car! Let me go!' Despite her best efforts to remain in command of her emotions, she failed to stay calm.

Amber, on the other hand, appeared to be more collected than she had ever known herself to be. She kept her hands at ten and two, with her eyes locked securely on the road in front of her, as she focused only on fleeing from the area.

Refusing to be irritated by Victoria's incessant panicking, she replied in a quiet monotone, 'You're wasting your energy. If you must know, I thought we would take a little trip together; you might want to fasten your seatbelt for this one.'

'Who are you?! What do you *want*?!'

The realisation had kicked in for Victoria. This was really happening. This, whatever it was, this kidnapping – oh God, she was being kidnapped! – wasn't just something that happened to movie stars in thrilling blockbusters. This was reality. It was *her* reality. Whatever she was supposed to do about it, however she was expected to act, she had no idea how to get herself out of this situation.

With only one thought on her mind, she fumbled for her phone to call for help. Amber was too quick for her though; she had observed her movements out of the corner of her eyes, and flung her arm out to snatch the phone. She didn't avert her gaze as she bashed it out of Victoria's hands and dropped it into the door by her right side. She knew Victoria would never try to reach over for it; such foolishness would have all three of them – Amber, Victoria, and the foetus – in a ferocious head-on collision.

She turned the corner onto the main street, and rolled up the windows all the way to muffle the sound of her passenger's ill attempt at crying for help.

'It's too late, Victoria. Nobody can hear you now.'

To see the shock on Victoria's face in that moment would have been such a thrill. Amber almost regretted not being able to summon the ability within her to look directly at her at that point.

The sound of silence, however, which blocked any squeak escaping from Victoria, was like sweet music to Amber's ears.

After the car twisted and turned down a few more

streets, Victoria in her panicked state had lost her bearings. She had no idea where she was, couldn't call anybody for help. This sort of thing didn't happen in real life, didn't happen to women like her. She was kind, honest. She told the truth, worked hard for her clients. She didn't even eat chocolate, for crying out loud. There had to be some mistake.

But then this crazy woman knew her name. She hadn't just been in the wrong place at the wrong time. Her kidnap had been premeditated, and, as they headed for the North Circular Road, where any hope of attracting the attention of an innocent passer-by sped away from her grasp, there was nothing she could do except sit tight and suffer the ride.

Chapter Twelve

It was quite possible that they had only been travelling for a short while, or perhaps they had been on the road for hours. Victoria had no idea how long she'd been trapped for. Not long after they'd headed away from the familiar district, very quickly her exhausting sobs took hold, forcing her heavy eyelids into a drifting state of consciousness. She was rather like a distressed infant being soothed to sleep by the motions of the car.

She'd battled to stay awake, but her mind had opted for flight over fight, and had removed itself from her surroundings. She began to stir though as the car was slowing down to pull onto the hard shoulder.

Amber steered the vehicle to the edge, then switched off the headlights. The intense whitish beams that had previously caused the rain to sparkle as it lashed down in front of the car now shut off completely, leaving them alone and out of sight

117

in the complete darkness.

There was a stiffness in the back of Victoria's neck, the least of her problems, as she lifted her head up. She blinked several times through sticky eyes before fully realising where she was.

'W-what are—?'

'Shut up.'

Only half registering the sound of her captor's agitated voice, Victoria reached out a weary hand to tug at the car door, but with no avail. Whatever fight she had left in her as she tried to process the situation had escaped with the remaining hours of the day. She was, for now, entirely drained and defeated.

Instead of pressing Amber further, she could do nothing but bow her head again and emit a long, low sob as the fear and frustration leaked out of her. She didn't open her eyes but could hear the sound of a seatbelt being unclipped as Amber released her own restraint. She felt her shift about beside her as she reached into the back of the car for her handbag, before bringing it to the front and dropping it into her lap. It was only when she began rummaging through it that Victoria, alerted by her own natural sense of curiosity, was able to lift her head again.

'What are you…you doing?' she sniffed. She was timid, but so baffled was she by the whole situation that a part of her, perhaps the most human part of all, couldn't help taking over.

Amber didn't answer her directly, but instead pulled out several pairs of tights from her handbag. She clutched them in her palm, then, without looking at her, angled them slightly towards Victoria. 'If you cooperate with me, this won't hurt.'

Victoria's eyes strained through the blackness that surrounded them and the car in the waxing night, concentrating until she was able to focus on the vague presence of several strips of nylon hosiery.

'I shouldn't leave them bunched up after I wash them,' Amber muttered to herself as she stretched out each pair of tights in turn. 'Stupid things become all shrivelled.'

A question lodged in Victoria's throat. She coughed it up with a quiver. 'What are those for?!'

'I said *shut up*, didn't I?'

The glare in Amber's eyes and the flare about her nostrils were easy to detect even in the dark. Although Victoria had awoken from her panic-induced exhaustion in the middle of somewhere entirely unidentifiable, she was confident with the thought that she knew she had nowhere to go, nowhere to run to. Still she couldn't relent though. That would mean this woman was winning. If winning for either of them was even an option at all.

She wiggled in protest as Amber stretched over and

fought with her wrists, twisting her arms around until her hands were clasped behind her back. It wasn't a straightforward task with the seatbelt getting in the way, which Amber had made her fasten after they pulled onto the ring-road, and which Victoria had done so reluctantly only out of fear, but it would have been a rookie error for Amber to unclip it to release Victoria from its grasp before she was positive that she had been successfully bound.

However, Victoria finally managed to release one of her hands from Amber's clawing figures, and flailed it around in an attempt to distract her. She became a victim of her own actions though when she lashed out and caught Amber's cheek with a sharp, manicured fingernail. It had been an unintentional attack, and, although she couldn't refrain from feeling a little pride when she saw Amber's own hand rush up to her face where now there appeared a faint line of crimson bubbling towards the surface of her skin, the fire in Amber's eyes was enough to persuade her that the ensuing punishment would be more than she deserved.

Just as quickly as she had released her clutched hands from Victoria's wrists to tend to the strike, Amber dismissed her minor injury as an occupational hazard, and finished securing a pair of tights firmly around her wrists. She retreated back into the driver seat, leaving streaks of deep red against Victoria's delicate skin in her wake.

With her head bowed forward again, the tears that tumbled down from Victoria's face were shielded from Amber's view. She fished for the other pair of tights, stretched them slightly, then turned back to her passenger.

'Lift up your head.'

Victoria sniffed, but couldn't summon the energy to obey.

'I said *lift up your head!*'

No time was wasted as Amber lunged forward, grabbing a wailing Victoria by the ruffled hair at the back of her head, and lifting her face upwards with a fistful of blonde strands. The second pair of tights were thrust in front of her, stretched over her eyes, and tied without hesitation in a robust knot at the back of her skull.

'There now, that wasn't so bad, was it?'

Exactly to whom Amber was speaking, it wasn't quite clear. At least she could relax a little more now; the rest of the night would be much easier now that Victoria's sight had been concealed and her mobility reduced.

She threw her handbag back onto the seat behind her, then glanced into her rear-view mirror. Her eyes met with the scratch on her cheek, which had smudged a little to smear and fleck drying blood against her flushed skin. She lifted a hand up towards it, then lightly pressed her fingers across its surface. She winced. Speckles of blood had transferred onto her fingertips.

'Bitch!' she snarled as she wiped her hand on her coat.

Victoria, who had in the last few minutes been too distressed for any motion, suddenly flung her head backwards. It was as if whatever energy she had remaining inside of her had rushed to the surface at once, with neither warning nor hesitation, in one final attempt to save herself from this unknown, degrading situation. Her mouth opened wide, and she screamed.

'Help! Please, somebody! Help me! I need hel—'

The slap of a heavy hand struck her hard across the cheek, lodging her breath in her throat and twisting her neck back towards the headrest. She yelped out in pain, but was too choked to continue her cries.

'Do you *want* me to muzzle you?!' Amber questioned through gritted teeth.

Had Victoria been able to see the venom in her stares, she would in that moment have been thankful for the blindfold. A tiny shake of her bowed head was all she could manage in response.

'Then I suggest you shut the fuck up. You really are an idiot! Who do you expect can hear you out here, anyway? There's nobody coming for you, Victoria.'

The sharp intake of breath was accompanied by the quivering of limbs as Victoria realised that the truth may well have been spoken.

There were people who loved her, who would help her. But that would be incredibly difficult if nobody knew where exactly they had to look to find her.

Thick tears soaked into the tights and dripped down her cheeks as she sobbed through her fear and confusion. Amber's own emotions, however, remained as neutral as her expression. Without wasting her time with any more tedious explanations, she fastened her seatbelt, set the car into gear, and slowly pulled away to continue on their way. The only sounds now came from the lashing rain against the window and the faint clicking of the right indicator as she turned around the corner, continuing their journey deeper into the night.

Chapter Thirteen

The house stood just as it did when Amber had left it last: in the darkness, surrounded by thick foliage, and isolated from the rest of the village.

She pulled the car up outside its entrance, parking as proximate to the front door as possible. The slowing motions of the vehicle caused Victoria to stir again beside her; she had cried herself into another exhausted silence, and had slumped over in a dreamless state of unconsciousness, with her head bowed and her back curved as far as her restraints would allow.

The rain had begun to soften some ten or fifteen minutes ago, just as they were leaving the North Circular Road to cross over the threshold into Highgate. By the time they arrived in Hampstead, it had stopped entirely, leaving the night to rest in near silence.

A faintly audible sniff was emitted from somewhere

beneath the hair that cascaded down the sides of Victoria's face. She was bound to be awake now, Amber realised, and at any rate she would soon have to prod her into action to get her out of the car; it would have been much easier if she could have conducted this while the bitch was still comatose.

She couldn't bring herself to look directly at her, but instead stared without blinking at the centre of the steering wheel. She opened her mouth, and penetrated the silence with a sharp command.

'Wake up.'

Victoria mumbled something, as if not entirely aware that she was conscious. She stirred, lifted her head, and muttered with bleary eyes. 'Where are we?'

Amber busied herself with stuffing things back into her handbag as Victoria's head inched towards her. She was just quick enough to remember to retrieve Victoria's phone from the bucket in the side of her the door before she could do anything about it.

An increasingly alert Victoria, whose eyes were now fluttering rapidly behind the blindfold, which was partly concealed behind wispy strands of blonde hair, was about to lash out in protest against her captor, when Amber thrust something out of her bag and pressed its tip lightly against Victoria's arm.

Her concealed eyes were a fearing wide contrast to

Amber's own penetrating slits. They fell down towards the blade of the pocket knife that was now poised a mere few inches away from her; the sharp, sudden pain of the knife's tip as it pricked against her skin was unmistakable. She may not have been able to see exactly what the weapon was, but she knew Amber wasn't messing around. Any chance, however slim, she may have had to fight for control over the situation was long since possible.

As Amber leaned closer towards the centre of the car, she spoke with a surprising calm. Her words were clear and confident, not once in doubt of her own authority.

'Now listen to me, and listen to me closely. In a moment, I'm going to unlock the doors. I'm going to get out of the car and walk around to the other side to help you out. After that, you're going to walk in front of me towards the house. I'll open the door, and you'll go inside. You're not going to say anything. You're not going to shout or scream or make any noise whatsoever. And there's no point in trying to run away; there's nobody around for miles, and nowhere for you to go. You got that?'

Victoria sniffed.

'Good. I'm going to take your blindfold off now. I suggest you keep your head still if you don't want this to hurt.'

Victoria could do only as she was told as Amber fiddled

126

with the pocket knife. She cut away at the knot at the back of the tights, releasing the restraint before throwing them onto the back seat.

Sensing Amber edge away from her, Victoria lifted her head a little, her movements slow as she strained to see through her puffy, watering eyes.

Her attention caught the knife that Amber was brandishing in her direction, revealing to her its identity. A small yelp lodged in her throat as she remembered her instructions, her eyes her only expression of her fear.

'Any wrong move from you, and you'll be finding out just what real pain feels like. Understood?'

Without bothering to wait for a response, Amber slid out of the car and slammed the driver door behind her. It was quite late into the night now, and, without any street lamps or other houses nearby to share the glow of their cosy family homes, she could rely only on the dim light from inside the vehicle that infiltrated its way outside to guide her. She shuffled her way around, then reached for the passenger door.

There was no time to protest, and certainly no time to plan any kind of feasible escape, as Victoria felt the tight clutches of Amber's grasp land on her shoulders. She pulled her out of the car and pushed her in the direction of the house.

'Walk.'

Amber nodded towards the front door. Her movements were fuelled by an almost military precision as she kept one eye on the door and the other on her victim; it was a stark contrast from Victoria's own stumbling attempts as she struggled to maintain control of her own balance.

She scuffled a few steps forward. Her every muscle and joint ached from being hunched over in one position for so long; how long exactly that had been though, she wouldn't have been able to guess. Her teeth chattered together ferociously, but whether that was more a product of the chilling autumn wind or of her immeasurable fear she couldn't be certain of *that* either. Right now, she knew absolutely nothing.

'Quickly!'

The order was barked through gritted teeth, and sent a shower of tears tumbling down Victoria's face. She had tried so hard to mask her emotions this far, to not give Amber the satisfaction of her pain, but it was no use. She was terrified. She had no idea what was going on, or where she was, or who this woman was.

And she was humiliated too. When Jason found out what had happened – *if* Jason ever found out – what would he think of her? What would her own child think of her? She was going to be a mother soon; she shouldn't allow herself to be this weak. If only for her baby, she had to stay strong.

As the emotion drained from Victoria, Amber jammed the key into the door and pushed it open. They both tumbled into the dark hallway before the door slammed firmly behind them, cutting off Amber and Victoria, and her unborn child, away from the rest of the world.

Chapter Fourteen

The naked bulb that swung from the ceiling illuminated the small room in a vibrant yellow. After spending so long in the dark outdoors, the light was almost too intense; if Amber had not in that moment been peering out from a gap in the curtain, it would have been easy for her to believe it was the middle of the day.

Instead though, she took pleasure in the pitch sky outside as it reminded her that the night was about to settle in. There was a lot that she wanted to get done tomorrow, and more importantly there were plans that had been made for in the evening, and she wanted to feel refreshed and look as alert as possible, so the sooner she got this over with the better. It wouldn't do for her to spend too long at the house anyway.

'You know,' Amber remarked as she drew away from the window, 'I'm quite surprised the rain's stopped. They said on the TV this morning that it was supposed to rain right through to tomorrow. I'd expected it to be lashing down right about now. Still, what do they know?'

She marched across the small room and disappeared out into the dark hallway. There was little risk in her leaving Victoria unsupervised now that they were inside; although it had been done not without thrashing and struggling, she'd managed to loop the tights that were tied around Victoria's wrists to the back legs of the chair. If she attempted now to unhook herself from the chair, it was almost certain that she would break an arm.

Ideally, she'd break both of them.

At any rate, it was enough to provide Amber with the peace of mind that it would keep her secured in the room while she took a few minutes away from her. Looking after Victoria on the journey up to Hampstead had been exhausting, and she needed a moment or two to herself to relieve herself of the stress.

Victoria's eyes scanned the square room as the clattering of metal on metal echoed in from the hallway. It sounded frightfully similar to the noise of rummaged tools. Sharp, heavy, and threatening.

There was little around her to offer her an escape. The room was sparsely furnished and barely habitable, offering just two chairs and a small circular table, all of which were unaesthetically positioned against one wall. It had once been a bright and airy space, often filled with smiles and laugher as Amber's grandparents frolicked over tea with scones and jam and clotted cream. The window was always open wide, with the occasional spring breeze providing respite from the golden warmth of the sun that had so often washed over them both.

The current emptiness of the foreboding space could not feel more imposing on that former happiness. The room had been verging on abandonment following the death of Amber's grandmother; with her grandfather unable to face anything that reminded him of the beloved past they shared, and it had been left to gather dust and the occasional cobweb. In its present state, it could not be any further removed from the joy with which it was once overcome.

Victoria may not have known what would happen next, but she knew she had to get out of there before it was too late.

She struggled and twisted her arms as she fought to loosen the knot, her wrists digging into the edge of the wooden chair as she tugged and pulled. In the hallway, Amber was still clattering around in the tool bag, searching in the darkness for some elusive object. To what detriment neither could know, but time was against them both.

'Aha! Here it is!'

The voice boomed intrusively, shunting Victoria into a frozen state of fear. The chair squeaked as the wood scraped against the edge of the table, just as Amber beamed in the hallway at whatever it was she'd been looking for.

She emerged in the doorway a shadow of a second later, clutching the object by her side. When she noticed that Victoria had shifted an inch, having disobeyed her earlier order to remain still, she stormed forward with hatred flaring in her eyes.

How dare the stupid little tart ignore her instructions!

'What the fuck do you think you're doing?!' Amber yelled in her face as a hand thumped against Victoria's shoulder. The chair crashed backwards against the wall.

'Please! Please let me go! Untie me! You've got the wrong person! I don't...I don't...'

Amber rolled her eyes as Victoria faltered, snot bubbling at her nose. She looked pathetic.

Closing her eyes, Amber took a moment to collect her thoughts. She exhaled with her mouth slightly parted, restoring herself to a former state of calm, then turned her attention back to Victoria.

'I'll untie your hands in a moment,' she finally said without looking directly at her. The handcuffs she'd retrieved from the tool bag moments earlier now swung down from one hand as she swayed them back and forth in front of

Victoria's face like some twisted hypnotist. 'But first I need to make sure you're going to cooperate.'

Victoria blubbered. 'Please! Oh, please! Whatever you want from me, whatever it is, just tell me and I'll—'

'We'll get to that in a moment. But, in the meantime, I can't be taking any risks now, can I? It would be seriously impractical for you to be running away from me. Especially after all the effort I went through to get you here in the first place.'

Amber concentrated all her attention on fastening the handcuffs around one of Victoria's wrists, manoeuvring beneath the tights as she secured the other end to the back of the chair, and all without once looking directly at the whimpering girl. A weak gasp escaped from Victoria's lips when Amber produced the pocket knife to cut away the tights from behind her, but she was too exhausted to put up any further protest.

'There now!' Amber said as she dropped her body down into the chair at the other side of the table. 'I feel much better now. Wouldn't you agree, Victoria?'

So preoccupied as Victoria was with flexing the feeling back into her one free hand that it had taken her a second for the words to register. When they did, her neck snapped round to face her captor.

'How do you know my name?! Who are you?!'

134

'We've been over this, Victoria. You'll find out in good time.' Amber puffed out her lips. 'God, I need a cigarette!'

She lifted up her handbag from where she'd dropped it by the window, and produced a packet of cigarettes and a lighter. An ashtray followed, which she dropped onto the table. It paid to be prepared.

'I swear every other week I say I'll quit,' she chatted as she flicked the lighter into action. 'I know fine well I never will though.'

Once her cigarette was lit and wedged between her lips, she proffered the packet in Victoria's direction. 'Want one?'

She shook her head.

'Suit yourself.'

The packet was stuffed back into the handbag before Amber took a drag. She exhaled with a long, deflating satisfaction.

'God, that's good. No, I don't think I could ever give these up,' she said, absently studying the butt of the cigarette. 'The devil's poison, my mother used to call them.'

'What do you want with me?' The words left Victoria's mouth as no more than a hoarse mutter. Amber didn't flinch, but instead nonchalantly flicked ash into the tray.

'It should have been mine,' she finally replied after a few more puffs.

Had Victoria anticipated any sort of response from this

woman, it certainly wouldn't have been that. A sudden bemusement threatened to override her fear. 'What?'

'Jason knew how much I wanted children. That baby you're growing? It should be mine. It *will* be mine.'

Another drag. More flicking of ash. The faint ticking of a clock somewhere deep inside the house was the only sound, until...

The penny dropped.

'You're Amber?!'

'He's mentioned me then. He kept *you* a secret from *me* for so long that I wasn't sure how much you actually knew about the whole sordid situation.'

Of course, suddenly it all made sense. This deranged woman was Jason's former partner. With all the stories she'd heard about her, about her clinging and obsessing and sheer inability to leave him alone, she should have known. And now the unstable former partner of her current lover, the father of her unborn child, had kidnapped her and locked her in a house in the middle of nowhere.

Something told Victoria she wasn't going to have the upper hand in this situation.

'I swear he never mentioned you,' Victoria spewed, making the snap decision to lie. Of course he'd mentioned her. She had been his mistress; she had known *everything* about the strains of their relationship. She had even become a source of much amusement, the punchline to private jokes, once Jason had finally freed himself from her clutches. 'Not while we were…If I'd known about you before he…before he…moved out, I never would have—'

'Fucked him?' Amber didn't notice, nor would have cared for, the rash of blush that rushed to Victoria's cheeks. 'It's alright. I don't blame you for the affair. Not really. The thing is though, Victoria, while I don't think it was your fault that the idiot couldn't keep his dick in his pants, I *do* blame you for the breakdown of my happy relationship. You know what you should have done once you *did* find that you weren't the only person he was screwing?'

A fleeting silence hovered in the air as Amber took another drag on her cigarette. She exhaled, then continued: 'You should have left him. Walked away. I would have forgiven him. Eventually. And we'd still be together, him and me, the way things were. The way things were *meant* to be. And you know something else?'

She smashed the cigarette into the ashtray then turned, for the first time since arriving at the house, to look directly at Victoria, whose own weeping eyes were fixed on her lap.

'It should be *me* carrying his baby. Not you. But no, you had to encourage him to leave me, didn't you?'

'I never—'

'And now I'm all alone! And you're partly to blame for

that! Do you know how that makes me feel, Victoria?!'

Silence. How could she possibly respond to that?

'Well?! Do you?!' Amber's eyes flared at Victoria's insolence. She leapt out of the chair and pounded her fist against the table, causing Victoria to jump back in her seat. The handcuff cut into her wrist as she cowered.

'I-I'm sorry, I ne-ever—'

'It's too late for your snivelling apologies, Victoria. Stand up!'

Victoria quivered as her legs turned to jelly. Her body became unresponsive. Even if she wanted to obey her captor, her mind seemed unwilling and unable to control her actions.

'I said stand the fuck up!'

The words were spat out in staccato as Amber's eyes met Victoria's. Mere inches hovered between them now.

Amber grabbed onto Victoria's sleeve and dragged her onto her feet, forcing a gasping cry to splutter out of her. She scrabbled for the key in her pocket and fiddled ferociously with the lock of the handcuffs.

With the cuff that had been tied to the chair springing free, she pushed her forward, steering her from behind as she stumbled into the darkness of the hallway.

'Where are you taking me?!' Victoria panicked. 'Stop it! Help! Somebody help!'

Amber was far too entertained by the screaming idiot.

Who did she think was going to help her?

'Oh, shut up. Nobody can hear you,' she muttered as she shunted her down the corridor. They stopped outside a door, and Amber fiddled with the knob.

The door creaked open, and both women seemed to look down to the bottom of the stairs that had appeared before them – Victoria riddled with fear for the unknown, and Amber taking a moment to confirm to herself the next stages of her plan. It was almost as if she was considering whether or not she wanted to go through with this after all.

It didn't take her long though to confirm to herself that, yes, she needed to go ahead with this. She couldn't afford to back out now.

'Down!' she barked without warning.

Victoria jumped as the order was shouted straight into her right ear. She felt Amber's heavy hand landing on her back and forcing her stumbling down the stairs. She put her cuffed wrist out to steady herself, the metal cuff dangling back and forth and clacking against the surround as she felt for something, anything, onto which she could hold.

They were encased only by walls and darkness until they reached the last few steps, at which point the rickety support of an old wooden banister could be felt by the most desperate of hands.

Victoria narrowly missed her footing as she was pushed

down the final step, before being forced into a halt when Amber's demanding hand grappled the material at the back of her coat.

She could have fought for the energy to whisk herself around, shove Amber out of the way, and tumble back up the stairs. Where she'd have run to after that she wouldn't have known, but she didn't need to worry about that now as she could do nothing but gawp at the room in which she now found herself. As Amber flicked on the bare light above them, the whole basement became dimly lit. Every corner, every crumbling brick and pile of dust, was washed in the weak artificial glow of the oft-flickering bulb that hung drooping from the precarious ceiling overhead.

All around them lay the discarded remains of the decades shared by two people alone together in their solitary home: an old rocking chair that once belonged to Amber's grandmother; a maple trunk that had undoubtedly housed the most treasured possessions belonging to her grandfather; the occasional sealed cardboard box with its contents mysteriously hidden from view.

The smashed remnants of the dresser were still scattered in the corner from when Amber had previously pulled it apart. Victoria's eyes scanned across the floor from the splintered wood, absorbing as if in slow motion the loose trail of shards until her attention rested at the end on the boarded-up window.

No wonder it had been so dark when they had first descended the stairs. It took a second for it to click, but then the alarm bells began to ring in an instant moment of realisation that she was unlikely to be freely allowed to leave any time soon. It became clear to Victoria that it was impossible for her to convince herself, for the sake of her sanity, that this was not simply a homely tour of the building.

Acting on a new surge of adrenaline, she spun around in her bid to flee, crashing straight into Amber. She would have tumbled straight down and smashed her knees against the corner of the steps if it wasn't for the fact that Amber's swiftness had triumphed over her, grabbing her by the arms and pushing her, after a momentary kerfuffle, deeper into the basement.

Victoria's arms flailed as she fought to maintain her balance. She stumbled backwards, tripping over a rogue object before twisting sideways and smacking her hip down onto the solid ground.

Her hand flung in front of her stomach to protect her child, but before her fingers had a chance to caress her navel she was already being dragged upright. She staggered backwards as Amber steered her, her hand clasped tightly around Victoria's wrist, and her body blocking out Victoria's vision as she forced her against the far wall.

A long wail emitted from Victoria's lips as she attempted to thwack Amber across the head with her free hand. Amber grunted but kept her focus, not letting the little bitch exacerbate the situation for her. She continued to fight with her as she tugged and pulled at the sleeves of her coat. Buttons popped off and pinged out into the darker corners of the room, until the garment was released and dropped to the floor. It was a luxurious, expensive affair; Amber didn't doubt that it would act as a comforting blanket for Victoria now when she would later drape it over her stomach to keep her baby warm.

'Aha! There!'

Amber panted through heavy breaths as the metallic clink of the handcuffs sounded against the pipe onto which they were now secured. She took a step back and wiped at her brow with the back of her hand.

Victoria tugged automatically at the restraint, yet knowing all too well that it wasn't going to slip away so easily, then yanked at it with more force as tears spilled down her face.

'You're wasting your energy, you idiot. They're fucking *handcuffs*.' The heavy sound of Amber's feet against the floor echoed throughout the room as she crossed over to the other side. 'And bloody good ones, as far as I can tell. Amazing what you can find online, isn't it?'

She crouched down to pick up a plastic bucket, one which looked like it had seen better days with its discoloured off-white faded appearance, then straightened back up with a smirk on her face. She had her back to Victoria, but could hear the sweet clinking of the resistant cuffs as they repeatedly clanged against the pipes.

Her smile dropped as she twisted around and headed back over to Victoria. She dropped the bucket onto the floor in front of her, letting it clatter down onto its side.

'Here. You'll be needing that.'

Victoria lifted her head up. She blinked away the tears that had settled on her eyelashes, then noticed the bucket that had landed beside her.

'I-I don't understand.'

'Well, I can't have you wetting yourself, can I? It won't be hygienic for the baby.'

Realising what Amber was implying, Victoria couldn't avoid contorting her face in disgust.

'I'm not going to the toilet in *that*!' she spat. 'I'm not going to the toilet in *anything* here! Let me go! Let me *go*!'

Victoria's voice raised into a shout as she helplessly watched Amber walk away from her. 'W-where are you going?! Come back and let me go, you crazy bitch! You can't leave me! You can't!'

Amber paused at the bottom of the stairs, one hand

poised on the banister. She glanced back in Victoria's direction. She looked like such a such a pathetic snivelling mess, all hunched up against the wall like that. If only she could see herself and realise just how much of a mess she had got herself into. Stupid tart.

'Don't worry, I'll be back soon enough. I've got plans tonight though so I can't just stay here and babysit you.' She glanced at her watch. 'Oh, hell. It's later than I thought. I look horrendous, don't I?'

She made an attempt to straighten out her clothes then ruffled her hair with her fingertips. 'Oh well,' she said with a sigh. 'It'll have to do. I'm sure he won't complain too much. Anyway, while I'm gone, you should probably try and get some rest. Keep your strength up. Right. I'm off. Sleep tight!'

Without casting a second glance at Victoria, she flicked the light switch to restore the basement to its prior blackness. She ascended the stairs with heavy footsteps, slammed the door shut behind her, and left in her wake only emptiness as the abandoned Victoria could do nothing except whimper alone in the dark.

Chapter Fifteen

The headlights beamed through the gloomy sky, illuminating the speckling rain as the car sped along the street. It swung into the side of the road and pulled up with an abrupt halt. The door flung open, and Amber jumped out of the vehicle.

She slammed the door behind her, pausing only long enough to check that it was properly locked, before charging down the path towards her flat. She fished in her pocket for her keys and prodded them towards the main door.

'Shit, shit, shit!' she mumbled to herself as she struggled in the evening darkness to find the lock. After a few more seconds of fumbling, the key slotted into the lock and turned with a satisfying click.

Leaving the outside world behind her, Amber emerged into her flat, flicking on various lights as she travelled through the hallway and into the living room. She threw her handbag onto the sofa, and dropped her coat over the armrest. She shook her head to cast away the droplets of rain that had settled in her hair, then glanced around her.

'Too quiet. Much too quiet,' she muttered as she picked up the remote control for the stereo. Without looking in its direction, she pushed the button to bring it to life. Despite being in control of the Hi-Fi system, she still jumped when the gruff voice of the radio DJ burst into the room, announcing the beginning of the late evening's 'ultra-energising playlist to keep you bouncing all night long!'

Something akin to wailing foxes over heavy metal filled the room, forcing Amber to finish piling the magazines on the coffee table and then lunge for the remote that she'd just deposited beside them.

'Oh God, what's that meant to be?! That'll never do!' she complained to nobody before stabbing the channel button. The next station filled the room in a pleasant mellowness as a classical concerto drifted into its first movement.

Content enough with the soundtrack, Amber returned to tidying up the flat, shuffling piles of books and plumping up sofa cushions. She had never had much time for housekeeping: when she was feeling inspired and spending most of her time behind her laptop typing out new chapters, it simply felt like an unnecessary excuse for procrastinating; and since being made redundant, being dumped by her beloved ex-partner, and then spiralling into the darkest depths of depression, she couldn't have cared less about a bit of dust here and there. Still, she had to make an effort tonight, at least if she wanted to make a satisfying impression, so she kept going until it looked at least marginally more habitable than usual.

While she tidied, outside, further down the street, Greig was sauntering along the path. He remained seemingly unaware of the smattering rain as he clutched a bunch of flowers in one hand, his other stuffed casually into his coat pocket. He whistled a gentle nondescript tune as he headed towards Amber's flat.

She still raced frantically around her home, trying to disguise months of abandoned clutter. Entering the kitchen, she glanced at the sink, which was full of dirty mugs and the odd plate decorated in buttery toast crumbs, then looked up at the clock.

'No time,' she decided, before ignoring the dishes. She made straight for the cupboard to hunt for clean glasses, then fished out a fresh bottle of wine and carried everything through to the living room.

A soft rap sounded from down the hallway. Greig had arrived, right on schedule.

'Oh God.'

She paused to check her appearance in the mirror. She looked so bedraggled, so washed out, with her exhaustion

147

after the day's exertion finally beginning to kick in as the adrenaline subsided. Still, what could she do? She pinched her cheeks to bring to them a little colour, shrugged at her reflection, then headed straight for the front door.

She smiled as she opened the door to her guest. It had been so long since she had felt the opportunity to create true happiness. As she welcomed Greig into her home, with all thoughts of the events from earlier that evening momentarily locked out of her present mind, she couldn't deny the strange newborn flutters of excitement that floated around in her stomach, promising to restore Amber to life.

Greig perched on the edge of the sofa, casting a glance around the living room. It was a small space, but Amber had managed to make it her own. He particularly liked the way she'd draped the curtains over their hooks rather than leaving them to hang loose; it was the little gestures that always counted most, even if it had only recently been done, and unwittingly for his benefit.

'Here we go,' Amber said as she entered the room. She was carrying two glasses of wine, and handed one to Greig. 'I hope red's okay.'

Despite her earlier attempt to get everything set up in the living room before Greig's arrival, she'd forgotten to bring in a corkscrew when she'd set up the wine on the coffee table, and had no choice but to return to the kitchen with the bottle in hand to prepare the drinks in there. It was such a rookie mistake, but so used to devouring alcohol that came in cheap bottles with screw tops as she was that she had to hide her embarrassment. She was sure Greig would be used to finer wine than that. She couldn't afford to disappoint him tonight.

Why she hadn't just retrieved the cork screw from the kitchen and brought it to the living room she wasn't sure, but she benefited from those few moments alone to ease herself into the date. She couldn't mess this up. Not if she didn't want to end up alone again.

'Red's perfect, thank you,' Greig replied. He accepted the glass and took a sip as Amber sat down beside him. 'I love what you've done to the place. Have you lived here long, or...?'

'Not too long, no. A few years. I had considered moving to somewhere a bit bigger, but...well, to be honest, I wouldn't know where I'd go, really!'

'Well it's lovely. And all those books!' He gestured towards the overflowing bookshelf that stood tall against the far wall. 'Do you use all those for teaching?'

Ah. She hadn't quite found the opportunity yet to inform him that she wasn't, as it happened, still teaching. It wasn't so much that she was keeping the truth from him; her redundancy simply hadn't come up in conversation. Besides, she didn't want him to think she was a layabout. She knew how quickly some people took to judging others, and she'd not yet had the time to work out whether or not Greig fell into that category.

Still, they *were,* or at least had been, for teaching, back when the sun always shone and the joys of educating was something she had taken for granted, so she didn't really need to lie to him to worm her way around this one.

'Some of them are,' she replied. 'Some of them I just like to read for fun.'

There was a brief awkward silence as they both sipped from their glasses, neither one particularly used to this situation, and each as desperate for the artificial courage as the other. Then, noticing out of the corner of her eye that Greig was watching her over the rim of his glass, Amber turned back towards him with a meek smile.

'Ouch, that looks painful! What did you do?!'

It took Amber a few seconds to realise that Greig was referring to the scratch on her cheek, which had been exposed after she'd brushed the fallen strand of hair back behind her ears. In honesty, she had completely forgotten all about it until now.

'Oh, this?' She put a hand up to her face, suddenly conscious of how deeply that bitch had cut her cheek. 'It's nothing. I just— '

What? What did you do? She couldn't exactly tell him the truth. 'I just turned around too quickly. Hit my face off the side of a door, didn't I? Probably not my most graceful moment!' She forced a breathy laugh before hiding her mouth behind her wine.

'I imagine not!' Greig replied with a light chuckle. 'Still, it does look quite sore. Have you put anything on it? Like antiseptic or something?'

'No. I'm sure there's no need. It probably looks worse than it actually is!'

'Are you sure?'

Amber nodded, but Greig decided that he could seize this moment anyway. He nibbled on the bottom of his lip, finding the confidence he needed to take the plunge, then leaned forwards. Lifting his hand to her face, he cupped Amber's cheek, and tenderly stroked the pale skin beside the scratch.

'Because if it *did* hurt, I'm sure I could make you feel better.'

He spoke more softly now, more sultry than he had ever done before in her company. Amber eyed his penetrating expression, her thoughts lingering until she finally caught his drift. Then, when she did, there was an immediate desire burning inside of her to play along.

'And how might you do that?' she whispered.

'Well, first of all I'd pour you something to drink— '

She sipped on cue, but kept her eyes looking over the rim of the glass, never taking them away from Greig.

'And then...'

He paused, his confidence threatening to slip away from him. But the sound of Amber's rasping breath by his side lured him back into the game.

'And then I'd do this.'

After taking Amber's glass from her hand and placing it on the coffee table, he stretched over until his body hovered over hers. His lips kissed hers, gently at first, and then more hungrily as her hands wandered to his hips, encouraged his gesture.

He pulled away, and, grazing his hand up her thigh, whispered in her ear: 'And all your worries will fly away and I'll protect you from all the horrible, nasty people in the world.'

His words faded as she pulled him on top of her, their lips locking as their hips moved in unison. As a faint moan escaped from Amber's lips as his fingers explored her curves, she knew that Greig was right. Whatever happened from now on, she would do whatever was necessary to make sure that, no matter the cost, nobody would be able to hurt her or prevent her happiness ever again.

Chapter Sixteen

Amber wasn't used to surfacing so early in the morning. The seven o'clock wake-up call may have been the one thing she didn't miss from her teaching days, and she didn't particularly enjoy being pulled from her rare peaceful slumber at such an unsavoury hour.

She rolled over and jabbed a lazy finger at the phone in a feeble attempt to silence it.

'Urgh!' she groaned when the ringing refused to stop. She rubbed at her eyes as she stretched over, but only when she noticed the caller ID did she feel herself becoming suitably alert.

Of course, she would have recognised the number anyway, even if it hadn't been programmed into her phone, but seeing the name of Doris Rae flashing across her screen had been absent from her life for months now. Confused, she swiped to answer the call.

'Hello?' she croaked.

'Amber? It's Doris! Doris Rae. I haven't woken you, have I?'

To tell the truth and admit to her former headteacher

that she now lapped up the luxury of sleeping in past nine o'clock wasn't an option for her. 'No, no, not at all,' she lied. She stifled a cough as she pulled herself upright, resting her back against the headboard.

'Oh, I'm glad! Look, I know this is short notice, but I have a huge favour to ask you, and I'm really hoping you'll say yes.'

A little under two hours later, Amber found herself standing in the familiar surroundings of the school staffroom. It had been so long since she had last found herself hovering by this counter, using this kettle, stirring her coffee in a miscellaneous mug plucked from that cupboard on the wall, and yet it somehow felt like she had never been away.

As Doris had explained to her that morning, one of the other English teachers had thought it would be a good idea to go skiing, and had subsequently fallen and broken a leg. Amber had expressed her sympathy for her former colleague, one in whom she had never really found kinship, but didn't hesitate to accept the offer of recommencing her old job again. Even if it was only on a temporary basis, it had to be a sign that she was stepping in the right direction.

She had also been informed that, following the staff layoffs at the start of the year, class sizes had significantly grown in size. It would mean more time spent teaching in the classroom, more hours marking in the evenings, and all for the same salary as before. But she didn't care; she was back where she belonged.

'So! Are you coming to the pub after work then? Down a few gins to celebrate your return?' Claire asked as she approached the kitchen area of the open-plan staffroom. She nudged Amber's side to greet her, narrowly avoiding sloshing Amber's coffee down the side of the mug.

'Can't, I'm afraid. I have far too much to catch up with. I don't even think I know half the kids I'm teaching this term. And the ones I do know have grown beyond recognition; so much facial hair!'

'And that's just the girls!'

Amber snorted. 'Don't get me started on the girls! I swear puberty wasn't so rapid when we were kids.' The elephant in the room – that Claire was a good decade younger than Amber – went unnoticed by the junior of the two, much to Amber's relief. She added, 'Plus, I'll need to catch up with Aisling's lesson plans to see where we're up to.'

'Never ends, does it? I've got a mountain of essays piling up on my desk that make my stomach turn whenever I think about them,' Claire sighed. 'Still, awful what happened to Aisling. I'd rather mark infinite homework about the history of French art than be strapped up in hospital like that.'

Claire shuddered at the thought, then took a moment to concentrate on straining her tea bag. She blew on the surface

155

of the hot liquid, then took a dainty sip. 'Anyway, on a more important note, how was the hot date with whatshisface? Did you...?'

Claire glanced over her shoulder to check if anybody was within earshot, then turned back to Amber with a raised eyebrow.

'You know!'

'What?'

Claire leaned in and lowered her voice. 'Did you shag him?'

'What, you mean *again*?' Amber smirked. Of course, such an escapade had been the substance of their first drunken encounter at the club, and couldn't really be considered any kind of romantic liaison. 'You know I don't kiss and tell, Miss Boyd.'

'Who said anything about kissing?! Besides, you don't need to say anything. I can tell by the way you're blushing.'

As Amber pressed a hand against a hot cheek, Doris idled over to where the two women were standing, sectioned off from the rest of the room. Doris Rae was a stout and rosy-cheeked lady who always wore pearls around her neck and a two-piece skirt suit in some vibrant colour that added a touch of faux youth about her.

'Why has Amber gone all pink?'

Claire was more than happy to jump to answer on

Amber's behalf. 'Things are getting serious between her and her new man. You know the one I was telling you about?' she beamed.

'Ooh, how exciting! Do I hear wedding bells?'

A nervous laughter escaped from Amber. 'God, no! Really, he's nice and everything, but marriage is the last thing on my mind just now. Besides, it's still early days.'

Which was true enough. Of course she craved her own baby, a family, the works, but the thought of walking down an aisle and being stared at by hundreds – oh, who was she kidding? – tens of people gawking at the bride as she approached her groom was too daunting for her to consider right now.

'Deary, it's never too early for a wedding! My Albus and I, we'd hardly been together a month when he proposed to me,' Doris explained. She was an emblem of her own era, with her permed hair and tweed suits that could have, and may well have, been born long before Doris Rae had risen to her current position at the top of the school. 'Still, things were different back then. Not like they are today.'

Before Amber had time to further protest, a teacher she'd never met before turned up the volume on the television set behind them. Everybody in the room turned around to see what was going on.

'Oh gosh!' Doris exclaimed as they all absorbed the

157

picture on the screen. The portrait shot that was positioned to the newsreader's left displayed a blonde woman in her mid-thirties, with her hair parted to one side, her grin wide and displaying a perfect set of straight white teeth.

Before anybody could say anything, the newsreader added to the text that was scrolling across the bottom of the screen.

'*Local artist Victoria Atkins was reported missing by her partner yesterday evening after she failed to return to her home on Friday. Ms Atkins was last seen on Thursday evening just after five o'clock. Police are currently scanning local CCTV footage, and they ask that any witnesses who may have seen Ms Atkins since then to get in touch by calling the number on the bottom of the screen.*'

'Oh, isn't it awful when it happens to the pretty ones?' Doris said as the picture disappeared, making way for the next story to take its place. 'It must be so awful for her to be out there all on her own somewhere, only goodness knows where, the poor dear!'

Yes, Amber thought, the poor dear indeed.

An idle murmuring smattered across the room as everyone returned to their previous conversations, with the odd speculation about the woman's disappearance added into the mix. It was always the same when somebody went missing; there was a great hubbub – for Amber could think of no more appropriate word to describe the influx of attention given in these situations - but soon enough another innocent victim would be stolen from their own safety, and the focus would shift. Besides, they would never be able to guess the truth. Only Amber could know what had really happened to the pretty blonde artist Victoria Atkins.

She nibbled on the ends of her fingers as Doris and Claire chatted to her side, wondering just how many of those uncountable missing people each year in London alone turned up, their captors captured and locked away. How had she not thought about this part of her plan? She had been so meticulous with making sure she had covered all of her tracks, but she had been foolish to not entertain the notion that there existed the tiniest of chances that it might not be executed so smoothly. Nobody had known where she'd been the night Victoria went missing though. She was confident that nobody had seen her, that nobody could accuse her. But she hadn't accounted for the fact that people would actually go looking for Victoria.

How nice it must be for one's absence to leave such a void in the lives of others. At least the lucky bitch knew what it felt like to be needed. She ought to be grateful for that; the time spent in the basement would hopefully teach her not to take things for granted.

The intrusive ringing of the bell flooded the staff room as the interval ended. Somebody, Amber didn't care to notice whom it was, switched off the television, and clusters of teachers started to drift out of the room to take charge of the impressionable minds that awaited them.

'Amber? Are you coming?' Claire asked with a furrowed brow when she noticed that Amber hadn't moved.

It took a moment for Amber to twig that she was being observed. 'What? Oh, yes. Sorry. Just thinking over what I'm supposed to be teaching now!'

She pulled her fingers away from her mouth and forced a smile. She didn't like being dishonest with Claire, but what other choice did she have? It wasn't the first lie she'd told that week, and it certainly wasn't going to be the last.

Chapter Seventeen

There was something indefinable about being in a public place that caused such time spent marking essays to pass more quickly. Claire had said that there was no way she could concentrate on dishing out pitiful grades with all those distractions around her, but for Amber it was the ambience that spurred her to work faster. Well, that and the fact that the café offered free refills for filter coffee purchased after five o'clock.

She had spent many an evening tucked away in the back of the café, surrounded by piles of paper displaying illegible handwriting and inky smudges. It had, in many ways, become her happy place. It was the place where she and Jason had spent many an afternoon together, sipping lattes and sharing plates of sweet carrot cakes. She had never really cared for carrot cake, but the frosting had been Jason's favourite, so she always made the effort to pretend to enjoy it.

Of course, after their separation she didn't need to worry about forcing anything down her throat for which she didn't care. Besides, apart from her first proper date with Greig, she hadn't been back inside the café in months, and thus had had no opportunity to enjoy their cake or otherwise. Now though, she had the perfect excuse to step back through its doors and enter the warm, inviting atmosphere of her happy place; after months of observing the café, and Jason as its inhabitant, through the window as she hovered across the street, she finally felt like she was ready to make a full return to the scene.

It wasn't entirely as it was before though. Amber was never one to miss an opportunity, and so decided to sit not in the booth as she used to, which was always vacant in the early evening, but instead took the last single table seat near the counter. Although displaying her in full view in the middle of the room, it did give her a much clearer view of the front door. Creatures of habit rarely changed their ways, and, if her observations over the previous few weeks had taught her anything, it's that Jason was still very much that creature.

Amber's eyes flitted between the essay in front of her and the entrance door up ahead. She was busy wading her way through a character study of Lady Macbeth when a buoyant waitress approached her.

'Would you like some more coffee?' she asked,

proffering a glass pot swirling with dark, steaming liquid.

'Ooh, yes please!'

She held out her mug for the top-up, which was delivered as the waitress studied the layout Amber had spread across the table. 'Wow, you look busy! Anything interesting?'

'Just homework,' Amber replied as she leaned back in the chair and cradled the freshly heated mug. 'I'm a teacher.' God, how good it felt to be able to say that again.

'That must be so lovely! What age?'

'Eleven to sixteen. I teach literature.'

'Oh, how amazing!' the waitress exclaimed with a shrill. 'Books are so great, aren't they? I just *love* to read!'

Something told Amber that this waitress was most likely not referring to the works as elitist as those stuffed on her own shelves. Just that morning she had, after many months of self-deterrence, decided to begin reading *Finnegans Wake*. Maybe Joyce's approaches to storytelling would inspire her own writing, which, she hated to admit, was still not going very well.

Before Amber had a chance to enquire about the waitress's literary tastes, she was distracted by the faint tinkle of the bell above the door. A customer entered, prompting the waitress to bound off to serve her.

Amber's eyes briefly followed the waitress to the counter, the wall on the clock catching her attention as they did so. If the time was set correctly, it indicated that Jason should be arriving through that entrance any minute now. She returned to her marking, but kept her thoughts firmly on the door.

Of course, she had entertained the thought that, what with Victoria's whereabouts currently unknown to him, there was always the chance that he wouldn't turn up today. But, as she had to keep reminding herself, Jason had visited the café almost every day after work for the last few years. He liked to catch up with the day's emails before retiring for the evening; it helped him to relax better if he knew that all correspondence had been filed away correctly. Surely he wouldn't change that now just because he didn't know exactly where his bitch was.

No, he had kept to the same unfaltering routine for years. Visiting this particular spot had turned into a group activity when Amber came into Jason's life; she would take whatever work she had to mark along with her, and they'd make a date of it. It became habitual for both of them, and, with so many fond and bittersweet memories attached to the place, Amber couldn't face it on her own after Jason had walked out on her. Besides, in those early days following their separation she had struggled to find the strength to travel any further than from her bedroom to the kitchen and back again; the café was on Jason's side of the town, not hers, and to reach it would have taken mental stability that she simply did not have. Still, once she was feeling a little better, and the distraught tears had dried up, leaving a mixed obsessive longing and bitter resentment in their place, she never needed to find an excuse to sit on the wall across the road and watch him from time to time.

The next time the bell above the door tinkled, Amber's attention shot upright. It was just as she had hoped: there he was, right on schedule. Jason entered the café, briefly sidestepping to let another customer leave, then headed straight for the counter. He looked flustered, Amber noted, before bowing her head to observe him over the top of her eyes.

Of course, he was bound to be unsettled. His supposed soulmate had just been kidnapped. Peering at him in the café like this, and at such close proximity, had summoned in Amber such a surge of memories that she'd almost momentarily forgotten all about Victoria.

Almost, but not quite.

Amber bade her time as she observed Jason from her distance. She watched as he fumbled through a stack of loose papers, struggled to suppress her grin as he handed one over to the waitress behind the counter, narrowly avoiding dropping the rest.

As Amber had predicted, it was just like old times. Jason

had visited the café after a day in the office, just like he did most evenings. Except this time he brought with him his fiancée's petite little features and perky smile paraded on a stack of grainy printouts. He'd really pushed the boat out for her with the coloured printing.

Departing more abruptly than would be typical, Jason was just about to head for the door again, no doubt to continue distributing prissy Vicky's mugshots across town, when Amber decided that this was her cue.

'Jason!' she shouted across the café. She needlessly shot her hand into the air as he twisted around to see from where behind him his name had been hollered. The rest of the diners in the small space glanced in Amber's direction to see what all the fuss was about, before carrying on with minding their own business.

'Amber?' He hadn't expected to see her there; to be honest, he hadn't really expected to see her ever again after the way she'd overreacted when he'd told her about the baby. 'Hi. Look, sorry, I'd love to stop and talk—'

Liar.

'—but now's really not a good time. I've got a lot to do, and I…I just…' he faltered.

'Jason, I know. I heard.' She slid out from her chair and sidled around to the front of the table, before resting her bottom against the tabletop. She pressed her palms onto the edge and let her arms relax. 'I heard about Victoria. I'm sorry for what's happened. Truly I am.'

Now who was the liar?

'Oh. Well, thank you.' He didn't know what else to say. A week ago, he'd have wished for nothing more than to have a civilised conversation with Amber, to bring her round to his point of view, but now his thoughts, oblique to his emotions, were strangers even to himself. Whatever this situation was, it was making him very uncomfortable. 'I really must be going now. I need to put up more of these posters.'

Amber gave a subtle nod. 'If I hear anything, I'll let you know. Don't worry, I'm sure she's fine.'

'I hope you're right,' Jason replied before making to leave.

'Oh, and Jase?'

He glanced back at Amber only briefly before carrying on his way. She smiled broadly at him, no longer feeling the necessity to compress her natural emotive response to the whole situation. It really did feel good to see him again, looking so dishevelled as he did, she added with a deserved satisfaction.

'Do take care of yourself, won't you?'

Chapter Eighteen

Given the condition of the rest of the old house, which was barely habitable and had no doubt been a hazard to the safety of its former resident, it was a surprise to find that the plumbing was still fully wired in. Perhaps the building had been partially serviced before the keys were handed over to Amber, but she hadn't been informed of any repairs or ongoing maintenance. No doubt it would have been carried out at her expense.

Not that she'd have cared; money never bothered her. It was one of the few benefits of trudging through life as a pauper – not actually having any money to begin with meant that there was never any need to worry about whether or not she was spending it wisely. Still, it was nice to have an income again, even if it was only until Aisling had regained full control of her limbs.

She stood in the narrow kitchen, leaning against the

worktop, and had drawn back a curtain to stare out of the window. The late evening had brought with it the sliver of a dull waning moon. She hadn't bothered to turn on the light in the room, so the only source of illumination came from the glowing tip of her cigarette. She fiddled idly with the sink tap in front of her, twisting it on and off again repeatedly, until finally giving up fighting for a distraction. She focused all of her attention instead on the blankness in front of her, the only thing she could see in the pitch of the night outside.

There wouldn't have been much to captivate her though even had the garden been visible. In recent years, it had grown into a backyard wilderness, with weeds overgrown and long grassy tufts in a disarray. It hadn't always been neglected though; there was a faint lingering memory there of trimmed turf and blooming flowers, picnic blankets and neatly varnished deck chairs. Her grandparents had spent a lot of time in their garden, and at some point in her childhood Amber must have been a part of that.

Still, there was no point dwelling on the past, she told herself as she dropped the cigarette into the plughole. She twisted on the tap and let it splash water down to extinguish the cigarette, then reached into her handbag on the kitchen table.

She produced from it a bulging plastic carrier bag, which she clutched tightly in her fist as she headed through the dark hallway and straight to the door at the top of the basement stairs. With only a brief hesitation and a small nibble of her lower lip, she creaked the door open.

No sound could be heard from down below. She considered calling out to coax a response, but she didn't want to give Victoria the satisfaction of unnecessary communication. She would be lonely down there, all on her own with only her bleak thoughts for company; why interrupt that any earlier than necessary? Still, perhaps Amber should have headed straight for the basement when she first arrived at the house. She had needed time to gather her thoughts though, to fully prepare for the next phase of the plan.

She reached out a hand and flicked on the light switch by the door. The stairs lit up beneath her feet, and she took a step forward, leaving the door to close behind her. Still no hint of life came from the bowels of the basement.

She glanced down to the bottom, then took her first step, bracing herself for the descent. With each movement the stairs beneath her creaked, an echo of the rasping door, each one yelling out in protest at the weight placed upon them. How old was the house, anyway? Amber had no idea, but made a mental note to endeavour to find out as soon as this was all over.

And it *would* be over soon. A few more months, no time at all really, and then all would be restored to how it always should have been.

Reaching the bottom of the stairs, Amber's nose twitched. The smell of human urine was strong and stale. The bucket, she noted, was still there, but had been tipped over onto its side. A small pale yellow pool had spilled out, and had trickled in the opposite direction from where Victoria was now cowering.

It came as no surprise to Amber to find that Victoria was right where she had been abandoned. She may have moved a little further along the wall, as the handcuff could slide back and forth across about a metre or so of pipe before it hit an obstacle that effectively screwed the pipe to the wall. Other than that small movement though, she was fixed in her position, entirely despite her best efforts to detach the chain from the handcuffs.

Victoria was awake, but made no effort to give any indication as to her state of consciousness. She didn't look up when Amber started across the basement towards her. Instead, she kept her head tucked into her knees, drained of effort as she huddled into herself. Even from her distance a few feet away though, Amber could tell that she was shaking.

Her lips twitched into a smile, allowing herself a fleeting moment to enjoy a brief triumph before forcing herself into action. She continued towards Victoria, then stopped directly in front of her in a tower above the hunched body.

Victoria only flinched when Amber dropped the carrier bag she'd been holding onto. It thumped against the floor, causing her head to jump away from her self-cradling arms. She coughed drily in between shallow breaths.

She kept her eyes low as Amber crouched down beside her, who then proceeded to rummage in the bag until she produced from it a bottle of water. She flicked up the handy sports cap then handed it over to Victoria.

Almost half of the bottle was drained in a matter of seconds as Victoria gulped it down greedily. The cool water soothed her dry mouth and rushed down her throat in a soothing stream.

'Drink the rest. The baby will need it.' Amber didn't bother to look at her as she spoke. 'I'll fetch you some more in a bit.'

'I can't…You have to…'

'Victoria, you're babbling. I would have been here sooner but, well, I was busy. Here, eat this,' she instructed as she plucked an apple from the carrier bag and dropped it in front of her. 'You'll need to keep your strength up for the baby's sake. There's more fruit in there for you, and I managed to get some of those little bottles of supplements too. I wasn't sure if you can swallow tablets or not – I know some people have issues with that sort of thing – so I made sure I got you some extra small ones just in case.'

Amber discarded the carrier bag and stood up, then turned her back for a few seconds as she checked on the tool bag on the other side of the room. It was a fruitless task, as she knew everything would be there – it would be only somebody completely heartless who would break in, steal her tools, and then leave without releasing Victoria – but she was too paranoid to leave them unsupervised and unchecked. It would take just one error, one mistake, to cost her the entire efforts of the whole operation.

When she turned back round, satisfied that everything was still where she had left it, she noticed that Victoria hadn't touched any of the fruit.

'Eat it then, you ungrateful little bitch!' Amber's eyes flared as she stormed towards her.

Victoria shook her head. She was starving, her stomach grumbling through the pain of hunger. She needed the sustenance. She knew she should eat it. But she felt nauseous, sickened at the thought of putting anything in her mouth. Besides, she didn't want to accept anything this crazy woman offered her. She had been too desperate to refuse the water, but it was impossible for her to trust that the food hadn't been tampered with

'I said *eat it*! Eat the fucking apple and feed my baby!'

When Victoria showed no signs of cooperating, Amber stamped her feet some more, then grabbed the apple from the floor and thrust it in Victoria's face. She snarled through her teeth, her lips curled, as she pressed it against Victoria's quivering mouth. Tears dripped down Victoria's cheeks as she twisted her head to the side, fighting to escape the bitter taste of the waxy skin against her lips.

Amber refused to relent, the apple following Victoria's face as she kicked and thrashed in a fruitless bid to push Amber away from her. On the cusp of doing herself – and the baby – more physical harm than good, she had no choice but to give up her fight. With the apple still firmly pressed against her lips, she parted them to take the tiniest bite. Her stomach lurched as she scraped her front teeth across the skin, the acidity of the apple spurting into her mouth.

'There. That's better, isn't it?' Amber said as she retreated. 'Now finish the rest.'

She grabbed onto Victoria's free, uncuffed hand and forced the apple into her palm, before turning her back on her to compose herself. She had hoped that she would play along with her; it made no sense that Victoria, who was incapacitated, would refuse her commands, especially when she had her best interests in mind. She needed to eat. She needed to feed her baby. How heartless of the bitch to fight against it!

Victoria couldn't say anything through her sobs and the dribbling of saliva that emerged as a response to the apple juice.

Facing the other way, Victoria was unable to see Amber's face as she lifted her head. Her hair had fallen down in front of her face, loose strands sticking to her lips. She wiped at her nose with the back of her hand, then burrowed her eyes into the back of Amber's head.

'Why are you doing this to me?' she asked in between sharp intakes of breath.

'You know why,' Amber replied, directing her response not to Victoria but towards the far wall. 'You robbed me of my happiness. You stole my child from me.'

'No! I never! You know that's not true! You can't treat me like this!' The coupling of fear and rage that boiled away inside of Victoria was poised to erupt.

'I don't agree with you.'

Amber continued to fiddle with random objects inside the tool bag, using it as more of a distraction than anything else; everything was going to plan so far, but she couldn't work out why she didn't feel as elated as she had expected to. Success was her favourite flavour, but with this it didn't taste as sweet as she had imagined.

Realising she couldn't waste any more time avoiding the situation, she grabbed something out of the side pocket of the tool bag then rotated to face Victoria again. She had dropped the apple back onto the floor and had returned to clutching her knees to her chest, marginally rocking herself back and forth.

That better not be harmful for the baby, Amber thought, as she scowled at the way Victoria had chosen to position herself. While she was down here in the basement, the baby was Victoria's responsibility; if she wasn't prepared to do everything with its care in mind, she would have to be punished.

Choosing to dismiss her actions on this occasion as not being a cause for concern, she addressed Victoria directly. 'The few days you've spent in here couldn't possibly match everything you've put me through over the past year. You'd be a fool to think otherwise.'

Victoria didn't respond, but kept her eyes on the floor as her toes tapped anxiously against the ground. Amber glanced around, puffed out her cheek, then let the air drift out of her mouth. It was now or never.

'Now,' she said as she stood in front of Victoria. 'I promised myself I wouldn't take too long with this, but…I don't know. Maybe it'd be better if I took my time.'

The lack of clarity in Amber's words was enough to coax Victoria to lift her head.

'Your time with what?'

'I guess I'll just see how I feel once I get started.'

Amber remained in her fixed position for longer than

required as she stared distantly as if lost deep somewhere within her own mind. It was only when Victoria was about to utilise this opportunity to examine the handcuffs now that she could see them more clearly with the light on that Amber sprung back to life.

'Right, let's not waste any more time and get straight to it, shall we?'

Energised by the prospect of the task, and by the fact that delaying it further would only increase the risk of her backing out completely, she dropped down to her knees. She remained angled to one side of Victoria, studied her for a moment, then came to a conclusion.

'Stretch out your legs.'

'What?'

'You're going to have to stretch your legs out. It's far too impractical for you to be sitting bunched up like that. I need to have easier access.'

'I don't…What are you doing?!'

It was only then that Amber unveiled the pocket knife from where it had been safely folded over in the palm of her hand. As she took it upon herself to pull down Victoria's legs so that her torso was left exposed, Victoria was too scared to speak. Too terrified even to take her eyes away from the knife.

'You'll be starting to show properly soon!' Amber

beamed as she observed the subtle hint of a baby bump around her naval. She couldn't wait to see her in full bloom, with her child blossoming in its eagerness to meet her. Time would pass quickly enough, and before she knew it she would be clutching the infant to her chest, cradling it in her arms and humming gentle lullabies.

There was no time to think about that just now though. She shifted a little closer to Victoria and chewed on the bottom of her lip as she weighed up her options.

'It would probably be easier for me to do this if I removed your handcuffs, but I think you'll agree that that's not going to be practical. You're just going to have to promise me you won't squirm around too much. It'll hurt much less if you stay still.'

Shimmying a little closer to Victoria, Amber repositioned herself more comfortably, then opened out the knife.

'You know,' she continued as Victoria struggled through her tears, tugging and pulling at the handcuffs in a wasted attempt to free herself from the restraints and from the clutches of this mad woman, 'I wasn't originally going to do this, but then I was sitting at home last night, and you know what I realised? It suddenly occurred to me that, while you'll be here with my baby, I'll mostly be at work, unable to bond with my child while it grows.'

'It's not your—'

Amber gently pressed a finger to Victoria's lips, silencing her with a surprising calm. She removed her finger, then continued.

'But then I had this fantastic idea! If you talk to the baby, and tell him – or her, we can't rule that out completely – all about me whenever I'm not here, then there won't be a problem, will there?'

She released a short, almost maniacal laugh. 'I can't believe I hadn't thought of it sooner, really. This way I can continue teaching for as long as I can and bring in the money I'll need to fix up the nursery, and, as soon as my baby's born, it'll know who its mummy is straight away. Clever, huh?'

'You're not its mother!' Victoria yelled into Amber's face. It didn't matter that she still had no idea what exactly Amber was talking about; there was no way this crazy bitch was having anything to do with her child.

A suddenly enraged Amber lashed her arms out, pressing Victoria firmly into the wall behind her. Through gritted teeth she snarled, 'Shut up! Shut your mouth, you fucking whore! I've put up with your tantrums so far. I've given you the benefit of the doubt whenever you've kicked off or refused to cooperate. But nobody – *nobody!* – tells me that I'm not the mother of my child! Don't you *dare*!'

As she relaxed her grip, Amber conducted herself

through a brief breathing exercise to diffuse her anger. It was a technique that her therapist had taught her for whenever she needed immediate relief from unexpected stress. It did the trick, restoring her focus.

'Of course, I had to do something to make sure that you'd keep your promise. We can't have you forgetting to mention me now, can we?'

Amber turned her attention away from the knife, and instead stared over the top of her eyes at Victoria.

'What's my name?'

Her tone had suddenly become unusually stern. When Victoria didn't respond, she tightened her grip around her arm.

'I said: *what's my name*?! Say it!'

Victoria quivered. 'A-Amber,' she whimpered.

'That's right.'

Loosening her grip, Amber repositioned her arm so that it rested on her own bent knees. Then, steadying the slight quiver in her own hand, she poised the tip of the knife on the taut skin of Victoria's forearm.

'If you stay still, this shouldn't hurt too much.'

'Don't! No! Please don't! I won't forget! Please, no!'

Amber's hold on her arm was too secure to relent against her resistance. She held on tightly, and glanced briefly up at Victoria.

A small dot of pressure was applied to the tip of the knife, just enough for Amber to test how firm she would need to be, but it was enough to send Victoria into a frenzy. She screamed, and attempted to pull her arm away from the offending object.

It was no use though as Amber wedged Victoria's arm in between her own knees, clamping it in place.

'Scream all you want, princess, but you're just wasting your energy. There's nobody around to hear you. It's just you and me here.'

It was fortunate that Victoria's head was flailing from side to side, as Amber's wide toothy grin would have imprinted in her the foundations of a relentless nightmare.

With the knife now penetrated firmly into the surface layer of Victoria's forearm, she continued to scream as Amber set about her work. If she could only pass out from the pain, Victoria thought as she wailed, she would be able to get through this. Jason would know she was missing. He would be looking for her. He'd find her. He'd stop the pain. It couldn't be much longer now, and he would bring her, and their baby, home to safety.

He had to. He was her only hope.

'Alright, I can hear you! It hurts, I get it! God!' Amber yelled over the noise as she continued to carve. Droplets of crimson blood oozed onto the surface of Victoria's pale skin, streaking out in uneven shades of pinky red as it collided with Amber's writing hand.

The curves were the worst. When marking in the straight letters – the A, the M, the E – the movements were fairly straightforward. But with the rounder letters, it took a little more concentration and control. Amber's hands shook as she concluded the final letter, the bend at the top of the R a little more jagged than she would have liked it to be.

'It'll do,' she said as she lifted the bloodied knife away. Victoria had not been able to look towards Amber at all in those minutes, with her eyes clamped shut to will away the pain while she remained very much conscious. But she had been unable to avoid seeing the mutilation of her skin now that it was finished; sensing that the grip around her arm had been released, she had quickly pulled it towards her torso, giving her eyes just enough time to register the name that had been engraved into her.

Each letter of Amber's name had been etched onto the surface in large, striking capitals, and now bubbled and dribbled with blood, causing each uneven cut to sting and throb.

As Victoria continued to yell out in pain, Amber fetched a cloth from the tool bag, then busied herself with wiping up the botched marking.

'Honestly, screaming like that won't help,' she insisted in

a flat tone as she began wrapping the cloth around the arm. She stroked the rag across each letter, taking care not to apply too much pressure to the fragile area. 'This'll only take a second. Think of a happy place. Like a meadow maybe. Or Jason's bed.'

She finished off by wrapping the cloth around the arm, and fixing it in place with a fraying knotted bow.

'There, now. That wasn't so bad, was it? That should heal quite nicely. You've got to promise me that you won't pick at it though or it could become infected, and we don't know how that might harm my baby. By the time I get back, it'll be ready for the cloth to come off, and you'll be able to see my name every single day. Only a fool would forget to mention me then. And you're not a fool, are you, Victoria?'

Amber hadn't expected any response and so she didn't pay attention to the ignorance, instead glancing around her before confirming to herself that she'd got everything she'd come for.

'It's probably a bit mean for me to leave you here on your own in the dark.'

'Then please! Let me go!' Victoria choked, leaning forward as she hugged her arm to her stomach.

'Don't be stupid.'

She'd considered not allowing Victoria the luxury, but decided a reward was due for not resisting too much while she was working on her arm. Not that the silly cow had much energy to do anything about it anyway, but still, it paid to be nice once in a while. Reaching into the tool bag, she produced the tall candle she'd packed in there earlier, then plucked out a box of matches from the side pocket.

After a moment of fiddling to strike a match, it finally lit up. The orange flame danced around as she drew it to the candle. Then, once a soft glow bobbed around on the wick, she blew the match out, leaving an oddly satisfying whiff of burning to linger in the air.

'There you go,' she said as she placed the candle in the middle of the room, away from anything hazardous. 'You can watch that burn down while I'm gone. It'll keep you occupied for a bit.'

After grabbing everything she needed to take away with her, Amber headed for the stairs, but paused briefly with her hand hovering over the light switch. Her attention went straight past Victoria's pleading eyes as she looked straight at her stomach. A brief flicker of a thought passed through her mind as she considered, if only for a second, letting her go. Just as quickly as it had arrived though she dismissed the thought entirely, then looked up at Victoria's sobbing face.

'Oh, and don't forget to eat up all your fruit like a good girl. We don't want you depriving my baby. Sleep tight!'

The light was switched off. Heavy footsteps sounded up

the stairs and out of the house until they faded to silence. Staring straight into the flickering flame of the candle, and with her thoughts only on the suffering of the flutter of innocence that grew within her, Victoria let out a long, piercing wail that would only remain trapped within the basement walls.

Chapter Nineteen

An early-morning start and a long day in the classroom should have been enough to coax Amber onto the sofa in the evening. However, with so much anxious energy pumping around her body, relaxing was the last thing she was capable of doing.

She had spent most of her lunch hour in the staffroom scrolling through the websites of numerous baby boutiques. It had initially been intended as nothing more than a little digital window shopping, more realistically a procrastination from scribbling down the notes for a chapter she'd promised herself she'd write that evening, but as she poured over the tiny booties and dainty mittens she failed to resist temptation. She placed an order before the afternoon was fully underway, just in time for same-day delivery.

By the time she arrived home after a quick stop off at the café – which had proved a waste of her time as Jason never turned up, probably too busy moping at home over the absence of his pathetic girlfriend – she was too anxious to do anything that required any kind of mental concentration. This seemed like the perfect opportunity for her to give her flat a long-overdue clean.

She threw on a pair of old jogging bottoms and a baggy t-shirt, slid her hands into a pair of buttercup-yellow marigolds, and set about cleaning the kitchen. She wiped down the surfaces, scoured out the microwave, and spritzed the oven. She scrubbed the hob, wrung out the mop, then blitzed the floor.

On her hands and knees with a bristled brush and a bottle of disinfectant, she sprayed and scrubbed and wiped until every nook of each door and skirting board was gleaming, and every slight hint of dirt and dust had been exterminated.

A quick glance out of the window disappointed Amber with no sight of a delivery van. She sighed in a brief interlude of melancholy, then raced through to the bathroom. She dropped to the floor, began scrubbing at the tiles and the plastic surface of the shower floor. She tidied up the clutter around the sink, whizzed a sponge over the medicine cabinet mirror, and wiped away the suds of soap to reveal her own reflection staring back at her.

She looked away as quickly as she had appeared in view,

but there had still been time for her to notice the paleness of her skin and the hollowing of her eyes that had worsened over the last few days. She had lost some weight in recent weeks too, and her hair had started to thin a little. There was no time for her to worry about any of that just now though. Besides, it would never do for her to dwell on something that remained, so she assumed, outside of her control.

She turned the shower on, and undressed while she let the water heat up. She toyed with the idea of turning on the little radio that hung from the caddy to numb her mind with the distraction, but decided against it; she needed to be able to listen out for the delivery driver. Leaving the bathroom door open ajar, she dropped her clothes into the washing basket and clambered under the stream of steaming water.

The plastic doors condensed all around her as she closed her eyes and allowed the water to pour over her. It soaked through her hair and washed over her skin with a comforting warmth. She lathered and scrubbed and rinsed and repeated, scouring at her shoulders and across her chest, over her torso and down her arms, not stopping until she was certain that every pore had been cleansed.

Her pale skin was mottled with a raw redness by the time she finally emerged from the shower into the moist air of the steamed-up bathroom. In the restored silence, she dried herself off with a fluffy towel, slipped into her pyjamas, and secured her dressing gown around her waist. With the towel wrapped around her head, she shuffled towards the mirror, and wiped at its surface.

She could see only a hint of her features through the fading condensation as she prodded at the skin beneath her eyes. In recent months she'd discovered that she was prone to dry skin as a result of stress, and this seemed to be resurfacing again after only a brief respite. Not that she was particularly bothered; it was an inconvenience only, and had no real impact on her daily quality of life. Or lack thereof. Keeping it under control brought only a mild improvement to her washed-out appearance.

Still, she tried to make the effort. As she reached into the medicine cabinet for her face cream, her hand brushed past the empty bottle that had once contained her daily little round pills. Perhaps she was too focused on retrieving the face cream, or maybe her brain had simply chosen not to register the bottle, but for whatever reason she didn't acknowledge it. It was almost as if she had decided to wash away all thoughts of her self-denied medication entirely.

After all, there was no point in wasting energy on something irrelevant to her routine. She was perfectly fine without them, wasn't she?

Half an hour later, Amber was perched on a chair by the

kitchen window, her hair lightly dried and hanging limp around her face as she sucked on the end of a cigarette. She flicked the dangling ash into the glass tray beside her then returned to staring out of the window.

Rain floated down in intermittent showers, but it was not enough to keep people indoors as the odd couple drifted from one side of the street to the other. Their chattering was faint and unintelligible as Amber watched them idly through the net curtain.

The street lamp on the path outside flickered, lighting up as the evening timer kicked in. Amber shot a glance at the clock on the wall to discover that it was almost nine o'clock. The delivery driver had ten minutes to arrive before he was outside of the day's final delivery timeslot.

She finished her cigarette, crushed it into the ashtray, then lit another one. She continued to stare out of the window as her foot tapped rapidly and rabbit-like against the side of the chair leg. She sipped on the cold dregs of her coffee then dragged on her cigarette, alternating between the two over the next five minutes. It was only when she could feel the tears of lost hope peppering in her eyes that the noise of a van door being slammed shut sounded from a little way down the street.

She jolted forward, spotted the white delivery van, then bolted to the front door. It didn't occur to her that the delivery could have been for somebody else on the street. She nibbled at the skin on the end of her thumb as she waited for the silhouette of the driver to appear behind the frosted window.

To her relief, saving her from a certain crippling agony that would have leapt onto her had the driver waltzed straight past her house with a parcel for her neighbours, the thud of footsteps up the front path was followed by a rapid knock at her door.

With as much haste as she could summon, she signed for the delivery, thanked the driver with a meek smile, then carted the parcel through to the kitchen where she deposited it on the table.

As she fished for a large knife from the drawer beside the sink, she kept her eyes on the box. Then, jabbing the knife into the sealed edge, she sliced the tape away from around the edges. She braced herself, took a step back as she returned the knife to the drawer, then leaned over to peer inside the box.

There he was, beneath several layers of bubble wrap, the first present she'd bought for her brand-new unborn baby. She could see patches of his golden brown coat as she unwrapped him, taking care not to pull too roughly as she removed each layer in turn.

He was gorgeous. Once she held him in her hands, first

at arm's length to study him, and then close to her breast, she knew she shouldn't have worried about spending so much money on a teddy bear.

He was the most precious teddy bear she'd ever seen. His fur coat was luscious and soft, and his thickly stuffed arms were jutted out in front of him, poised at all times for a loving, comforting hug. His beady buttoned eyes were shiny and black, and on one of his velvet paws was stitched the unique inscription for which Amber had paid quite a bit extra to have it made up and finished that day.

'Oh yes! You're very beautiful, aren't you?' she said as she stroked the fur between the bear's ears. She ran a finger over the inscription, tracing the fine letters as she admired the handiwork. She had chosen to have stitched onto him the bear's name, and she had decided he was to be called Jason. It suited him well, the perfect name for such a beautiful little bear.

She held him close, and whispered in his ear, 'Baby's going to love you. I just know it.'

As she continued to caress the bear, clutching its head to her chest and rubbing up and down its back as if soothing it to sleep, she stared into the distance with a gentle smile. She thought only fondly of how her petite baby would sleep every night in a dainty new cradle with the bear watching over from a nearby perch. The child would adore him.

'I can't wait for you to meet my baby. In fact,' she said as she clutched the bear tightly to her chest, realising that for the first time in months she finally had hope and joy and meaning in her life, 'I'm looking forward to it more than anything in the world.'

Chapter Twenty

There was a blustering wind circling around the park on the following Saturday morning, which promised to become very wet as the day progressed. Every now and then the occasional child would skip through the gates, bundled from head to toe in coats and hats and scarves and mittens; it was a wonder they could move at all. Weary-looking parents would flop down onto a bench for five minutes and observe their little cherubs shooting down the slides and swinging from the climbing frame, before quickly ushering them away to seek out warmth.

Most of the children protested when instructed to leave. It was such a beautiful quality, Amber thought as she gently rocked herself back and forth on the swing by the entrance, to be involved in such innocent fun without a care for anything as obtrusive as the numbing temperature. As an adult, the weather was often the cause of frequent whining. It was almost a shame to grow up and leave behind that carefree existence.

A few more minutes passed by as she swung gently, her expression vacant as a scattering of thoughts drifted in and out of her mind. It was only when another child dashed with a squeal of delight towards the climbing frame that she snapped out of her trance.

She threw a glance at her watch.

Shit!

Jo would kill her if she was late. It was too easy to envision the therapist's spindly fingers clamped around her throat as she leapt up from the swing and dashed across the road towards the glass building, narrowly avoiding the oncoming traffic as a bus blasted its horn. Charging through the revolving doors, she disappeared from the outside world into the building.

'Well, I must say, Amber, you definitely seem a little more positive than usual. I wouldn't go as far as saying you're particularly *chirpy* – I wouldn't want to lie to you now, would I? – but it's definitely an improvement.'

With a subtle nod, Jo displayed the hint of a smile, as if genuinely impressed, and almost certainly shocked, that Amber had at last showed some signs of improvement. She leaned back in her chair, one leg crossed over the other, and doodled random shapes in the corner of her notepaper as Amber relaxed on the sofa opposite her.

'Do you *feel* happier?' she pressed as she leaned forward, unfolding her legs to shift her weight.

Amber shrugged. 'Yeah, I guess so. I suppose I do feel a little more positive than usual.'

'And what do you suppose is the cause of this new-found happiness?'

It was always the same questions from Jo: why do you feel like that? When do you think you started feeling like that? Why do you think you've started to feel differently? Amber had always assumed she would be paying for the therapist to give *her* the answers, not the other way around. Still, she puffed out her cheeks, slowly released the air through slightly parted lips, then summoned the first plausible response that came to her.

'I dunno. I suppose I'm just getting used to not being around him. Not having that constant reminder, you know? I'd been with Jason for so long that I'd kind of forgotten how to cope without having somebody there all the time.'

She paused only briefly as she considered leaving it there, but decided finishing her response would satisfy Jo enough to keep her off her back a little, if only for a short while. 'I mean, I'm not completely alone. I've started seeing this guy, but—'

Jo paused her doodling, suddenly interested. She raised a curious eyebrow. 'Oh really?'

Amber found herself blushing, instantly regretting her decision to mention Greig. She had never been very good at divulging the intimacies in her life, and had not prepared herself for follow-up questions. 'Yes. But don't get too excited. It's nothing serious.'

'But you're happy about this new relationship in your life, yes?'

A sliver of doubt briefly halted Amber's speech. To admit that she was happy, and particularly to Jo who had been trying to drag such sentiments out of her for months now, was not something she had expected to be doing so soon. Maybe even not ever at all. But she *was* happy, wasn't she? Certainly happier than she had been in a long time. Surely Greig must have something to do with that.

'Yeah,' she finally decided. 'Yeah, I suppose I am.'

When Jo refrained from making any effort to respond, Amber knew that she was being encouraged to elaborate. Well, in for a penny, in for a pound. 'I don't know, maybe it's a good thing that I'm not still constantly moping after my future with Jason.'

'Or lack of,' Jo muttered under her breath.

'I mean, it can't do any harm for me to see somebody else, can it?'

'That's the spirit!' Jo just about managed to resist the urge to punch the air in celebration of her long-overdue triumph. How rare it was for her patients to take her advice; the fact that this seemed to be paying off for this particular one was, if she dared to admit it, rather miraculous.

Jo kept the confession to herself, and continued, 'Now, since you're in a reasonably good mood today, I think this would be the perfect time for me to try something a bit different with you. It might help you to progress even further. I'm not sure how you'll find it, since I've *technically* never tried this on a human before, but I definitely think it's worth a shot. See if we can get you over another hurdle!'

'What's the next hurdle?' Amber asked as Jo left her notepaper on the coffee table, and shimmied across the small space between them to join Amber on the sofa.

'Well, now that you're starting to accept the fact that you're perfectly capable of living a strong, independent life without Jason, we need to…Oh, how should I put it?' She pretended to think, then finished bluntly: 'Get over him.'

This wasn't where Amber thought this session was going. Hadn't she already explained to Jo that she was managing fine with Greig in her life? Why was there cause for further meddling?

'But I…I don't know if that's even necessary. I mean, I just told you I'm seeing somebody, and I—'

'Amber, just because you've started dating again, it doesn't mean you've put the past – or the future, the plans you had, whatever way you want to look at it – behind you. It was always going to be a long road. You knew that. Will this work? I don't know. But is it necessary for us to at least give it a chance? Yes, I'd say it is.'

As Jo held her hands out in front of her in preparation, the room suddenly became hot and stuffy. This felt like it was going to be so much more invasive than anything Amber was sure she'd signed up for. The thoughts about Jason that she had locked away from view were her own; she couldn't possibly relinquish them to her therapist.

'Now I only read about this on the internet last night, so I'm just going to think of you as my little guinea pig. I should probably get you to sign a waiver or something but…' Jo glanced around her, as if waiting for the consent form to magic out of thin air, then turned back to Amber. 'Oh, never mind. I can't see there'll be any harm done.'

Amber raised an eyebrow as Jo placed her hands by the side of Amber's head. Her fingers brushed lightly against her temples.

'I need you to close your eyes for me.'

Reluctantly, Amber did as she was told. She stole a quick glance through a partially opened eye, only to find that Jo too had closed her eyes. She clamped them shut again, now more bemused than frustrated.

'Right. I'm going to place my forefingers against your temples. Just lightly though. There, does that hurt at all?'

Amber shook her head.

'That's a good sign. Now, you keep your eyes closed, and I'm going to count backwards from ten to zero. With each number, I'll be removing my fingers from your head just enough so that you can no longer feel them there, then reapplying the pressure on each count. While I'm doing that, I need you to think about Jason. Think about all the things you hate about him.'

'What, like the fact he cheated on me?'

Jo shook her head in dismay. 'No, no. That'll never do. It has to be something light. Like the way he constantly whistled. Or how he would always wear too much hair gel,' she explained. Then, a little more aggressively, 'Or how he would constantly leave his wet towels in the middle of the bedroom floor after every shower, and expect me to pick them up after him despite the fact the washing basket is right there in the corner!'

Amber squinted open an eye, and raised an eyebrow in Jo's direction. Whatever kind of existence Jo was trudging through outside of the office, it was probably best that Amber didn't enquire further.

'Eyes closed.'

'Okay, I think I've got something,' Amber finally said once she had control of her inner focus.

'Good. Try and control your breathing with the rhythm of my counting. Here we go then!'

After taking a deep breath to get her started, Jo did just as she had explained, counting slowly from ten to zero, and adjusting the pressure of her fingertips on Amber's temples accordingly. Once she reached the end, she removed her hands from about Amber's person and placed them in her lap.

'You can open your eyes now.'

She did so.

'Did it work?'

Amber wasn't sure how to respond. 'What was supposed to happen?'

'The negative thoughts are supposed to be pulled away every time that I removed my hands from your temples. You're not supposed to be thinking about Jason anymore.'

'But you're asking me about him. I kind of can't help thinking about him.'

'Yes, well. It'll probably take a few attempts for it to have any lasting effects anyway. Do you *feel* any different? Perhaps like you want to avoid him from now on? Any thoughts of resentment or loathing?'

Amber was lost for words. Was this really the kind of

treatment she was paying for? She looked quizzically at her flippant therapist, finding herself unexpectedly amused. 'Where did you say you read about this technique?'

'Shit, shit, shit!'

Amber muttered under her breath as she dashed along the road, using her handbag to shield the pouring rain away from her head. She swung the garden gate open, not bothering to close it behind her as she charged up the path.

Sheltered beneath the small canopy above the front door, she glanced at either side of her to make sure nobody was watching, then bent down towards the ground. The plant pots were still there, just beside the coir mat, sporting some half-dead faded greenery. She sifted through a few of them, upending each inner plant pot until she found what she was looking for.

'Idiot,' she grumbled, then fumbled with the spare key as she crammed it into the lock. She was relieved to find that the overhead light hadn't switched on to illuminate her path – it had always done so before, but no doubt the bulb had gone since last winter, and nobody had bothered to replace it yet – but the darkness did make it more difficult to see what she was doing.

Finally the key slid into place. She twisted it, listening to the satisfying click as the door unlocked. With a final glance around her, satisfied that nobody was watching, she slithered through the gap in the door and shut it softly behind her. At last she was concealed inside Jason's home, ready to prepare the commencement of the next phase in her plan.

The only noise came from the dripping tap in the kitchen as it plinked into the sink, out of sync with the beats of the silent hand of the clock on the wall above it as it creeped its way through the hour.

The drips grew louder as Amber emerged in the kitchen, swirling around the contents of a wine glass with one hand. She turned the tap to silence it, then rested her elbows on the worktop. She glanced around her, taking in the atmosphere that had once been so familiar to her.

Months had passed since she had last found herself in Jason's home. He had cooked her a meal, put on some gentle music. They'd enjoyed their pasta in the fragrant ambience, content in one another's company. There had been wine then too, and sex afterwards. Lots of sex, she remembered. They had always been compatible together that way, like the only two pieces of one raunchy, carefree puzzle.

Now though, everything seemed wrong. As a third, unwelcomed piece of their puzzle had forced its way into their life, with it came a bitter sense of unfamiliarity. The crockery was still stored in the same cupboards, the fridge still stocked with similar produce. The walls were still the same colour, and the carpets throughout still blotched with the occasional smudgy stain or loose fray, a product of a home in which one had lived happily and without worry. But it just felt weird, alien somehow. Could a few months apart really make this much difference?

Sauntering back through to the living room, she sighed as she headed for the mantelpiece. The same ornaments were still there, a small selection of figurines he had inherited from his late grandmother, but there was something new there too. In the centre of it all was a silver photo frame. She picked it up with her free hand, and scowled down at the happy couple. Jason and Victoria were unnaturally close to the sunlit foreground as they grinned at the camera, displaying equally sickening sets of immaculate teeth.

'Bitch.'

A car door somewhere outside slammed shut, causing Amber to jump. Keeping her eyes on the window, she discarded the photo, and headed over to peer outside.

It was only the neighbours, much to her relief. She could feel her heart pounding in her chest as she watched them enter their own home across the street, not paying attention to anything or anyone else around them.

Amber let the curtain fall back into place, then shuffled her way through into the kitchen. The cupboard on the wall was, as had always been the case, lined with bottles of whiskey and vodka and wine. Jason had never been a big drinker, but he did like to entertain. Amber had attended several of his gatherings, but rather chose to avoid them when she could; she hated seeing Jason pouring himself over his colleagues, paying her no attention most of the evening.

Dismissing the memories, she reached for the bottle of claret, and topped up her drink. She drained it greedily in a string of satisfying gulps, then glugged out some more into the glass.

She looked up at the clock. It was almost half past the hour. He would be home any minute now. She drank deeply, wiped at her mouth with the back of her hand, then slammed the glass down on the worktop.

It was show time.

Chapter Twenty-One

Out in the street, Jason pulled up into his designated parking space in front of his home. In the darkness of the evening there would have been no reason for him to notice the familiar car of his former partner parked a few houses back. Nor could it have been expected for him to acknowledge that his garden gate was open as he headed up the path to the front door; he was on autopilot, carrying out his daily routine, while his mind was focused elsewhere, searching for answers about the disappearance of his fiancée. It was only when he put his key in the lock and realised that it was already open that he considered that something was amiss.

He froze only briefly, certain that he had locked it. Then he started to consider that he had in fact forgotten to lock it when he left the house in the morning, rushed with the stress of searching for Victoria piling on top of him.

Victoria!

That had to be it. She'd returned, escaped her captor, regained her way, whatever she needed to do to find her way back. Of course she would go straight to Jason's house; she knew he'd be out of his mind with worry.

Gingerly, he pushed the door open, and stepped over the threshold with a cautious foot.

'Victoria?' Her name came out quieter than he had expected. He closed the door behind him, and stood in the centre of the hallway.

'Victoria?' A little louder now. 'Are you here?'

He paced towards the living room, worried about what he might find. His mind raced with all kinds of terrifying notions. What kind of state would she be in? Would she even look the same? It hadn't been very long, barely a week had passed, but he'd heard so many horror stories about missing people being tortured and mutilated beyond recognition.

'Vick? Is that you?' He entered the living room. 'The door was unlocked, and I—'

He halted. He wasn't disappointed. Maybe he was a little surprised. Most of all, however, he was confused, unable to fathom why Amber was lounging on his sofa.

'Hey,' she said coolly. 'Want a drink?'

She gestured to the now-empty vessel as she pulled her body upright. She returned to the kitchen, a baffled Jason in tow, and reached for a fresh bottle of wine.

'What? No, I don't want—why are you—what—how did you get in?!'

Amber fished the key from her pocket and dangled it in front of her. 'Plant pot. Some things never change, Jase.'

As Jason rubbed his hands through his hair, she kept her back to him as she poured out two drinks. She returned the key to her pocket, and pulled out after it a small packet of white powder. She tipped it into one of the glasses, stuffed the empty packet out of sight, then twirled the liquid around. A drink was proffered to Jason.

'No. No, I'm okay.' He shook his head.

'Go on. You look like you need it. I bet you've not had much sleep recently, have you? You look exhausted.'

It was true: he'd hardly slept, and felt like a zombie dragging himself through the day. He gave a subtle nod, accepted the drink, and stared absently into it, as if searching for answers in its bottom. His stubble looked oddly amusing as the creases of his chin folded downwards as he bowed his head. He hadn't shaved in days, probably hadn't washed much either. He really did look like shit.

He sighed. 'I just don't understand. Things like this shouldn't happen to…to good people, you know?'

That's right, Amber thought, they shouldn't happen to *good* people.

A brief silence fell between them as Jason disappeared

into his own thoughts, running a fingertip around the rim of the glass. Then, as if suddenly being pulled back into the present situation, he looked straight up at her. 'Sorry, Amber, what did you say you were here for?'

Amber inched a little closer. 'I just thought you could use a bit of company. Some moral support. I know things must be difficult for you at the moment.' She sipped at the wine, smiling at him over the top of the glass.

'But you hate Victoria. And what happened between us—'

'Is all in the past. I still care about you, Jase. What with everything we went through together over the years, this is the least I can do.'

She locked her eyes on his as they widened, her grin broadening as she drew the glass away from her face. With more sincerity than Jason ever could have feared, she asserted over him her reassurance.

'Don't worry, I'm not ever going to abandon you, Jason.'

Too wearied to think beyond the moment, it hadn't taken much effort for Amber to lead Jason into the living room. It had almost been *too* easy, as she dropped down into the sofa opposite his armchair. She relaxed, at least that was how she appeared outwardly, as she leaned against the armrest; she was a stark contrast to Jason, who had perched on the edge of his chair, his leg jigging up and down, unable to rest as he fiddled and fidgeted and glanced around without cause.

'So what do you think happened? Have the police said anything yet?' Amber asked. She kept her eyes on Jason's glass as he occasionally lifted it up to sip at the liquid. It tasted slightly vinegary, strong enough to mask the taste of any foreign ingredients.

'No, nothing. They're just as clueless as I am. They didn't say those exact words, of course, but it's pretty obvious they've nothing to go on.'

'And you're sure something bad has definitely happened?'

Jason scrunched up his face.

'I mean, there's no chance she hasn't just gone off and left you? Maybe she wanted to get away from everything? I imagine her emotions are all over the place just now, what with the baby and all.'

Jason shook his head, kept his eyes to the floor. 'No. She wouldn't do that. Besides, all her stuff's still there. Her clothes. Her artwork. And her handbag. Her purse. Her phone's missing, but she always kept that with her if she was nipping out anywhere. But…No, she was excited. We were supposed to be moving in together next week!'

He placed his glass on the coffee table, dropped his head into his hands, and let out a low groan.

'She was supposed to be in the house all day. Working from home. It's possible she popped out for a bit though. I know she started to take a stroll most evenings, said the fresh air would do the baby good. Oh God, the baby.' He rubbed at his forehead, growing increasingly frustrated. 'I just don't understand what could have happened in such a short space of time. How much can go wrong between her leaving the house and taking a walk around the block?!'

Amber, who couldn't quite bring herself to offer him the reassurance he needed that his girlfriend was okay, and decided instead to gesture instead towards his empty glass. 'Want another one?'

'What? Oh. No. Actually, I don't feel too good. Must be the lack of sleep. I think you should go home now, Amber. I need to lie down for a bit.'

Jason stood, intending to lead Amber towards the front door, but instead of leaving the room he found himself swaying on the spot. His vision blurred, moving in and out of focus as he tried to concentrate on Amber. She remained faint and faded as he wobbled, staggering a step forward. He tried to move sideways, to start for the door, but his motions were disoriented.

'Are you sure you don't want me to stay and help you with things?' Amber asked. Her voice was distant and distorted, almost muffled behind the tinny ringing sound that had flared in his ears. 'I've got plenty of time if you need anything, and I'm sure I—'

'No, no, I just…I can't…'

The words left Jason's mouth in a slur as he tried to reply. He hadn't been able to formulate the rest of his sentence though, nor could he witness the toothy grin spread across Amber's face as she observed his struggle. With no further warning or time to release his internal cry, his eyelids dropped, his legs collapsed, and he crashed down to the floor. With his eyes shut, everything black, the silence was restored.

Chapter Twenty-Two

There was a faint hum in the air, like static, some sort of white noise that always seemed to exist but which nobody could ever quite work out where it was coming from or what was causing it. It vibrated subtly as Jason's head drooped forward, slowly bringing himself out of an induced slumber.

He hadn't been immediately aware, following his dreamless sleep, of the situation in which he now found himself. In those few seconds of blissful ignorance, as his mind crossed from the land of nod to his living nightmare, he may easily have been back home in his bed, a soft sun trickling in through the window, Victoria's warm body delicately pressed against his side with her arm wrapped around his chest.

Victoria! She was missing. He had to find her.

His eyelids flickered as he began to regain consciousness. He squinted into focus, fighting to shield out

213

the bright light of the room. A few more blinks. His eyes opened fully. With the sudden rush of confusion that washed over him, he almost wished he couldn't see at all.

He didn't know where he was or how he had got there, but he was definitely not at home in his own bed. He wasn't in a bed at all, in fact, but instead found as he attempted to pull his arms forwards that his wrists had been strapped to the back of a chair. There was something else too, something that he'd been too dazed to notice before; a thick wedge of cloth had been secured over his mouth. It hadn't been tight enough to suffocate his breathing, but now that he was aware of it panic rose from deep within him, and escaped out of his mouth in a muffled grunt.

'Hrrrrlp! Hrrrrlp!'

He thrashed about as he tried to scream. The chair swayed, rocking slightly on its legs as it threatened to tip Jason over. Still he continued to struggle, with the combination of his yelling and the clattering of the chair dominating over the sound of approaching footsteps.

'Alright, alright, I'm coming!' a voice called from somewhere outside of the room. He heard it, and froze. Whatever was going on, it did *not* sound like the rapid response of somebody coming to free him.

When Amber entered the room, he was too lost for words to produce any kind of response. Of course, she had never expected him to leap into song and dance at the sight of her, but it would have been nice if he had at least made a little effort to show *some* kind of emotion.

She gave him a moment to let it sink in, then walked across the room to where she had abandoned him earlier. As soon as she reached towards the back of his head to fumble for the knot that held the cloth in place, he began screaming again.

'Seriously, you're making enough noise to wake the dead! Will…' – she found the knot and fiddled with it blindly – 'you…' – untied it as her fingers clasped at the strands of material – 'be quiet?'

She let the cloth fall loose, then rubbed at her forehead. 'You're going to give me a headache!' What with all the wine she'd consumed, it was surprising that she wasn't suffering one already. In fact, it was a wonder that she was alive to feel any kind of pain at all, given the fact that she had somehow managed to drive from south of the river up to Hampstead while heavily under the influence. Had she been stopped by the police, there would have been so much about that situation that she wouldn't have known how to explain.

Yes, officer, I have *been drinking. What? Oh, him? I just spiked his drink, then bundled him into my car when he was unconscious. Nothing to worry about, I can assure you.*

She wiped away the thought, counting her blessings,

215

then whipped the cloth away from Jason's face. She dropped it onto the floor just as he regained his breath enough to bark at her.

'Amber?! What the bloody hell?! What's going on?!' He jerked back and forth in a fruitless bid to remove his restraints. When she showed no signs of moving to help him, he stared up at her and panted through the exertion. 'Get me out of this fucking chair!'

'No can do, I'm afraid.'

'What do you mean?! Let! Me! Go!'

With a heavy sigh, she shuffled forward, then knelt down in front of him. She kept a small distance between them, not willing to give him the satisfaction of sensing her closeness. She didn't refrain from addressing him directly in the eyes though. He needed to learn who was boss.

'There's no point in wasting your energy. You're not going anywhere. And we're miles away from anyone else, so yelling and shouting like that won't do you any good.'

She straightened up, and angled away from him. It was not too long ago that she was saying almost the exact same words to Victoria. 'It's not really déjà vu though, is it?' she said out loud.

Too worked up to focus on whatever it was that Amber was muttering to herself, Jason continued to struggle for his escape. It was only when he had to accept that there was no way the ties around his wrists were going to loosen that his effort relented. His face was beetroot red as he seethed through his growing anger.

'Not important. Won't make a difference,' Amber continued to babble away to herself.

'Difference to what? How did I get here?!'

Amber hesitated before answering. 'What do you remember?' she asked coyly.

He thought about it for a moment. His memory was still fuzzy, but bits of the previous few hours were coming back to him in disjointed fragments.

'I came home from work. You were there.' He was almost nodding along to his own words, trying to convince himself that this wasn't some sort of insane nightmare. 'We had a drink and I…Oh God. I felt sick. I was going to go for a lie down.'

'Well you definitely did end up lying down. I'd never seen anybody hit the floor so quickly!'

He clocked Ambers grin, and his voice escalated as the truth suddenly pelted him full force. 'Did you…did you drug me?! Did you put something in my drink?! Oh God, that's how you got me here, isn't it? That's kidnap!'

Amber said nothing. There was no point in denying the truth. It was much better to watch him work up a sweat.

'What the bloody hell is wrong with you?! Is this because

I left you for Victoria?'

Victoria, who was now missing. Victoria, who had the life Amber had dreamed of. Victoria, upon whom Amber had on more than one occasion wished a slow and painful death.

'Victoria. Oh Christ, she's here, isn't she? What have you done with her? And the…the baby…shit, the baby!' He spoke almost in disbelief, not quite understanding the words that left his own mouth. Then he raised his voice, projecting it somewhere out of the room, and bellowed, 'Victoria! Victoria! I swear if you've laid one finger on her I'll fucking kill—'

The slap fell hard against Jason's cheek as Amber's hand came down, striking fast without warning. He was stunned into a brief silence as he regained his breath.

'You fucking psycho,' he snarled, attempting to mask the pain of his throbbing cheek, which had reddened with a prickly heat at the point of impact. 'All this time you pretended to care that she was missing, but it was all your fault in the first place. You're insane, you know that? What have you done with her? You better tell me *now*, or I'll—'

'You'll *what*, exactly?'

Jason groaned as Amber sauntered over to the room's only window, the ties cutting into his struggling wrists as he wiggled.

'You won't get away with this.'

She chose to ignore the comment, and instead made a

small gap in the curtains so that she could peer out into the night.

'It's so dark outside. Quite cold too,' she remarked nonchalantly. 'I reckon it'll snow soon. Thank God for central heating, eh?'

Bored of the outside world, she returned to Jason, and crouched down in front of him. His head was bowed forward, and his eyes were struggling to stay open as exhaustion took hold.

'I've missed you, you know.'

Her fingers brushed forlornly against the side of his face. He snapped his head up, curling inwards at her touch.

'We're over, Amber. Finished! Just accept that. As soon as I get out of here, I never want to see you or hear from you again! You're dead to me, do you understand that?'

'You think this is about you?' She failed to swallow a short burst of booming, almost maniacal, laughter. 'Oh, Jason, how misguided you are! This hasn't got anything to do with you, my little sausage! No, not one tiny little bit, I'm afraid. You're only here because I couldn't risk you finding out where your prized bitch was while you were still free to roam the streets. Don't worry though. As soon as my baby's born, you won't be hearing from me again.'

'You leave my baby alone!'

'It's not *your* baby. Well, not really. Sure, you got that

cow knocked up, put it in there for me, but I'm accepting the child as compensation for all the hurt you've caused me. I thought you'd ruined my life, you know. But now? Well, just as soon as I have my baby in my arms, I reckon I'll be able to forgive you.'

She stood up and walked over to the door to the hallway, but paused before leaving as she let her own words sink in. 'Well, maybe not *forgive*,' she corrected herself as she cast a look in his direction. 'But ignore, perhaps.'

'You keep away from Victoria, you hear me?! You don't harm my child either!'

'Harm? Oh no, Jason. That's the last thing I'd want to do to my baby.'

She flashed him a grin, then waltzed out of the room, leaving Jason to yell and shout after her. She pushed his voice away from her mind, and whipped Victoria's phone out of her back pocket, before scrolling through the photos. Most of them made her stomach turn, but there was one she simply adored, and caught herself gazing at it rather frequently. She looked down at it now, her eyes wide as she admired the little shape. Right in front of her on the screen, there he or she was, the little outline of her unborn child in its first sonogram.

Unable to control the secret smile she shared with the grainy image of the foetus, she stroked the phone with an extended finger.

'Not much longer, my precious angel. You'll be with mummy soon. Just you wait.'

There was an uncanny spring in Amber's step as she bounded down the last few stairs to the bottom of the basement. She had already flicked the light on up at the top, and now the room was lit up from the naked bulb overhead.

Unsurprisingly, Victoria was huddled up against the wall. She was fidgeting, shifting restlessly back and forth when Amber jumped down from the last step, landing both feet together with a thud.

'Hey, you!' Amber chimed to the unborn child. 'Mama's back!'

'What have you done to Jason?!' Victoria demanded. When Amber didn't answer, she lurched forwards as much as she could, causing the handcuffs to cut deeply into her flesh. 'That's him, isn't it? I can hear him shouting!'

Amber twisted her neck sideways, pointing her ear towards the ceiling. 'Oh yeah! You know something? I think you're right!'

When Amber showed no signs of providing any further information, Victoria retreated, hunching inwards. 'Why are you doing this to us?' she begged. Her voice was hoarse, her throat dry from the sparse water.

'You know why.'

Amber's boots clumped against the floor as she began to pace around, fiddling with this and that. Her own meddling blended in with the natural whirring and humming of the pipes, but it was still not enough noise to drown out the faint and fading cries from Jason up above.

Victoria's eyes followed her around the room, until at last Amber had tired of her own company, returning again to stand directly in front of her. Only then, as she towered above her, did she notice that the cloth she'd secured around Victoria's forearm had been tossed aside. No doubt the silly cow had used her teeth to undo the knot. Hadn't she expressly told her to keep it covered up so that it could heal? Still, it wasn't looking too bad.

'That's scabbing up quite nicely,' she remarked as she gestured in the general direction of her engraved name. At least she was pretty sure that's how it was supposed to look at this stage. A couple of crusty bits had formed on a few of the letters, and there was a weird pale yellow colour dried into patches of skin around the cuts, but it was probably just the body's way of healing itself.

'I suppose I should be thankful,' she continued. 'At least you're the one ruining your figure at my expense. Not that I don't wish I could carry my own child, but every cloud.'

She sighed, then patted out a nondescript tune against

her thighs with her palms as she wandered around in a circle. She was restless, and most likely wouldn't sleep tonight. Probably just as well since she'd need to babysit this pair of idiots for a bit, make sure they didn't do anything stupid.

'Still, it doesn't make up for the fact that you took from me what I wanted. What I *had*. He was mine. But now every time I look at him, you know what I see?' It wasn't a question that needed a response. 'I see you. *You* and your vile, thieving, disgusting little face. We were going to be married. It wouldn't surprise me if that ring on your finger was the one he'd planned to give to me.'

She snarled in the general direction of Victoria's hand, then, without warning, snapped around and marched up towards her. 'Show me it.'

Victoria didn't move, leaving Amber no choice but to lunge straight at her. She scrabbled at her hands, tugging and pulling in a bid to prise her hand away from where she had tucked it into the crease of her other arm.

Victoria cried out as her fingers twisted backwards. She couldn't let her win, wouldn't give in to her demands. The pain soared up her arm though, making it difficult to resist. She fought on, refusing to give her any satisfaction, but a clear cracking sound, which was followed by a brief crunch, generated an instant shooting agony that spread rapidly from her fingers, travelling all the way up her arm.

Her stomach lurched, threatening to make her retch, as Amber twisted and yanked the ring away from her broken finger. The severity of the pain had lodged any cries in Victoria's throat as she clutched the throbbing, purpling finger to her torso.

Amber had already leapt away from her to examine the ring in the stronger lighting directly beneath the bulb. The artificial glow reflected off the band as she turned it around in her hand. 'I must say, it's quite pretty, isn't it? Looks a bit cheap though, maybe a bit too small, but then Jason isn't exactly known for throwing his money around, is he?'

She slid the ring onto her finger, thrilled to find that it was a near-perfect fit, then stared at Victoria with narrow, jealous eyes. 'Not that you'd know. You've only been with him for – what? Five minutes?'

'Please…Let me…Let me see him…' Victoria begged in between sharp breaths. Tears now poured down her cheeks. She had tried to fight it and she had lost. She was drained of all energy, and longed for fresh air away from the heavy, repugnant basement. If she could get to Jason, he would know what to do. He would be able to help her.

'Why should I?'

'Because I love him! And I—'

'You *love* him?! You barely *know* him, you silly cow!'

She stormed over to Victoria, her fists clamped into

balls, with the ring clenched against her finger securely by her side. It may have boasted a rather more petite stone than she had hoped it would, but still it was going to take all of her strength to refrain from slamming it straight into this stupid bitch's face.

She halted, steadied her breathing as she looked down on her. Counted to three. In and out, in and out.

'Show me it,' she demanded as calmly as she could.

Victoria didn't understand. She had already taken the ring from her, as the soaring pain of her throbbing finger refused to let her forget.

'W-what?' It came out as more as a squeak than a question. If Victoria started to show her fear now, then Amber would know she was winning. She mustn't let her see her weakness. She *had* to stay strong. Or, at the very least, she had to learn to fake it.

'My baby. Show me my baby!'

'I…I don't understand.' Truly, she didn't. Her baby wouldn't be born for months yet, if they both made it out of there alive at all.

No, she couldn't start doubting herself now. She would find their escape. She just needed more time. Needed to think harder. 'What do you—'

Another slap fell across her cheek as Amber's impatient rage took hold. 'Take off your top, you stupid bitch!'

Momentarily stunned, Victoria kept her head to the side, waiting for the tears to blink away. Then, with thoughts only for the innocent life growing inside of her, she sniffed, and lifted her head back up to meet Amber's eyes. She would fight to save her baby, but she'd need to cautious; she knew one wrong move could cost her the life of her child.

How much she'd be able to relent and do whatever Amber asked of her, while all the time concentrating her energies on winning her over, maybe even falsely befriending her, in an attempt to persuade her to let her go, she wasn't sure. At the moment though, it was the only plan she had, so it was simply going to have to work.

She gave a subtle nod. 'Okay, but you'll have to untie me first.'

A short, snarled cackle hissed out of Amber's parted lips. 'Nice try! You still have your free hand. You're not entirely incompetent. Hurry up!'

Okay. Fine. She would cooperate. Lifting up the edge of her t-shirt with her one free hand as Amber had demanded, Victoria started to pull it up over her torso. The flesh that pulled tightly across her small bump was exposed to the cold of the room. She struggled as she lifted the t-shirt up higher over her naval, her wrist bent awkwardly and her movements slow but obeying.

Time was precious though, and Amber was too

impatient to wait for her to struggle with it any further. She lunged forward, dragging the t-shirt up over her breasts and around her neck, tugging at it until it finally escaped from Victoria's squirming body. She had pulled at it so aggressively that it had torn, ripping completely away from the handcuffs as the metal shredded the seams of the fabric. She tossed the scrapped material to the floor, composing herself while Victoria, having been thrashed about in the haste, did the same.

Once she had mellowed, she turned around to find Victoria crouched on the floor. She had her arm clasped around her torso and her chest, the latter of which covered only by a flimsy bra.

As Victoria fixed her hazy stare in the distance, silent tears pooling in her glassy expression, Amber kept her attention firmly on her naked stomach. Her fingers twitched greedily as they hovered over her naval.

'My son. My daughter,' she whispered to herself as the tips of her fingers lightly caressed just above the belly button. She drew the outline of a loveheart across her stomach, and kept her eyes on the small bump as she asked, 'What do you think it is?'

'I don't know,' Victoria answered truthfully. She didn't wish to know either; she knew it was a such a cliché when expectant mothers said they didn't mind as long as it was a healthy baby, but she did feel that way. She grew up with a younger sister, and would love to have a little girl, but then raising a strapping young boy, the image of his father, would be wonderful too. Jason, on the other hand, had expressed an interest in learning the sex of the baby before he or she was born, so perhaps it wouldn't be left unknown for too long. They were still to reach a concrete decision on that one.

Oh, Jason! She would have given anything to be with him right then, idly debating about trivial things like whether or not they should have a gender reveal party of if they should be painting the nursery ivory or cream when they move in together. He was so close to her, the occasional sound of his yelling managing to infiltrate through the heavy basement door and floating down through the ceiling, and yet she had never felt so alone.

'I bet it's a boy. I always wanted a little boy. Jason did too. Did you know that? Of course you didn't. You don't know anything.'

Then there was only silence as Amber grinned down at Victoria's bare naval, stroking her flesh as her mind wandered to the near future when she would be able to cradle her little cherub in the protective warmth of her arms. It was difficult for Victoria to not recoil at the touch of her captor, but, at least with Amber distracted, it gave her time to consider her own next move.

'I can tell you,' she finally responded after a moment of inspiration. 'I can find out for you if it's a boy or a girl. I…I have an appointment. Please, just let me go, and I'll—'

'When?'

Victoria hesitated. She *did* have an appointment soon, but it wasn't time to find out the sex. Never any good at lying, she would have to tread lightly.

'Monday,' she replied.

'Hmm. Well, it's a shame you'll have to miss it, but I'll find out the sex soon enough anyway. No harm done, so I wouldn't worry too much about it.'

'But you have to let me go!' Victoria's frustration rose as she struggled to hide it shaking in her voice. 'They'll wonder why I haven't turned up! They'll try to phone me, and then they'll worry about me if they can't get hold of me! They're bound to send somebody looking for me.'

Her words increased in pace as she became more frantic. This wasn't how this was supposed to go. If she didn't make that appointment, then…Well, then what?

She'd still be trapped here. Wherever exactly that was.

Amber suddenly sprang forward, as if somebody had just slapped a hand across her back from behind. 'Shit! You're right. I hate to admit it, but you've got a point. People are already looking for you, of course, but we can't let anyone else get involved—'

'They're looking for me?'

What a stupid question. Of course they were looking for her; she was a missing person, for crying out loud. Didn't she watch crime shows at all? 'Yes. That idiot upstairs was handing out flyers with your precious face on them.'

She pushed the pads of her fingertips against her teeth, nibbling at them, then thrust her head into her hands, rolling her shoulders over as she barely remembered to keep her balance.

'Argh!' The sound came out as a muffled groan before she threw her head back, her arms locked straight, palms splayed and thrust out by her sides. 'This isn't how this was supposed to go! You stupid bitch, you've managed to ruin my plans all over again! I hope you're fucking happy!'

Happy? She was securely handcuffed to an ancient wall, and was growing weaker by the minute as she struggled to stay strong for her unborn child. She was sure she was starting to forget what fresh air tasted like, what sunlight looked like, and her only hope she had of escaping this insane nutcase and her makeshift prison was suffering somewhere upstairs and struggling through goodness knows what. How could she *possibly* be happy?

Amber paced back and forth, oblivious to the clinking of Victoria's frugal attempts to snap her restraints away from the metal pipe. There had to be a way out of this setback.

She halted, poised her hand out in front of her, bracing herself for the oncoming thought. Yes, if they were careful, it might just work.

'You're going to have to phone them,' she declared.

'Wha—?'

'The clinic. You're going to need to phone them. Tell them you can't make the appointment. They'll have heard about your disappearance, of course, so you'll need to pretend to be a friend or a sister or something.' It seemed like such an obvious solution now that she had thought of it. Really, Amber amazed even herself sometimes.

'I don't have a sister! They'll know it's me. I won't do it! I won't—'

Another slap snapped Victoria's head to the side. It was always the same cheek; if Amber continued to resort to violence to have her own way couldn't she at least mix it up a bit, maybe give her throbbing left side a break?

'You will!'

Nothing more was said on the matter as Amber pulled out Victoria's phone from her back pocket. She checked the signal, and groaned, then thrust it up towards the ceiling. She waved it around a little until the bars crept up enough to suggest a reasonable reception, then dragged Victoria up onto her feet.

Victoria didn't utter a sound as she huddled into herself,

231

only slightly resisting Amber's rough manhandling. She couldn't stand straight as her arm remained cuffed to the pipe, and she was contorted unnaturally as Amber steered her as best as she could towards the phone's sweet spot.

'Almost…there…perfect!' Amber glanced at her watch. 'They should still be open just now. Here, hurry up before I lose signal again.'

She offered the phone to Victoria, who could do nothing but stare at it.

'Take it!'

A soft thud sounded from upstairs, causing them both to look up towards the basement ceiling. No doubt Jason had discovered another bout of energy, and was now fruitlessly trying to escape again. Still, as much of a failure as he always would be, Amber knew she'd need to speed things along if she wanted the rest of the evening to plan out as she had intended. Reaching into her other pocket, she fished out the pocket knife, unfolded it, and brandished it in front of Victoria.

'I said *take it*,' she demanded in staccato through gritted teeth.

A whimper escaped from Victoria as she gingerly reached out a shaking hand and took hold of the phone. She noticed Amber had already gone to the trouble of opening up her list of contacts, so all she had to do was scroll through them. She reached the entry titled 'DR ASHFIELD CLINIC RECEPTION', pushed it once, then jumped as Amber's eager hand rushed forward to hit the green phone icon. It started ringing.

It continued to ring for a few seconds as Victoria, her eyes constantly twitching towards the knife, lifted the phone up to her ear. Amber was pressed against her side so that she could listen in. She tried not to recoil at the touch as she waited for somebody to answer.

'Good afternoon, Sunshine Clinic!'

The voice that chimed from the other end was almost nauseating, Amber thought as she stuck her tongue out in protest. When Victoria didn't immediately rush into the conversation, she elbowed her in the side, forcing her into action.

'H-hi, this is…'

'Say you're your sister!' Amber hissed in her ear.

'Th-This is the sister of Victoria Atkins. She's one…one of your patients. Dr Ashfield's patients.' Both Victoria and Amber held their breath while they waited for some kind of indication that the sickly sweet receptionist had been informed of her disappearance.

Nothing.

'I'm just phoning to say that…that I…' Victoria closed her eyes as she stumbled over her words, her cheeks burning and blushed, with nobody except Amber to see her failing. 'I mean, my sister – that's Victoria Atkins – won't be able to make it to her appointment on Monday.'

She swallowed the lump in her throat as the receptionist screwed up her face down the line. '*Oh. Is everything okay, Miss…?*'

'Everything is…'

This was her chance. All it would take was one word, a single cry for help, and they'd know she was still alive. Amber must have sensed her tense up beside her though as the blade of the knife suddenly pressed its flat edge against the bare skin of her arm. Just beside where Amber had already left her blood-encrusted mark.

She could scream down the phone and beg for her rescue, but she had learned very quickly that Amber wasn't somebody with whom she would be wise to mess. Something told Victoria that it wouldn't do her any good, would doubtlessly only lead to more harm. Besides, she didn't even know where she was. She couldn't give an address, or even offer any kind of indication as to where about in the country she was. She knew nothing except that, if she stepped one toe out of line, Amber would punish her before anybody had time to work out where she was being held.

She knew there was only one answer that she could give. She had to lie, if only to protect her unborn child. She sniffed, let the fat, salty tears tumble from her eyes and down her cheeks, then parted her mouth.

'Everything is fine.'

'Well that went better than I had expected,' Amber admitted a few minutes later. 'She sounded a bit too trustworthy, if you ask me. Still, it's sorted now.' Rummaging in her tool bag, she had her back to Victoria, who had slumped back down onto the ground, her knees tucked up to her chest as she stared blankly at the empty space in front of her.

Sure enough, the receptionist at the Sunshine Clinic had accepted the story. For whatever reason – perhaps she lived with her head in a fluffy white cloud high up in a milky blue sky – she gave no indication of having heard of the missing person case, and had accepted the story that Victoria was simply feeling too unwell to leave the house. Her local doctor had recommended a few days of bedrest, she'd lied in the guise of her fictitious sister, but would phone to reschedule the appointment once she was feeling better.

It had been as simple as that.

As Amber busied herself with reorganising her tools, Victoria rocked herself from side to side, swaying with her one free arm wrapped around her knees. She should have said something. She'd been given the chance to do something. And now she had no idea what would happen next. One thing was certain though: with no signs of a way out of this, and with Jason upstairs as another victim to Amber's prey, she had failed at saving her family when she had been given what she was certain had been her only chance.

No. It couldn't be the end of it. It was just a setback. She couldn't give up now. They were all in this together, Victoria and Jason and the baby, and whatever it took she would make sure they escaped Amber's clutches, and as alive and unmarked as possible.

She lifted her head and burrowed her eyes into the back of Amber. She was whistling some faint tune that drifted across the room. How could she possibly be so ferocious, so dominating, one minute, and then seem so placid the next? It didn't make sense. Surprisingly, Victoria found herself more angry than she was confused at such a dichotomised single personality. With the frustration growing immensely inside of her, no longer could she hold back the high-pitched, deafening scream that escaped from somewhere deep within.

'Let me go!'

The unexpected outburst had taken Amber by such surprise that she jumped, scratching her hand with an unidentified metal object inside the darkness of the tool bag. Partly embarrassed by how easily she had been startled, and partly outraged that Victoria had dared to make such an ugly noise, she stormed back across the room and pushed Victoria by the throat until she was firmly pressed against the wall behind her.

'Listen, you stupid little fool! You're not going anywhere. You're going to sit tight, you're going to make sure my baby is looked after until it can be in my arms, and you're not going to say another word. You got that?'

The grip around her throat loosened just enough for Victoria to release a subtle nod.

'Good.' Amber let go of Victoria, who whimpered as she slid down the wall into a weary heap.

Retrieving a bottle of water and a cloth from the side pocket of the tool bag, Amber headed briefly back over to Victoria. 'I'll be back in a minute. In the meantime, I think you should give your face a wash. You look a mess. I won't be long.'

With nothing else to add as she stared down at the prim slut, she deposited the goods beside her, then disappeared up the stairs, slamming the basement door shut behind her.

Having fought to hold it together as much as possible while in Amber's presence, now that she was alone the floodgate erupted in Victoria. The tears poured out of her eyes, snot blubbering at her nose, as she struggled to breathe through the grasping intensity of her grief.

Agony soared through her as she tilted her head up towards the ceiling, trying to follow the noise of the unsettling clattering on the ground floor above. A heavy thud, something akin to a solid furnishing being tossed to one side, was quickly followed by heavy footsteps as they made their way across the floor in a scuffle.

The door at the top of the stairs flung open, crashing against the wall, before the two sets of footsteps trudged and stumbled down the steps. A moment later, Jason appeared at the bottom, his hands tied behind his back as Amber pushed him from behind.

'Jason!' Victoria yelped as she lurched forward, her wrist twisting sideways as she'd briefly forgotten about her restraint.

There was no time for him to reply. Amber thwacked him on the back, sending him reeling across the room. With his hands affixed behind his back, he only narrowly avoided tripping and falling flat on his stomach.

He dropped to his knees in front of Victoria, who embraced him as best as she could. The scarring on her arm was hidden only briefly behind his neck until she brought it down again.

'What has she done to you?!' Jason gasped. He turned to yell something, anything, at Amber, only to find that she was standing right beside him, with her knife threateningly close to his jugular.

'Leave her! Get over there. Touch her again, and I'll use

this.'

The knife pointed to the other end of the pipe to which Victoria was attached, sectioned off further down the wall. Jason hesitated, knowing by the sickening state of his fiancée that Amber wasn't messing around, and tried to weigh up his options.

But what options did he have? He looked towards Victoria as if searching for the answer, but she could only nod at him to obey.

Without turning her back, Amber edged towards the tool bag to retrieve a longer length of rope. Then, with the knife still poised in front of her, she steered Jason into his corner.

'Flinch and I'll stab you,' she said flatly as she crossed over to him. Before Jason had time to respond, she had already hacked off the thin rope from around his wrists. She twisted at his arms, pressing her knee into his groin to prevent him from using his weight against her, and knotted the new rope to his wrist. The other end was swiftly secured to the pipe; she gave it a tug, satisfied that it wasn't going to come loose, then sprang away.

With Victoria slumped to her left, and Jason struggling ferociously to her right, she couldn't help admiring her own handiwork. She had them exactly where she wanted them.

'Amber, I swear to God, if you don't—'

'It's getting late,' Amber interrupted him as she clocked her watch. 'I suppose I better be heading off. School in the morning. You know how it is. But if I find that either of you two has moved more than an inch by the time I return, there'll be trouble.'

That knife was becoming a firm friend, she thought as she brandished it again before closing it and returning it to her pocket.

'Amber, for fuck's sake! Let us go! You can't get away with this. My work will wonder where I am. Your name—'

'My name is perfectly safe, Jason. I'm no longer part of your life, *remember*. I'll leave you and your precious fiancée alone together for now, but I'll be back soon enough.'

'Let! Us! Go! No good will come of this, Amber!'

'Oh, shut up, will you?! You're such a broken record!' She trotted to the bottom of the stairs, then paused as she glanced back. 'Sit. Be quiet. Move and you're dead.'

Well, Jason would die, at least. She'd not harm Victoria, not while she was looking after her baby, at any rate. Still, it wouldn't harm to make her sweat in the meantime.

Ignoring the repetitive shouting that followed in her wake, she headed up the stairs, locked the basement door, and scooped up her handbag from the hallway. She didn't stop to think about anything until she was outside in the driveway with a lit cigarette poised in between her fingers.

She inhaled deeply as smoke spiralled out into the darkness. A solitary tear escaped from her eye and dripped down onto the end of her nose. She wiped it away with the back of her hand and blinked back the rest that threatened to follow it. A few more puffs on the cigarette before she crushed it into the ground and headed for her car.

As she drove away, leaving the house growing smaller in her wing mirror, she left behind with the building her emotions and her baby. It wouldn't be much longer now. The pregnancy was bound to fly by, and then it would all be over. The waiting was painful, and it would undoubtedly intensify once she was able to feel her baby kicking. But she was closer to it than she had ever been before. Yes, not much longer. In the meantime, she was just going to have to be brave and strong.

Chapter Twenty-Three

If there was one thing that could ruin an otherwise perfectly good day, it was having to deal with a catfight. Teenage girls were so mean to each other; Amber was certain she hadn't been like that in her own youth. And fighting over a boy? They were so naïve at that age, so confident that the boy they'd hooked up with the previous night was their charming soulmate. It was all she could do to refrain from telling them both that a quick shag in a cupboard at an underage party didn't constitute real love. God, girls were so much hard work. She really hoped she was having a little boy.

Of course, that's not what she was *meant* to say as an expectant mother, was it? She should be wishing only for a healthy little baby. The sex shouldn't matter. But it did to Amber, and she didn't believe for one second that every other mother wished not for one sex over the other. Not that she wouldn't love her child if it turned out to be a girl, but a baby boy whom she could dress up in pretty pastel blue colours and little bibs decorated with choo-choo trains would be perfect.

Oh well. Que Sera, Sera, as her mother used to sing to her when she was a child. Perhaps she would sing it to her own baby in a few months' time. She hummed the song in a gentle lullaby as she reached into the takeaway parcel she'd dumped onto the kitchen table. She fished out a chip, blew, and popped the vinegary morsel into her mouth. It was so refreshing to be able to enjoy some proper food for a change; for so long she had felt too nauseous to stomach anything more than dry toast, the stress of all the rapid changes in her life building up on her. At last though she felt on top of things, and could enjoy the little things that life had to offer.

A few more chips immediately followed before she leaned back and rested her weight against the worktop. She reached for the phone in her trouser pocket and began flicking through the photos. Why Victoria didn't protect her mobile with a password, she had no idea, but then she didn't seem to be the sharpest tool in the toolbox.

She'd taken it upon herself to reorganise the images. Oh, she'd definitely entertained the notion of deleting them, threatening to banish the sickly snapshots of the happy couple into the digital ether, but that would have been callous. She liked to think that she still had a little heart left in her; ever since Jason had tried to steal her first son's cardigan from her though, that inability to live without him had shattered in a tiny heartbeat.

Now that she thought about it, perhaps it wasn't simply because of her consideration that she hadn't deleted the photos of Jason and Victoria after all. She chewed contently on another chip as he scrolled past the folder of Victoria's personal photos displaying all the irrelevant junk she snapped pictures of each day – artwork, immaculate architecture, the occasional fluffy white dog – and headed straight for the folder where she'd reorganised the smiling selfies of her former partner and his bitch.

No, it wasn't just out of kindness that she'd decided against deleting the precious pictures. She'd become surprised to find that she actually enjoyed looking at them. They encouraged her, spurred her on whenever she felt like her plan was lagging. There was something so infuriating about the way they both flashed their perfect smiles and their glistening wide eyes for the camera, their arms entwined and their heads pressed together. It was disgusting.

They were fuel for her motivation. It had become an obsession, a nightly ritual to coax her into a sound sleep after a long day. She would flick through the photos after waking to silence her alarm clock, instantly stretching over to retrieve her phone from her bedside. She curled her lip as she swiped

244

through a few more, wondering where a particular candid shot of Jason had been taken. Most likely she was looking at Victoria's front room. It was sickeningly organised, with lilac walls and pink scatter cushions. And she called herself an artist!

She snarled, then rubbed at her forehead as she abandoned the phone. Her sleeping may have improved over the last few nights, but she was still battling the bleary eyes of exhaustion. She blinked several times in quick succession, then turned around to face the sink. There was a heaviness at the front of her head that she hadn't expected, as if a great weight was being pressed down on her forehead. After stopping her medication cold turkey, she had experienced a little fuzziness, with a weighted sensation around her head now and then, as if it were imbalanced, but this wasn't the same. The pain was louder, more intense. She went to reach for a glass from the cupboard to pour herself a drink of water when a woozy sickness hit the pit of her stomach.

She had been foolish to think she could stomach the pleasures of a greasy takeaway. She had had nothing to eat all day, and with her sparse diet over recent weeks the harshness of the combined chip fat and acidic vinegar bounced around her empty insides.

Straightening out her torso with her palms pressed into the worktop, she breathed in slowly through her nose, exhaled calmly through her mouth. In, out. In, out.

She opened her eyes. Ran.

She made it to the bathroom just in time, narrowly avoiding throwing up on the carpet.

Later that evening, Amber found herself unable to summon the energy to do anything that didn't involve lying on the sofa beneath a blanket and cuddling into her baby's teddy bear. The sickness had subsided, no doubt because she'd vomited up all of the chip grease until there was nothing left inside of her except self pity.

She kept herself distracted with something dull and mind-numbing on the television. She had no idea what she was watching – some show about rich drama queens in Los Angeles who threw tantrums because their ten-billion-dollar car wasn't the right shade of black – but she was too lethargic to reach for the remote, instead remaining comatose as she felt her brain cells dying one at a time.

She lay there for a few more minutes, wallowing in her own setback, but was forced back into reality when she was interrupted by a rapid knock at the door. She glanced in the direction of the hallway, then back to the living room, before finally hauling herself upright and fishing for the remote to mute the television. Before she had a chance to shuffle her way towards the door, there came another, more urgent knock.

'Alright, alright. I'm coming,' she muttered as she made her way through the hallway, the blanket draped over her shoulders and clutched to her chest with one hand. She unlocked the door and opened it to reveal a young woman: she was blonde, short, and dressed in dark jeans and a faux leather jacket, with a thick woollen scarf wound around her neck.

It had been the last face Amber had expected to see. Years had passed since they had last spoken, and they'd certainly not been in touch since Jason abandoned her. The girl looked flustered, and had clearly been crying.

Of course, despite her flustered experience, Amber recognised Carrie instantly. The last time she'd seen her, her hair had been a little shorter, now falling down to her shoulders, and she'd dressed a little more edgy back then as she was going through her teenage punk phase. However, there was no denying that the visitor before her, with that similar narrow nose and round hazel eyes, was Jason's little sister.

'Carrie?'

Carrie sniffed, forced a weak smile, and then let herself into Amber's home.

Perched on the edge of the sofa, Carrie tucked one leg

beneath the other. She was restless, fidgeting with the tassels of one of Amber's scatter cushions. She turned her neck to see Amber returning from the kitchen, carrying two cups of tea, with a packet of tissues wedged underneath her arm. She handed one of the cups to Carrie, who accepted it gratefully before reaching for a tissue. She dabbed at her watering eyes as Amber sat down at the opposite end of the sofa, keeping her distance.

'I just don't know what to do!' Carrie declared. 'First Victoria, and now Jason! I've been up all night worried sick. He *always* returns my calls, especially if he's not at home, and I don't—'

She paused to blow her nose.

'—I don't know where he could be. It's too much of a coincidence for him to go missing so soon after Victoria, and I...well, I didn't know who else to turn to. I hope you don't mind?'

Amber was about to open her mouth to mumble some spiel about it being fine, and that she understood how she must be feeling, but Carrie was quick to continue.

'I know you and Jason haven't been together for a while now, but, I don't know, I guess I just always thought you two were good together, you know?'

'If only your brother thought the same.'

'Yeah, it's a shame that things just didn't work out for

you two.'

It was more of a shame that he couldn't keep it in his trousers when he had everything and more waiting for him at home.

'Oh, don't get me wrong – Victoria's great! Have you met her? She's so sweet, and she's really talented too! She does these drawings of animals – wildlife and stuff, you know? – and she did one of Fluffy for me for my birthday. Fluffy's my cat.'

'Hmm,' Amber replied, not bothering to attempt to get a word in edgeways as she ran a hand through her hair. She diverted her rolling eyes away from Carrie, who had paused for breath while she sipped at the sweet tea. When she lowered her mug, she clocked Amber's vacant expression.

'Oh, I'm babbling, aren't I?' she rushed in a pitch that could only be described as squeaky. 'It's just that I'm so nervous, and so scared, and I...I don't know what I'm supposed to do!'

'I understand.'

God, she needed a cigarette. Would it be a problem if she lit one up with this distraught mess of a girl beside her?

Sod it. It was her home, after all.

'You do? You were always a great sister-in-law to me,' Carrie gushed as Amber reached onto the coffee table for her cigarettes. 'Oh, don't worry, I do know you and Jason were never married, but I always thought of you as a big sister. Did you…did you feel the same way about me?' A short chuckle escaped from her lips. 'Not as a big sister, of course! But as your little sister. I hope you did! Did you?'

Amber sparked the lighter and ignited the tip of the cigarette she'd wedged in between her lips. She took a drag, and exhaled. 'Sure.'

'I knew it!'

Whatever sentiments Carrie was about to divulge next were interrupted when her mobile phone sounded from inside her jacket pocket. Her eyes widened as she leapt up to unzip her pocket.

'Ooh, that'll be them!' She spoke with an unusual excitement, given the circumstances, as she fumbled for the phone before it stopped ringing.

'Them who?'

'The police! They said they'd phone me around this time with an update.' An idea flashed before her. 'Oh, *say* you'll talk to them!'

'No. No, I don't think so.' Why didn't she just shut up, and hurry up with answering the phone before they hung up?

'Why not?'

'I…my therapist won't allow it. She says I'm not allowed to involve myself in Jason's life anymore.'

'Oh. Okay then.' She didn't sound too concerned as she

replied to Amber, before whisking around to take the call.

Amber had actually surprised herself with that spot of quick thinking. If nothing else, it was just nice to think that her time spent with Jo had finally been put to good, albeit brief, use.

As she continued to enjoy her cigarette, she could see Carrie out of the corner of her eye; her broad smile perfectly matched her sickly sweet voice. There was no way the police had any information on her. She'd covered her tracks well. Hadn't she? She tried not to show any emotion as she listened to one side of the conversation.

'Hello, Carrie speaking. Hi, yes. Now's a perfect time! You've not heard anything at all?'

Relief washed over Amber, who released a breath as she flicked ash into the tray. 'But I don't understand where he could have gone!'

Leaving Carrie to her conversation and to her developing hysteria, Amber stubbed out her cigarette, lifted herself out of the sofa, and carried her mug and the teddy bear through to the kitchen. She settled him down on the worktop and took a sip of the tea. She had left it to sit for too long, and it had now become tepid and unappealing. She stuck out her tongue before pouring it down the sink, then turned back to the bear.

'Well, fuzzy Jason, it looks like things are going to plan.

All that worrying over nothing – that was silly of us, wasn't it? We still need to be careful, of course we do, but it looks like everything is going to turn out just fine after all.'

Chapter Twenty-Four

It was never sunny in the cemetery. The rest of the town could be illuminated by a silky yellow sunglow, but the clouds above the headstones were always dank and grey and overcast. The once-luscious grass was almost colourless, and the path weaving above the corpses was streaked with the early morning's rain.

Amber stuffed her hands inside her sleeves as she crossed through the graveyard. Although she could think of better places to spend her time, she had never really been disconcerted by death, and so she didn't mind passing through as she took the shortcut from her home to the high street.

Not that she was in any hurry. After an unexpected restless night, she gave up tossing and turning and dragged herself out of bed all bleary eyed not long after four o'clock that morning. She was washed and dressed and pacing around the house before the sun had forced itself to warm up the bitter November morning, and in the end, after a brief failed attempt at concentrating on marking homework, she decided to set off earlier than necessary for her lunch date with Greig. Otherwise, if she hadn't, she would have ended up driving herself crazy.

The saunter through the streets had been pleasant enough; few people were around as most had had the sense to stay wrapped up warm indoors, with the exception of the occasional dog walker or newspaper enthusiast popping out to pick up their mid-morning read. However, that calm atmosphere was quickly threatening to diminish, as a fat raindrop landed directly on Amber's forehead.

'Shit,' she muttered to herself as she stopped beneath a tree to rummage in her handbag. In her haste for fresh air she had foolishly left her umbrella at home. She glanced around her, weighing up her options. Her coat was long enough to protect her down to her knees, but she was still a little way from any shops or cafés into which she could escape should the weather worsen.

As another drop fell from the sky, then another, and another straight after that, she knew she needed to hide inside somewhere until it lessened if she wanted to avoid resembling a drowned rat when she finally met Greig for lunch. She glanced around her, and that was when she noticed that the door to the church at the end of the pathway where the cemetery blended into the churchyard was ajar. She cast a look up towards the sky, then back to the door, before rushing along the path with her handbag over her head to protect her hair. As she approached nearer, she noticed that the sign on the door indicated that the pre-lunch service was about to begin. With no other option in sight, she lowered her handbag, and slipped inside the church.

A few moments later, after dropping some loose change she'd managed to salvage from the bottom of her bag into the collection pot by the doorway, she had found herself a lone seat on an empty pew. There were a few people dotted around, but nowhere near the volume that she would have expected. Maybe it was too wet for people to worship that morning. Either way, she was relieved to find that those who had turned up for the service did not stare at her or pay her any attention at all. It was almost as if each churchgoer was oblivious to the presence of those around them, each absorbed in their own problems and their own prayers.

She fidgeted uneasily for a few minutes, fiddling with her phone and checking it several times to make sure it was on silent; the last thing she needed was to draw attention to herself if Greig happened to call her during the service.

Finally, the priest walked out and took centre stage at

the front of the pews. Amber tried to recall the last time she'd seen anybody wearing a clerical collar. Come to think of it, she couldn't pinpoint the last time she'd been inside a church either.

The priest began speaking, and Amber found her mind zoning in and out of focus. She picked up odd words of his speech though as she retreated back and forth from reality.

'—and karma is a word we find so often thrown around, whether we are addressing somebody directly, or overhearing a conversation—'

Her expression remained vacant as she was lost deep inside her own empty thoughts, remaining unaware of the words that were infiltrating to the back of her mind.

'—I ask you this: on whom does the responsibility to issue such punishment lie? Is it yours? Is it mine?—'

The voice was faint as the temperature rose in her head. She should have removed her coat. It was so stuffy in there, that suffocating density that seemed to weigh down the air whenever a storm was brewing.

'—Our Lord God of the Heavens has such power as to decide the fate of another. But we have faith that those who are evil will have evil done unto them in return. But it is not our responsibility to issue this—'

She had been stupid for thinking she could do this. She needed isolation, not to be trapped inside an invasive room with strangers all around her. She should have kept on walking in the rain. There was fresh air outside. She would be able to breathe outside.

Snapping out of her transient trance, she sprang out of the pew, grabbed onto her bag, and rushed up the aisle towards the exit, her shoes squeaking on the wet floor as she ran. As she charged through the first door and headed for the second that would lead her to the vast freedom of the outdoors, the priest's voice trailed behind her, latching onto her thoughts before continuing in her wake.

'—As the Bible reminds us, 'eye for eye, tooth for tooth, hand for hand, foot for foot…"

The sound of the flushing toilet whirred around Amber's head as it echoed inside the bathroom. Once she had restored herself to a state of balance, she flicked off the light and headed to her bedroom, rubbing at her temples as she walked. She entered the room in its darkness, and kept it that way as she glanced momentarily at her bed, before realising that she had neither the energy nor the inclination to pull back the bed covers and crawl inside them. Instead, she let the weight of her body flop towards the floor, and sought out the support of the solid wall behind her as she firmly pressed her back against it.

Her lunch date with Greig had been pleasant enough,

but now, as the contentment faded with the remainder of the day, her head throbbed, she felt like somebody had poured a vial of washing up liquid into the pit of her stomach, and with each move her muscles screamed out with a burning strain. Her brain was still fuzzy too, awash with a cloudy faintness every time she moved her head to the side; starting to convince herself that she was dying, she had Googled the symptom to put her mind at rest, and, according to the trustworthy doctors of internet search engines, it was a common side effect of abandoning those specific antidepressants she'd been prescribed.

But what was she to do about it? There was nothing she *could* do now. Even if she wanted to start taking them again – which she most certainly did not, as she had never felt so alive, and refused to give up being able to feel like herself again – she had thrown them down the sink. Almost two months' worth. There was no way she would be given any more just now, not when she wouldn't be due another batch for quite some time. She was just going to have to suck it up.

But that was easier said than done, she realised as she curled her knees up to her chest, leaning forward to rest her forehead on them. Through the fog of her mind she sought some comfort, some kind of mental image to which she could attach these darker feelings of weariness and self pity.

It was no use. As she groaned and curled further into

herself, she failed to barricade the moving pictures that flashed in succession behind her eyes.

Jason and Victoria at a restaurant. Laughing and smiling, drinking champagne in a candle-lit booth. The happy couple in their eternal honeymoon period.

Jason and Victoria holding hands. Strolling through the park, giggling as they disappear behind a tree. Eager, greedy kisses. Not a care in the world.

Jason and Victoria in Amber's bed. Hot, clammy, naked. Nibbling ears and soft moaning. Hips dancing rhythmically until they both climax in unison.

Jason and Victoria in a pastel-blue nursery. Looking over Victoria's shoulder as she watches out the window, Jason fixing a mobile to the cot in the corner. He crosses over to Victoria. She turns. In her arms she cradles a newborn baby boy. Tiny fists, puckered lips, button nose and beady eyes. The perfect vision of innocence.

'Aargh!'

Amber let out a cry as she beat her palms against the side of her head. 'Go away! Go away! Go away!'

She slapped her hands onto the ground, beating out an intense rhythm in an effort to exorcise her pain.

She leapt up from the floor, and pounded her fists into the wall. 'Leave me alone! I can't…I can't *stand* it!' she moaned. Dropping her weight against the wall, she surrendered to her pain, before crumpling down to the floor.

As she curled up in a ball, hugging her knees to her chest and weeping through the agony and the nausea, she knew that there was nothing that she could do except accept her need to suffer the existence of the sickly couple as best as she could until the time arrived for her to claim her prize and bring her baby home. She would only be alone in the world for a short time longer. Then she would be able to smile at last.

Chapter Twenty-Five

Despite the struggles and the hardships that tormented the mind and tore apart the soul, the human body remained a marvel. Jason had only been trapped for a little over twenty-four hours, and had yet to be struck with the full force of sparse food and little hydration; for now, all of his thoughts were focused only on escaping. Victoria, however, who willed for whatever small intake she did have to travel straight to the baby, had entered a state of survival. What little food she did have was now being stored as her emergency supply, as if she were a mother bear in hibernation with her cub through winter. It meant she had little energy with which to work, but it did increase her chance, if only marginally, of escaping the basement alive.

The only silver lining, if she dared to think of it as such, of spending the passing hours in complete darkness was that her eyes had become accustomed to her surroundings. After a few days her pupils had learned to adjust, allowing her to take in the room a little more clearly. Still she had not successfully sought any feasible method of escaping from her restraints, but at least she did not cease her search.

For now though, they slept, both of them propped up against the wall, Jason stretched out flat on the floor with one hand dangling limp, while Victoria curled foetal with her legs tucked inwards.

She stirred, but did not wake, as she rotated slightly. Her handcuffed arm twisted a little, stopping her from moving any further. It clanked against the pipe as it whirred, more alive than either of the inhabitants chained to it. A hand went to her stomach as she dreamed about her baby; it was a happy dream, with only soft colours and large, open spaces. The air was pure and her baby, wrapped snugly in a fresh cotton blanket, was safe in her arms.

Her arm wrapped itself around her torso as she hugged onto her unborn child. She would remain sleeping for as long as she could; any dream, however far removed from her present reality, would be better than the truth.

Chapter Twenty-Six

Birdsong could brighten up even the dullest of days. The sun shone unseasonably in the early evening, allowing a rare autumnal warmth to lighten the park in its final hour before closing at dusk. The air was calm, with only an occasional breeze serving as a reminder of the approaching winter.

As Amber and Greig sauntered side by side along the path, they chatted idly. Greig stuffed his hands casually into his coat pockets, but Amber, who was enjoying the freedom of the fresh air, found herself leaving her arms to swing loosely by her sides. Apart from the crick in her neck she'd gained from falling asleep on the floor the night before, she didn't feel quite so unwell today, restoring a little of the spring in her step.

'I told her it would be impossible,' Greig explained as he continued the story that he'd been telling since they were back at the park entrance. Amber walked silently along beside him, content with doing all of the listening. 'There was no

263

way I could pick up her shopping for her before the supermarket closed. But you know what exes can be like. Always full of unreasonable demands, you know?'

'Mmm.'

'Don't get me wrong. She's the mother of my child, so I'll do anything to help her out when I can, but sometimes people don't really see the wider picture.'

A small group of children giggled loudly as they swung from the monkey bars in the nearby playpark. Amber glanced around her to cast her gaze across the pond in their direction, squinting over the shimmering reflection of the setting sun on the water's surface. She could hear them screeching as they played and tumbled in their carefree innocence. Never had there been a happier sound.

Having finished his story, Greig had turned to meet her face, but was greeted instead by the side of her handbag, out of the top of which protruded a small furry paw.

Bemused, and with Amber still observing the children, he prodded at the object.

'Hey, who's this little guy?' he asked, pulling Amber back to reality.

She glanced down to see what Greig was referring to. 'Oh, that? It's…it's nothing,' she rushed.

To convince him that it was indeed nothing of any concern, she removed the teddy bear from her bag and held it limply. Inside, she wanted to clasp it to her chest and shield it from the world around them, but how could she possibly explain that to Greig?

'It's just a present for my friend. My friend's kid.' How easily the lie rolled off her tongue.

'And you carry it around with you in your bag?' With a childlike curiosity, he slipped the bear from Amber's grasp. He made it wave at her, then tumbled it about in his hands as if it were performing somersaults in the air.

'No! No, I must have forgotten to take him – *it* – out of my bag.'

Greig stopped twirling the bear to inspect it more closely. His eyes met with the personalised stitching on the bear's paw. 'Who's Jason?' he asked with a furrowed brow.

Oh God. She'd not mentioned Jason by name to Greig, had kept as much of her past – if she could call it that – suppressed from their relationship, and intended to keep it that way for as long as she could sustain it.

'The…the bear.'

It was the first answer that came to her as she rushed for an explanation that concealed the truth without further interrogation. But then Greig couldn't possibly have found out about Jason, and should have had no need to press her further. Why was she worrying?

'Oh. I assumed it was the name of your friend's kid,'

Greig replied, before handing the bear back to Amber, having tired of playing with the toy.

Amber emitted a short burst of nervous laughter as she accepted the bear and returned it gently to her handbag. 'Y-yeah! That would have been a good guess!' Why hadn't she thought of that?

They continued down the path in silence until they turned the corner towards a small cluster of eateries. Greig halted, craned his neck, and sniffed inquisitively.

'Do you smell that?'

'What?'

'Warm doughnuts, that's what! I used to love them when I was a boy. Oh, let's get some!' He turned towards her and clasped his hands like a small child pleading for a treat. 'I haven't had warm doughnuts in years!'

'Er…sure! Yeah, alright then. I mean, it's nearly dinner time, but what the heck!'

'Brilliant! Be right back then!'

Greig planted a swift kiss on Amber's cheek, checked his wallet was still in the back pocket of his jeans, then skipped over to the doughnut stand. Amber sauntered in his wake, stealing a glance into her handbag to ensure she'd placed Jason back inside without any damage to his fur.

She glanced around as a gentle breeze whipped around her. It carried the pungent mix of aromas that drifted from

266

the food stands, with the sugary sweetness of the doughnuts blending with the penetrative scent of sizzling onions and grilled hotdogs. If she was honest, the thought of such gluttonous food was making her feel a little queasy, but she decided to keep quiet, not wishing to dampen Greig's spirits.

He returned a few moments later, clutching two paper bags of squishy hot doughnuts. He handed one to Amber, then wasted no time tucking into his own.

'Ooh, ooh! Hot! Hot!' he warned as he blew on the piece of doughnut he'd shoved straight into his mouth. He chewed, then finally swallowed. 'God, that's good!'

He reached into the bag and wedged a hearty chunk of doughnut in between the paper, blew, then took another deep, fulfilling bite. 'I know they're so bad for you,' he mumbled with his mouth full, 'but it's great to be a little wicked sometimes!'

Before Amber had a chance to respond, her phone sounded from inside her handbag. Glad for the distraction, she handed her paper bag to Greig as she reached to answer it.

'Who is it?' Greig asked with sugar-speckled lips.

'I don't know,' she replied truthfully, staring at the number she didn't recognise. 'Sorry, I better take this.'

She answered, and listened to the voice on the other end as Greig mimed running amok with Amber's paper bag.

Distracted, she turned her back to concentrate on the call.

'Carrie? How did you get my number? His phone? Oh. No. No, I don't mind. What do you mean, you've found something? Yeah. Yeah, I'll be there in about an hour. Okay, sure. Bye.'

She hung up, and turned back to Greig, who was happily munching away. He looked up at her, his eyes glistening with glee, but dropped his grin when he noticed her concerned expression.

'Something up?'

She shook her head, not sure whom she was most trying to convince. 'No, I…It's nothing. It was just a friend of mine. She's going through a bit of a relationship crisis at the moment, and I said I'd go round and see her in a bit. You don't mind, do you?'

'Not at all. You do what you've got to do. You really do need to taste these doughnuts, by the way. They're incredible.'

He returned her paper bag and recommended stuffing his face. With her eyes glazed, staring into the distance as she tried to fathom what exactly Carrie could possibly have found, Amber nibbled at a small piece of lukewarm doughnut. When she was faced with the sweet sugar though, she could taste only bitterness.

The car sped along the road, only slowing down to let

another vehicle pass as it headed towards her from the other direction; the narrow street had been lined with impatient drivers after the rush hour, all settling in the for the evening and turning it into little more than a one-way lane.

Amber waited for the car to pass. She drummed her fingers on the steering wheel as Beethoven's *Für Elise* blasted at an obscene volume from one of those classical radio stations as she attempted to drown out the buzzing of her own brain. The driver waved a polite thank you, then allowed her to continue on her way.

She knew where she was going as she hurtled towards the end of the street. She had been in Jason's home many times, of course, and several times in recent months she'd hovered outside of it too, but she had not intended on returning so soon after her previous visit. The journey itself was unpleasant enough, but she should have known it would have been this cramped and difficult to find a space to park at this hour.

Finally she found enough room a few houses down from Jason's front door. She squeezed her car into a tiny claustrophobic space between a monstrous Range Rover and a flash new Mini, then slammed off the radio. The silence was brief as she leapt out of the car, banging the driver-side door shut behind her, and headed straight up the path to the garden gate. If she faltered, even for a second, she risked losing her wit completely, and then everything would threaten to unravel out of her grasp.

'Bloody hell!' she exclaimed more loudly than intended as she threw her handbag over her head, narrowly avoiding stepping in a puddle. Of *course* it started to rain as soon as she got out of the car. Struggling to suppress her fear of whatever it was Carrie was on about, she would have been a fool to expect things to go any other way for her that evening. Still, she could have at least remembered to pack an umbrella to ease the misfortune a little.

She sped up the front path and pushed against the front door. Carrie had unlocked it with her own spare key and had left it that way, allowing Amber to escape from the rain without hesitation. Once inside, however, after she shut the door over slightly to block out the wind, and tousled the rainwater out of her hair, she paused before stepping any further into the house. She needed to brace herself for the potential of an oncoming storm.

In and out, in and out, she breathed deeply. If only marginally, she could manage to reduce the twitching in her hands as they fiddled restlessly by her sides. She glanced in the mirror that Jason had hung on the wall by the door. Her pale skin was blotted with patches of red where the rain had attacked her even in those few seconds she spent outdoors, but aside from that there was nothing about her expression that could possibly give anything away.

Okay, she was ready. Reaching a hand out behind her she slammed the door firmly shut, as if suggesting she had just entered the house, then made her way down the hallway to locate Carrie. She had been careful, had covered her tracks well. Whatever Carrie had found, there was nothing for her to worry about. She had everything under control.

'What do you think it means?'

Carrie pointed an accusing finger at the two empty glasses on the coffee table. They sat side by side, right where Amber had left them.

Oh shit. She had been in such a hurry to bundle the barely conscious Jason out of the house and into her car that she had forgotten to wash up the evidence first.

'I don't think it means anything.'

Carrie drew her hand away from her mouth, then marched over to the table. 'How can it not mean anything? It clearly wasn't *Victoria* he was drinking with, was it? And look!' She picked up one of the glasses and thrust it towards Amber, desperate for it to be the clue to her brother's disappearance that she had been seeking.

In that moment Amber couldn't work out what she was supposed to be feeling. On the one hand, Carrie had just freely handled the evidence, contaminating it with her own fingerprints. On the other, however, she was staring at her own faint pink lipstick smudge on the rim of the glass.

'It *must* have been a woman he was with!' Carrie proclaimed. Then, more distraught, she cried, 'If I'd only noticed it the first time I came here, when I let the police in, we could have found him by now! Who was it, Amber?! Who could she be?! He would never have cheated on Victoria!'

Ah, of course. Carrie had never been informed about her brother's own dark affair with the bitch in question. To her, he was forever a saint.

Amber considered entertaining the notion of explaining to Carrie everything that went on between Jason and Victoria while she was still sharing a bed with him, but then what good would it do? No, it would only give her a motive, and the less negative attention she drew to herself the better. Besides, it was more crucial that she obtained the glasses from Carrie to decorate them with her own fingerprints while in front of a witness. That way, if they were tested, Carrie could back her up. Of *course* Amber's fingerprints were all over them; she had been ever so helpful to the young girl, and was there to help her clean up the mess Jason had left behind. Not only was it plausible, but it was also, broadly speaking at least, the truth. It was the perfect deterrent.

'Here, let me see,' she ordered with an outstretched hand. She took the glass from Carrie, and picked up the one from which Jason had been drinking. She had, after all, handled both of them already, and needed to cover her tracks.

'What are you doing?' Carrie asked as she watched her turning the glasses around in her hands, pretending to inspect them for any incriminating marks.

'Just seeing if I recognise the colour of the lipstick.' Which she did: it was 202 Winterberry Blush, her favourite.

'And do you?'

She feigned dissatisfaction. 'Don't think so, no.'

'Oh! We must tell the police! Whoever that woman was, she'll know where my brother is. Even if she's not...'

'Guilty?' Amber offered. The word slid out of her mouth like ice, sharp and jagged as she stabbed it towards Carrie. She had nothing against Carrie personally; she was a nice enough girl if a little juvenile, but a part of her was enjoying watching Jason's own sister sweat like this.

Amber returned the glasses to the table, then moved closer to Carrie as she burrowed her eyes into the vulnerable girl. 'The police will have already seen them,' she explained. Which was likely, though why they had left them there she had no idea. Perhaps they too, just as Amber had tried to convince Carrie, had jumped to the likely conclusion that Jason had left to find his missing fiancée. 'They came here, remember? You told me so yourself. If they thought they were important, they would have made a note of them.'

She placed an arm around Carrie's shoulder and drew her in closer. 'In fact, I bet they're investigating the swabs they took from them as we speak.'

'You think?'

'I *know*.' God, she hoped she was wrong. 'I'm sure they'll be in touch if they find anything, but for now you just need to put it out of your mind. Worrying about things isn't going to help matters, and you'll only make yourself ill. You need to trust me on this one. I was almost your sister-in-law, remember. I wouldn't lie to you, would I?!'

Carrie pondered this for a second, then released a heavy sigh. 'I know. You're right. But…how can I not worry when I just *know* something bad has happened to him?'

Amber considered her reply for a moment as she searched for the perfect response. There had to be a way to distract the girl from the truth.

Finally, she leaned in closer towards Carrie's face, and said, 'Look, Carrie, I didn't want to have to mention this, but I think I know where your brother's gone.'

Carrie's eyes widened. 'You do? Where?'

'Yes. Well, not where as such, but why. All the signs are there. I think – and brace yourself, as you're not going to like this – but I think he's been having an affair.'

Carrie gasped. She was falling for it, hook, line, and

sinker.

'I know. It's not great. But everything points to it. The lipstick. Victoria missing. Isn't it possible that she found out about this other woman and left him?'

'But—'

'Carrie, I've been through this sort of thing before.' There was no point in explaining to her that many of the same people had been involved in that affair, nor did she need to know that Jason had been the one to walk away from that relationship. 'I know what this looks like. It's not pretty. I know it isn't. But you need to trust me on this one. I'm almost certain that this is what's happened here.'

'Really?'

'Yes, really.'

'Then we must tell the police that!'

'Tell them what?!' Amber snapped as she pulled away from Carrie, threatening to lose her cool. The girl had a seriously unhealthy obsession with the police; it couldn't be good for her. 'That Jason's a sleazy adulterer? No, there's no point. It would only tarnish his name. And you don't want that for your own brother…Do you?'

The question was met with only silence and a strong shake of the head. That was the last thing Carrie wanted. The last thing in the world.

'Me neither. Then I suggest we wash up these glasses,

ignore the fact that Jason's morals are a little loose, and trust that everything will work out for the best. Agreed?'

Carrie slowly exhaled. She trusted Amber. She knew she wouldn't lead her astray. Finally, she nodded. 'Agreed.'

'Good. Right, I'll do the tidying up here, so why don't you head off home? Get some rest. You look exhausted!'

'You're too good to me, Amber. I don't know what I'd do without you!'

'Don't mention it.'

No, really don't mention it. The sooner she got the girl out of her sight the better.

Retrieving the other glass from the table, Amber turned her back on Carrie and headed through to the kitchen, leaving her to gather her things and let herself out. She blasted on the hot water and let the glasses fill up beneath the tap, before reaching under the sink to where Jason always kept the bleach.

She knew she would have to be more careful in the future. She had been so sure she'd left nothing behind. She had been mistaken though, and now she would have to remain alert of her actions at all times. It would be exhausting work, but the reward would be worth it. As she scrubbed and washed and wiped at each glass, she cleansed them of all their invisible marks, rinsing away any evidence that suggested she had ever been near Jason at all.

Chapter Twenty-Seven

'So, has anything interesting happened since our last session that you'd like to tell me about?'

It was the way Jo liked to start every therapy session, inviting her patients to steer the conversation in the beginning. She decided it made them feel like they were in control of the situation, and that they could escape the discussion at any time if they felt it was becoming too uncomfortable. She always managed to drive things back to where she wanted them though, plucking out the information she needed to push their progress further.

However, as she observed Amber, who perched rigidly on the edge of the sofa, something told her that today wasn't going to be that straightforward. Her eyes were blank, her expression giving nothing away; it was as if she had built an invisible barrier between her emotions and the outside world, preventing Jo from tapping into them at her will.

'Not really,' Amber murmured with a weary shrug. Her

shoulders felt heavy from a sleepless night of tossing and turning and lying awake at awkward angles in an attempt to achieve any respite from her growing fear of being caught. Whatever confidence she had previously had in her ability to sail through her plan with few obstacles was now lacking, causing a great pressure to weigh down on her. Coupling that with the nausea that frequently washed over her, a product of some underlying guilt that she unknowingly fought each day to suppress, things weren't going as smoothly at this stage as she had hoped.

If Jo thought she was going to share any of that with her though, she was gravely mistaken. She noticed she was still staring at her, encouraging her to continue.

'I got a new desk at work,' Amber finally added to satisfy the therapist's silent prompt.

'Well that's riveting,' Jo replied flatly before glancing down at her notes. 'What about your grandfather's house? Have you decided what you're going to do with that? I expect it's keeping you quite busy.'

Amber didn't flinch, conscious of her movements. She couldn't afford to give anything away, especially not now.

'I've thought about it a little,' she said, 'but I've not been up there recently. I'm probably going to sell it though; there's no point in me keeping it to myself when there'll be some family out there who could turn it into a loving home.'

Was that what Jo would want to hear? For good measure, she added, 'I could put the money to good use, do a bit of travelling or something. I'm sure that's what my grandfather would have wanted.'

'I didn't know you were interested in travelling?'

Amber didn't respond. There were only so many lies a person could tell in one hour.

Thankfully, Jo didn't care much for pressing the matter, and swiftly moved on to a subject the therapist found more appealing. 'I must say, Amber, you definitely seem to be handling things much better than I ever would have expected from you. Do *you* feel like that's the case?'

She shrugged by way of response. Truthfully, she didn't know how she felt. One minute she was up, and the next she was down. Like the grand old Duke of York and his ten thousand men. The thought made her smile, which was timely as Jo was staring right at her, but she quickly brushed it away again. If she appeared too positive, too upbeat all of a sudden, she risked Jo becoming overly suspicious.

'I guess so,' she replied. 'I suppose I've just let things naturally dry out on their own. They say time's a healer, don't they?'

'Perhaps, but you've got a long way to go, don't you? I still don't think you're ready to stop seeing me just yet. It's important that we get a handle on things to make sure you're

279

fully on the road to feeling like your old self again. I once had a patient with severe depression who terminated our sessions earlier than I had advised, and two weeks later she was found dead in her bath. Crazy or what!'

Nothing like patient confidentiality.

'I feel fine—'

'Often people can feel okay one minute, and then all of a sudden something can trigger buried emotions, and then *bam*!—'

Amber jumped, startled, as Jo clapped her hands together, her volume rising. She carried on, however, completely unfaltered.

'—all that angst comes flooding back!'

'I don't think that'll happen to me. I really do—'

'Have you seen Jason recently?'

The question was so unexpected that it stumped Amber into silence. What did Jo know? Could she know anything? It wasn't possible.

'What? No. I mean, I did what you told me to do. I stayed away from him. I no longer feel the need to go down that street with the café he usually visits.' It wasn't completely a lie. 'That was what you suggested, wasn't it?'

'Yes, yes, very good. I'm very proud of you,' Jo muttered with a hint of patronisation. 'But there's something else you need to think about, Amber. What would you do if you saw him again? This is a free country, after all; he can come and go wherever and whenever he pleases. You can't safeguard yourself against his existence entirely; you may bump into him when you least expect it. And how would you feel then? Angry? Upset? Enraged?'

'Fine. I'd feel fine.'

'You really believe you'd feel *fine*?'

Well, yes. She did, didn't she? After all, she had seen Jason very recently indeed, however unbeknownst to the therapist that may have been, and the encounter hadn't elicited any kind of heightened emotions in her, had it? She hadn't overreacted. Quite the contrary, she had been rather calm, she thought.

'Yes, I do think that,' she replied. 'I'm working through things now. Channelling my energies elsewhere. Working on other projects, you know?'

'What sort of projects?'

Another shrug. Why was Jo always so inquisitive? 'Just things. Work stuff. I'm still seeing Greig too. Keeping busy, just as you recommended.'

'Listening to my advice is a good start, I'll grant you. I'm full of the stuff—'

She was full of *something*, at any rate.

'—and you're right to listen to it. You could learn a lot! In fact, one of my other patients was telling me that they find shopping to be really beneficial whenever they're feeling overly anxious. Why don't you give that a go? Personally, I can't see any fun in it, but apparently it really works for some people. They even find it quite soothing, though Lord knows why.'

For the first time in…Well, possibly the first time *ever*, Jo had actually said something that Amber agreed with. She hadn't browsed the shops on the high street in a long time; she'd been too preoccupied with the redundancy and the depression and the anxiety and the isolation. Then, once all that had calmed down, she had channelled all of her energy into carrying out her plan. But she'd worked hard on it all, hadn't she? She'd pulled herself out of the worst of the darkness and had put her efforts into something positive. Perhaps she should allow herself a little retail therapy.

After all, there was still so much she needed to buy for the baby, and it would be in her arms before she knew it. It would never do for her to not be prepared.

'You know, I think that might actually be a good idea,' she remarked to Jo, whose face twisted in surprise. Clearly she wasn't used to her patients agreeing with her so freely.

'Well…good! Yes, very good,' she said, failing to entirely hide all of the emotion in her voice. 'Treat yourself! But still, I cannot stress enough that a new handbag or a new pair of shoes or whatever it is you're into isn't going to cure you overnight. I think we better book you in for another session.'

Jo flicked through her diary, then glanced up at Amber, looking over the rim of her glasses as they perched on the edge of her nose.

'How does next Thursday grab you? What about Friday too? Same price as usual, of course.'

'Do I really need two sessions in a row?' Amber asked. Then, scoffing, 'You're not exactly cheap!'

'I know exactly how much I cost, I can assure you. I'll put you down for the same time both evenings. You'll be my last appointment of the day.' Jo looked unnaturally elated as she filled out the details.

As Amber made no effort to hold her fake smile, Jo closed the diary and leaned over, her eyes locked on Amber's. 'You must remember, Amber, it's as I always say: you can't put a price on sanity!'

Chapter Twenty-Eight

Victoria snored softly as she hunched up in a disjointed ball against the wall. Her arm had reassumed its position around her waist as she slept, her chest rising with each gentle breath.

She sounded so at peace, Jason thought as he cast a glance in her direction. He squinted through the darkness, now quite accustomed to the black space around him, and could make out her figure further along the wall. If he closed his eyes, he could just about pretend they were back at home, in his comfortable bed with its freshly washed sheets, and not trapped in a damp and dreary suffocating basement.

He should probably count his blessings though that it was only suffocating to the mind; enough air seemed to infiltrate the room from the gaps around the door at the top of the stairs. It was, for now, enough to keep them both alive.

No, he corrected himself, enough to keep all *three* of them alive.

It wasn't truly enough though, and he couldn't let himself think that. It was his responsibility to make sure that his fiancée and his child made it out of there with their future intact. He was exhausted, and every muscle in his body burned with soaring pain, but he couldn't rest. There was no time for that.

And yet, time was the one thing of which he now had an abundance. A person could go crazy being stuck down here alone; he had no idea how Victoria had coped for so long. He supposed she *hadn't* coped, not really; was it selfish of him to now consider himself thankful that she was down there with him? He had never been fond of the dark, and rather feared enclosed spaces too. At least – at the very, very least – he wasn't alone.

Having Victoria beside him also gave him the motivation he needed when he felt his efforts lagging. He wanted nothing more than to curl up and drift into a solid, if not eternal, sleep. But he had to go on, for her sake if nothing else. With the sound of her puttering breaths near his ear, he once more recommenced tugging at his restraints, desperate to weaken the knot.

As he continued to pull and yank at the rope, confident that it must be doing *something*, if only making a millimetre of a difference with each effort, the noise of his struggles caused Victoria to stir. She turned around, bleary eyed, to face the blurry shape that was her lover.

'Jase? What are you doing?' she asked sleepily.

'What do you think I'm doing?!' he snapped back. He continued to tug, ferociously grunting and thrashing about. Finally, he relented, and slumped over with an exasperated sigh. 'Sorry, I didn't mean to speak to you like that.'

'I don't blame you,' Victoria replied softly. 'Keep trying. Don't give up!'

She was right, of course. He mustn't give up. He couldn't afford to. He pulled some more, his wrists taking most of the strain as he struggled to clasp his hands around the awkwardly positioned rope.

'It's no use, Vick. The knot's tied too tightly,' he said as he shifted back onto his bottom, fully drained. 'She's got us well and truly trapped.'

'But we can't let her win!'

'Win? Victoria, this isn't a competition. It's not a game we're playing here. You've no idea what she's capable of.' He sighed, deflated and defeated. 'Quite frankly, neither do I.'

There was only silence between them for a few minutes as they both became absorbed in their own agonies. Then, finally, Victoria spoke:

'Well we have to do *something*. She's a psycho! If we don't get out of here, she'll only hurt us more, won't she? She's going to kill us.'

The words left her mouth as little more than a soft whimper. It was a statement that sought out correction, some kind of response that suggested she was mistaken. She wouldn't really hurt them. Everything would be fine. In the end, everything always turned out alright.

But Jason, who was rapidly losing the strength to find any hope, could only turn to face Victoria, and reply gravely, 'I know.'

The radio station that had fired up when Amber had started her car had dedicated the entire evening to a non-stop playlist of cheesy upbeat Eighties classics. They had kept Amber in delightful company for the first ten minutes of her drive away from the high street. She couldn't help smiling to herself as she drove up behind a queue of vehicles waiting at the traffic lights; whether the music was the reason for her chirpiness, or if Jo's advice had actually had more of an effect on her than she'd imagined, she wasn't sure. Whatever the cause, she wasn't going to let anything bring her down tonight.

As a few more cars piled up behind her, she took the opportunity to turn her attention to the little gift bag on the passenger seat, its pure white design printed with the elegant black department store logo. It was the ultimate symbol of taste; she would only ever accept the best for her baby.

As much as she hated to admit it, Jo had been right.

Amber had never really been too fussed about shopping before, and certainly anything that involved cowering behind a changing room curtain or lowering her self-esteem as she tried to squeeze into a dress size she wished she was rather than the size she actually was proved to be nothing more than a living nightmare. But shopping for clothes for her baby? That was a whole different story.

She had floated trancelike around the first floor of the department store, feeling almost as if she had entered a daydream. Of course, she had been there before; with her first baby she had been so anxious to have everything ready that she had begun gathering his little essentials almost as soon as she had discovered that she was pregnant. This time though she had decided to wait, had held off as long as possible, but she could wait no longer.

As she picked up each delicate garment in turn, turning them around in her hand to admire the tiny patterns and soft colours and sweet cartoon characters, she knew she wouldn't be able to buy everything she wanted for the baby all at once. Her income was looking a little brighter now since she'd returned to teaching, but she didn't know how long that was going to last. She shouldn't go crazy with spending for her child. Not now, at least. And, not knowing the sex yet, she wasn't keen on buying anything that could be considered gender specific. Sure, there would be no problem in dressing a little girl in blue or a little boy in pink – wasn't that how it used to be anyway, once upon a time? – but she was so fond of the idea of donning her picture-perfect baby in colours that would instantly hail them as her dashing prince or her pretty princess.

In the end, she had lingered over a tiny babygrow, small enough to fit only the most delicate newborn, with a matching white hat and teeny scratch mittens. It was so pure and innocent, everything she knew her child would be. Without further hesitation, she'd bundled the outfit into one arm, and headed straight to the till to pay for her child's first outfit.

She peeked into the bag now while the static traffic allowed her the chance. It looked so soft and delicate, all neatly folded over at the bottom. He or she would look so adorable in the tiny outfit. She was so anxious to dress her newborn, but she would need to be patient. It would arrive for her soon enough. Not long now.

A car horn blared from somewhere behind her, forcing her to lurch upright to find that the lights had changed back to green. She launched the car back into gear, and slowly continued down the road. As she headed along a straight route towards the north of the city, her mind wandered away from her surroundings and instead focused inwards on the giggling gurgles and the button nose and the tiny wide eyes of the baby on whom she could not help doting. A hand wandered of its own accord away from the steering wheel and towards the front of her stomach as she manoeuvred through another street, protecting the infant inside of her that would never really be there.

'These handcuffs are practically welded shut. You're our only hope. Please, Jason. Keep trying!'

Victoria relented as she rolled over onto her side as much as she could manage, before sipping at the remaining drops of water left for her in the plastic bottle. On the other side of the room, Jason continued to tug at the ropes, all too aware that, after hours of struggling, it was going to make no difference.

'If only I had nails, I could probably try and open up the knot a little. Are you sure there's no way you can slide the handcuffs any further along the wall?'

'Jason, I can't. The pipe, it connects to another one about half a metre away. It's impossible for me to come any closer. I promise you, there wouldn't be this distance between us if I could do anything about it.'

Of course, it had been a stupid question. The only thing he wanted right now, or at least as much as he longed for an escape, was to hold Victoria in his arms. It was his responsibility as her future husband, and as the father of their child, to protect her. And he was failing at that miserably.

'Urgh!' he grunted as he lost his grip on the rope. It was beginning to cut into his wrist, and had burnt across his palms as what little grasp he did have on it proved to be faltering. 'This is not going to work like this. It's too resilient; it's impossible to snap. I need something sharp, something to fray it with to weaken it.'

'I'll just go grab my handy tools, will I?' Victoria snapped.

'No need to have a go at me either, Vick. I'm trying my best here. I feel guilty enough as it is.'

Silence was restored as neither knew what to say, or do, or even think. They were both trapped, and, as much as neither of them wished to admit it out loud, they both knew their chances of escaping were becoming increasingly less favourable.

Jason wasn't lying though. If he hadn't turned up uninvited at Amber's door to ask for the cardigan back, none of this would ever have happened, would it? He and Victoria would be cuddled up at home on the sofa, watching some trash on the television, while they talked and laughed and basked in one another's company. Instead, he was trapped in a dark room, fighting the thought that, if it were necessary, and even possible, he would have sawn off his own hand in order to save his family. After all, such a desperate act had worked well in that movie, hadn't it?

After a while, Victoria spoke. 'It's not your fault. Yes, she has every right to be angry. I know you cheated on her. *We* cheated on her. You left her for another woman. But think about the alternative. You would have been trapped with that maniac. So don't you ever feel guilty for getting away from her. She has no right to be treating us like this. *Nobody* should be treated like this! She's insane!'

Jason patted his hands on the floor around him as he replied, 'I've never known her to behave like this before. It's as if something inside of her has just flipped.'

'Or stopped working altogether,' Victoria retorted. Then, noticing through the darkness that Jason seemed to be shifting around a lot, she arched an eyebrow. 'What are you doing now?'

'I'm trying to find something to help me get this bloody rope off.' His voice was strained as he stretched out an arm as far as he could manage, threatening to pull all the muscles down one side of his body. 'There's all this old junk around us. I can see cardboard boxes over there, and there's some furniture over to the side of me, but it's just out of reach. There has to be something nearby though, something I can use to get this stupid thing off.'

Victoria joined in as she pushed her limbs to the limit, twisting her torso around to reach over to the far wall. 'There doesn't seem to be anything around me. She made sure of that when she first left me here.'

'Careful, don't exert yourself, Vick—'

'I've got something!' Her words were followed by a short, spluttered, guttural laugh. 'Ha! The stupid cow! It turns out she's not as clever as she thinks she is.'

'What? What is it?'

She held up the object in Jason's general direction. 'Her knife.'

'She left it lying on the floor?'

It seemed a little too good to be true. Would she really have been so careless? But then she had appeared to be quite scattered, as if her mind was always working one step ahead of her actions. It was possible.

No, there wasn't anything *possible* about it. The pocket knife was there. He could see it, if only slightly, as Victoria brandished it in his direction. For whatever reason, Amber had dropped her guard, weakened her concentration, and had forgotten to retrieve the knife after her last visit to the house.

'Silly bitch would lose her head if it wasn't screwed on. Here, catch.'

Victoria folded the blade back into its sheath and slid it across the floor towards Jason. It landed a little way from his feet, but not so far away that he couldn't bend forward a little, testing the resistance of his restraints, and scoop it up from the ground.

He flicked open the knife, pausing to study the blade only for a second, before he began hacking at the rope. He sawed it back and forth, the rope cutting into his wrist as he pulled it taut, until it showed some sign of cooperation.

'It's working!' he cried as it started to fray beneath the chopping blade.

'Oh, thank God!' The words were music to Victoria's ears. Freedom was so close she could almost taste it. She could hear Jason grunting as he hacked away on the other side of the room. 'Come on, keep going! Hurry up, Jase!'

'I'm hurrying! Almost there…Almost…Ah!'

The rope gave. It snapped in two, sending Jason toppling backwards at the release. The knife clattered to the floor as he lifted his wrist up towards his chest, rubbing at where the rope had cut deeply into his skin. Then, almost not quite believing it wasn't some sick and misleading dream, he pushed himself up off the ground, and rushed over to free Victoria.

A little further away, in West Hampstead, Amber steered the car through a quiet residential street. She hummed along to some vaguely recognisable pop song on the radio, tapping her finger rhythmically against the steering wheel as she meandered onto the next turning. The roads were peaceful in the early evening, the sun low and warm as it crept towards the horizon.

With her sunglasses poised on her nose to shield her from the glare, nothing was going to dampen her mood. She couldn't let it do so; after the threat of retreating back into her own darkness, she'd managed to claw her way back into the unseasonal sunlight, and it was there that she planned to remain.

She continued driving across West Hampstead and into Frognal, before winding her way through several short streets up towards the Heath. A few minutes later, after curving her way along the narrow path, which was concealed at either side by tall, swaying brown-leaf trees, she pulled the car up outside the house.

She jerked the handbrake, then killed the engine as the radio clicked into silence. With the motions of the vehicle ceased, the queasiness in the pit of her stomach that she'd managed to suppress all the way there began to rise again. She sat for a moment as she rested her head against the steering wheel. She breathed deeply as she pushed fresh air down into her lungs. It was probably just a response to her giddy excitement; she knew they were going to love what she'd bought for her baby, and she could hardly wait to show it to them.

Finally, she lifted her head up, and titled it towards the

bag that still remained peacefully beside her on the passenger seat. She lifted it up, peered into it, and at the same time placed a hand on her stomach.

'Mummy's coming, baby.'

Back inside the house, down in the depths of the basement, Jason embraced Victoria in a tight, almost suffocating hug.

She pushed him away. 'Let me out of here! Hurry!' She wanted nothing more than to remain in his arms, but there would be time for that later. Right now, she needed to concentrate only on escaping. And quickly.

Jason glanced around him. 'Where's the key?!'

Shit. She hadn't thought about that. She racked her brains, sifting through the last few days as she tried to recall where Amber had put the key to the handcuffs.

'Try the tool bag,' she suggested. 'I'm sure I saw her put it in there.'

'Really? She didn't take it with her?' Jason queried as he rushed over to it.

'Yes!' Victoria displayed an unexpected excitement as a new memory surfaced. 'That's it! I remember thinking that exact same thing when I watched her leave it in there! God, she's a stupid bitch.'

Jason rummaged around, metal clanking and zips opening as he sought frantically for the small object.

'Can you see it?'

A bright light suddenly beamed across Victoria's face. She squinted, the light harsh on her eyes after spending so long in the dark. Once she had readjusted her vision, she saw that Jason was crouched over the bag, sifting with one hand, and holding a torch with the other.

'Found it!' he replied a moment later, jumping up into the air with the key thrust out in front of him. The torch beam traced his footsteps across the floor has he bounded straight for Victoria.

'Can you hold this?'

Victoria nodded and accepted the torch, the scabs on her arm itchy and sore as she reached for it, then angled it towards the handcuffs as Jason fumbled with the tiny lock. His hands shook as he fiddled with the mechanism.

'It's so…fucking…argh!' He almost dropped the key, before grasping at it just in time to save it from clattering to the ground.

'Careful!'

'I *am* being careful! It's a tight lock, and I…there! Got it!'

Victoria wasted no time in shaking herself free from the restraint. She flung her arms around Jason's neck, oblivious to the pain that soared through her infected skin when it came into contact with the fabric of his shirt. Locked in an embrace together, Jason took the time to slip her ripped shirt back

.

over her head after he'd retrieved the torn bundle from the ground. He pulled it over her shoulders as best as he could manage without breaking free from the hug.

'What has she done to you?' he asked meekly as he pulled away to straighten out the garment so that it just about managed to cover her exposed chest and stomach.

It would have been easy enough for Victoria to lose herself in the sorrow reflected in Jason's eyes. They couldn't stall though; they had to keep moving.

'Come on, we can worry about other things later,' she said as she stepped away from him. 'Right now, we need to get out of here before she comes back.'

She was right, of course. They charged up the stairs, Victoria guiding the way with the torch as they wasted no time in observing their footing. With the doorknob lit up by the thin beam of light, Jason twisted it furiously.

'Fuck!'

It was locked. There was so much about this escape that they hadn't considered. Amber may not have executed her own plans flawlessly, but at least she always seemed to be one step ahead of them. Always able to snuff out their latest successes on the road to freedom.

'Watch out of the way,' Jason instructed, placing an arm in front of Victoria's stomach to steer her to the side.

'What are you—?'

Victoria's words were interrupted by a thunderous crash as Jason stormed his weight into the door, attempting to shoulder-barge it open.

'Stop! You'll hurt yourself!'

'Fuck!' Jason grunted as he dropped his weight against the door. 'It's too solid.'

'What are we supposed to do now?!' As much as she fought to mask the whimper in her voice, she knew Jason would be able to see straight through her. 'She'll kill us if she finds out we've tried to escape.'

Unable to hold it together any longer, she burst into tears. It was the first time in all the months they'd been together that Jason had seen Victoria truly weep like that. She had shed a few tears when they'd discovered she was pregnant, but never had the floodgates opened so freely. It unnerved him.

He made to place a lingering arm around her, but she pushed him away before he could get any closer. 'Maybe there's something in the bag we could use,' she suggested instead with a sniff as she started back down towards the basement, turning her back on the exit.

'No. Stay here,' Jason ordered as he squeezed past her to take the stairs two at a time. There was no point in her wasting what little energy she had left, especially not when she had the baby to think about too. No, Jason would take responsibility for this. It would be him who had to exert himself for their escape.

Victoria continued to struggle with the doorknob, until Jason returned a moment later with a hammer he'd managed to locate amongst the other tools in the bag. God knows what Amber had intended to use it for.

He decided not to think about that as he lifted the hammer high in the air, poising it briefly over his shoulder as he prepared to whack it down onto the heavy wooden panel.

The thud that sharply followed though came not from the hammer against the door, but from somewhere else inside the house.

Both of their eyes widened as they registered the sound. Jason lowered the hammer to his side as Victoria whispered hoarsely, 'What was that?!'

Her question was met by the slow repeated clack-clack-clack of low-heeled boots against the solid floor. Breaths were held as the footsteps wandered towards the basement door, growing louder with each step as if counting down to an uncertain threat, before fading as they headed back through the house.

'Shit, it's Amber!' Jason hissed as she headed towards somewhere in the back of the house, as if there had ever been a possibility that it was somebody else, arrived in the nick of time to defy the bitch with an attempted rescue. 'Quick, get back down! Down!'

It wasn't easy to rush down the steps so speedily, both racing to reach the bottom, both hobbling and swaying with aching bones and weary strength.

'What do we do now?!'

Neither attempted to refrain from panicking. If ever there was a time when panicking was the acceptable response to a situation, it was now. They glanced around them frantically, searching for something, anything, that could help them.

Before Victoria had the chance to voice her thought of stealing tools from the bag and bludgeoning Amber to death, Jason's eyes clocked the panel Amber had fashioned from the back of the dresser.

'The window!'

They rushed over to it, aware that Amber was still stomping around overhead. Jason reached up to tug at the panel covering the window, the butt of the lit torch wedged between his teeth to guide him.

It didn't budge.

'If I can just get this off,' he said through his strained effort as he tried to slacken the thick nails around the edges, 'I'll be able to hoist you up, and—'

So preoccupied as they were with trying to loosen the panel from the wall that neither of them noticed that Amber's footsteps had grown increasingly louder. No longer were they muffled, but instead clear and echoing as she took each wooden step down to the basement in turn.

'What the fuck are you doing?'

Her unnaturally calm voice sent shivers through Jason and Victoria. They froze, hands still grasping at the panel, neither one willing or able to turn around.

Jason was the first to look his predator in the eyes. He rotated, the beam from the torch casting an ugly glow across Amber's contorted face. In a split-second decision, with only the protection of his family at the front of his mind, he lunged forwards with no real plan. But it wouldn't have mattered whether he would have decided in the last second to crash into her or barge past her; she had anticipated his movement, and reacted much too quickly for him to respond.

Dropping the gift bag onto which she had been so fondly clutching, Amber charged into him, sending him flying into the wall as she wrestled Victoria to the ground. Even in her speed she managed to avoid placing any pressure on her baby as she twisted Victoria's arms behind her back. She struggled, not concerned about the disoriented Jason behind her, and dragged her back over towards the wall. It was a short distance, but required all of her strength, until finally she retrieved the handcuffs from the floor and clamped them around the wench's wrist.

Only a brief respite had been granted to Amber though as she panted through the struggle; having regained his balance, Jason was now pushing himself up onto his knees.

'Get off her!' he yelled as he staggered upright.

The previous moments had unfolded so quickly that Amber now found herself taking a calm step in front of Victoria. Jason, weakened from lack of sustenance and swaying slightly for want of regaining his composure, stood before Amber. He seethed, his fists clenched by his sides as he fought to suppress his rising anger. Even in the darkness, with the torch smashed against the floor amid the kerfuffle, Amber could detect the flare in his eyes.

She could hear Victoria whimpering as she quivered behind her, but she paid her no attention. Instead, she focused only on Jason. 'You've made things really difficult for yourself now,' she said. She spoke plainly, as if void of all emotion.

'You're a fucking maniac, you know that?!' he spat.

'I'm going to give you two options.'

'You're not going to give me anything, you stupid bitch. You're going to release my fiancée and our unborn child, and we're going to get the hell out of here.'

The maniacal laugh that flew from Amber's lips curdled the pit of Victoria's stomach.

'Oh! Oh, you are too funny, Jason. But then you always

303

did make me laugh. It was one of the things I loved about you.'

Amber caught her own words as she acknowledged her use of the past tense. She wasn't lying this time, found she had no need to. She had loved him, once upon a time. But now? Now she was sickened by the very sound of his name.

'Of *course* I can't let her go,' she continued. 'I need to make sure that my baby develops nice and healthily, and it's crucial that nobody interferes with that while it grows. Nobody must know about it until I have my baby in my arms.'

'You're not a midwife! You can't provide the care she needs! The care they'll both need!' He was struggling to not throw a punch directly at Amber's face. Oh, he wanted to, more than anything he wanted to kill her right there and then, but he knew it wouldn't do any good in the long run. 'And how the fuck are you expecting to explain to people that you've had a baby all of a sudden without ever showing any signs?! You're off your fucking head! Victoria and I are together now, and we're much happier than you and I ever were. We're over. This is over! Now let...us...g—'

The sentence gargled as it lodged in his throat. During Jason's little rant Amber had remained unresponsive. She had found it quite amusing to watch him ramble on like that, knowing full well he was speaking nonsense. Let him have his hope, she thought; it would make ripping it out from under his feet all the more enjoyable.

But when he moved through the darkness to help Victoria, she wasn't prepared to let him have his own way any longer. She hooked out her foot in front of him as he made to push her out of the way. He stumbled forwards, but not so swiftly that Amber couldn't grab onto the back of his t-shirt before he fell to the floor.

She let him pull her to the ground as they both fell. He was strong and she struggled against his wrestling weight, but she had the upper hand as she dropped her body down on top of his groin. She straddled his waist, squeezing her legs at either side of his hips to prevent him from thrashing around too much, and pushed a hand against his throat as she stretched over with the other towards the tool bag that lay just within reach.

The bottle had been lying in there, on its side, for several weeks on standby. She hadn't envisioned needing it, at least not this early on into the game, but desperate times called for drastic action. With Jason still squirming beneath her, she popped up the sports cap, and forced it into his mouth. She squeezed the bottle, and a cloudy water gushed out, spilling down the sides of Jason's mouth and down his neck.

He coughed and spluttered as it filled his mouth and forced its way down his throat. As Amber released some of her weight, he thrashed about beneath her, until he faltered, then stopped moving completely.

'What have you done to him?!' Victoria screamed as Amber stood up, wiped at her brow, and stepped away from Jason's still body. By chance she had noticed the pocket knife lying on the floor; how could she have been so foolish? That must have been how the idiot had loosened his restraints. She would need to keep a closer eye on the knife from now on, she instructed herself as she swooped it up and stuffed it into her pocket.

'Oh, relax! He's not dead. It'll wear off eventually.' Amber nudged his leg with her foot, then, satisfied that he wasn't going to stir, strode over to Victoria. She thrust the bottle towards her. 'Drink it.'

Victoria squinted, tears streaming down her cheeks, at the half-full murky liquid. It was too dark for her to make out what it was, but she knew there was no way she was going to cooperate.

'No! Let me go now!' she demanded. It was a fruitless request, and she knew that, but with her fiancé unconscious and her wrist once again handcuffed to the pipe, what else was she supposed to do?

'Drink it, or I will kill him.'

She wasn't lying, and Victoria knew that.

She said nothing as Amber placed the bottle down on

the floor beside her. She gave her a few seconds to pick it up, before retrieving the pocket knife.

'Hang on,' she said to herself as she reached for the light switch. Without warning, the room flooded with the sickly yellow brightness from the bulb overhead. Victoria's eyes squinted, before widening a split second after once she spotted the flexed knife in Amber's hand.

'That's better. I can actually see what I'm doing now!'

Amber dropped down beside Jason's body, and stroked an outstretched finger across his throat. She could feel his Adam's apple, unmoving yet prominent beneath his skin. Keeping her menacing eyes burrowed firmly into Victoria's terrified expression, she positioned the tip of the knife against his windpipe. She pressed down only lightly, but from where Victoria cowered on the other side of the room it would have been impossible for her to tell how much pressure she was applying. One slip would be all it took, and…

'You think I won't do it, don't you?' Was she addressing Victoria, or speaking to herself? She wasn't quite certain. 'Drink it,' she instructed with a nod towards the bottle, 'or you'll find out just what I'm capable of.'

How much worse could things possibly get? She had already hit rock bottom. But then Victoria was just beginning to learn exactly what Amber was capable of; if anybody was able to make things worse, it was Amber. Amber too was learning just how far she was willing to go to get what she wanted. She never failed to surprise even herself.

After a brief hesitation, Victoria reached for the bottle. She sobbed heartily as she reluctantly drew the bottle to her lips. She glugged, her eyes clamped shut.

She wailed as she curled into herself, a long, high-pitched banshee screech. Amber fought to block out the irritating sound as she pulled herself upright, and retrieved the gift bag from the floor. By the time she had propped it up against the tool bag, allowing herself a quick glance at the tiny garment in which she would soon be able to dress her baby, Victoria had fallen silent.

She shot a look towards Jason, who was still motionless, then crouched down in front of Victoria. She prodded her in the chest, causing her body to rock slightly. She didn't open her eyes though, emitted no sound as the weight of her body dropped back against the wall.

Perfect. The mixture she had prepared was meant to be only a precaution, not something she thought she would have needed. The fools. If they had only cooperated then this never would have happened. Still, the drugs would wear off soon; she would have to act fast if she didn't want them to mess this up for her.

With a quick sip from a separate bottle of pure, uncontaminated water, she wiped at her brow and set to work. This was going to be mentally treacherous and physically laborious, but she had a duty to carry out. They had disobeyed her, and that meant they had to be punished.

It took Amber no time at all to set the scene. Satisfied that there was still plenty of time before either of them woke up, she'd unfastened Victoria's handcuffs, hung them limply over her own arm, then dragged her into the centre of the room. She proceeded to roll Jason towards her, until they both lay by one another's side.

Gently placing the handcuffs on the ground by her feet, Amber allowed herself a moment to hover over Victoria. With her stomach exposed, she could detect the subtle milky-white bump that protected her growing baby.

She lifted up her a finger and softly ran it across Victoria's naval. The sensation would have tickled a wakened Victoria as Amber spelled out the letters of her name in turn.

'Hi, baby,' she whispered with her face close to the stomach. 'Stay safe in there for me please. I'll never hurt you, I promise. I'll always protect you. Mummy can't wait to meet you.'

With her hands positioned either side of Victoria's still body, she leaned forward and pressed a light kiss against the flesh of her naval. Then, with an unexpected speed as she felt her head fogging up and the increasing dizziness from her withdrawal resurfacing, she forced herself upright and jumped across towards the tool bag.

She lifted out the cordless electric drill, and, wasting no time, switched it into life. It whirred proudly as she angled back towards the bodies, then strode over to them with unwonted zeal.

Soon after she'd set about conducting this next stage in her plan – which, she had to admit to herself, was more of a new development than it had been a concrete step – she struggled to relax her grin. She smiled widely to herself as she worked, realising that, as long as she didn't falter, and worked quickly, there was no way this wasn't going to work.

She'd already positioned Victoria's hand on top of Jason's as she simulated a motionless representation of the holding of hands. After fumbling with the handcuffs and reaching the conclusion that they wouldn't bind them tightly enough, she'd wound rope around their wrists to secure their hands in position, then bound each hand on the outside of their body – Jason's right hand and Victoria's left – to their thighs. It had been challenging to manoeuvre their heavy, unconscious limbs, but she wasn't prepared to take any chances. If she wanted this to go smoothly, she would have to ensure they remained entirely immobile.

She muttered to herself to help her remain focused as

she tested the strength of the bindings. 'They thought they could escape and continue playing happy families together. Idiots!' she smirked.

Her breath, quickened and short, wheezed out of her as she worked frantically to securely tie their feet together. It was dustier down here in the basement than she had remembered; she would need to give it a thorough clean before she moved into the house to create a family home with her baby, and she would also need to thoroughly disinfect the stench of sweat and piss and decaying hopes that seemed to protrude into her nostrils.

As she prodded around their ankles, finishing the last of the knots, she was too focussed to notice Jason's eyelids flicker. The light bled into his pupils as his eye turned into narrow slits. Disoriented, he glanced down. His vision met with the top of Amber's head.

'W…Wha's going on?' he muttered. He felt drowsy, and his limbs were heavy as he struggled to lift them.

Amber glanced up to acknowledge his voice, but returned to work without a word. As she finished off the final binding around their ankles, Jason's consciousness restored with his senses.

'A-Amber! G-Get the fu…fuck off!' Everything flooded back to him now that he was conscious of his surroundings. How he had managed to become tied up on the floor, he wasn't sure, but it was likely that she had drugged him.

Again.

He tried to thrash with his remaining strength, but even if his limbs hadn't been numb it would have been no use. The ties around him made it impossible to move.

As Amber finished off her work, she dusted off her hands and stood up. Jason continued to attempt to sit up, but refused to move himself too forcefully with Victoria strapped beside him. Unable to twist his body around to follow Amber's movements, he remained unaware, perhaps blissfully, as she reached into the tool bag behind him for a roll of duct tape.

It was only when the coarse sound of the tape ripping as she yanked at it between her teeth that his eyes widened in recognition.

He had no time to scream out in response. Amber stormed up behind him and slapped the tape over his mouth, pushing it down onto his cheeks and against his jaw as he yelled a muffled cry.

Ignoring Jason after checking he could still breathe through his nose, she shimmied to the still unconscious Victoria. She secured a strap of tape to her mouth, then slid down to her stomach. She leaned in, and whispered with her lips to the naval, 'Don't worry, baby. This won't hurt you one little bit. You'll soon be safe with me.'

She kissed Victoria's stomach, then crossed back over to the tool bag. The only sounds in the basement were Jason's whimpering and the slight rummaging as Amber reorganised the contents of the bag.

And then, ricocheting off the walls and bouncing directly into Jason's ears, came once more the brief but certain penetrating noise of the electric drill as it was flicked into life.

Amber's footsteps echoed on the ground above the noise as she stepped back across the room. She moved slowly, never taking her eyes away from the supine bodies.

She stood over them, and Jason's incalculable fear was unmistakable as the drill whirred back into action. It was angled towards the conjoined hands as Amber crouched down to the ground, and positioned the drill over them.

The force of Jason's thrashing as he screamed fruitlessly pulled Victoria into a mild state of awakening. She surfaced just as the tip of the drill pushed into the back of Jason's hand.

Even over the dominating volume of the drill, the sound of crunching could be heard as the drill slipped through the metacarpal bones of Jason's hand, spurting blood concentrically as it penetrated through his palm and deep into Victoria's.

Neither of them had remained completely flat, as the soaring pain had caused them both to involuntarily bolt upright, contorted in opposite directions, as much as their restrains would allow them. Victoria's head had thrust backwards in her near-silent scream, but Jason had doubled over, straining the rope around their wrists so much that Amber had to steady their hands with her own free hand. She worked the drill with the other, and didn't stop until she could see the wet crimson of their mixed blood dripping from the spinning head.

The room returned to an almost deafening silence as she halted the tool, tearing it away from the gaping holes she had formed in their hands in the process. She stood, and wiped at her forehead, smearing blood from the back of her hand onto her face. It had spurted onto her chest and her torso in rich red blots, and right now she longed for nothing more than a steaming hot shower.

There would be time for that soon enough though; she wouldn't be much longer, and then she could rest for the night.

It had surprised her that the screaming had stopped almost in unison with the silenced drill. Jason still whimpered, but Victoria had become comatose from the shock of the pain, and from the loss of the blood that now seeped out of their palms.

Unmoved by the emerging sickly sweet scent of the sticky red pool that was expanding around them and soaking into the clothes beneath them, Amber shifted further down to their feet. She kneeled, slipped off the boots from Jason's feet, and retrieved the drill.

It was a blessing for Amber that he was now drifting in and out of consciousness; his lack of squirming made it so much easier for her to drill a neat hole straight into the sole of his foot. The wet crunching was nowhere near as satisfying though if she thought he, not fully conscious, wasn't receiving the full extent of pain through which he was supposed to be suffering.

Still, she couldn't have everything her own way. She moved on from Jason's left foot, heading straight for Victoria's right foot, continuing with her work until both inner feet had been drilled. It was a messy job, with blood spurting across the floor and across all three bodies. And, with little knowledge of what lay beneath the skin of the human foot, Amber had only to make an educated guess as to where would be the most practical place to penetrate.

Still, she thought to herself as the drill slowly rotated to a halt, it looked like she'd made her decision wisely. The holes had been formed, and would allow her to proceed.

The silence was absolute now and the bodies still as Amber fetched some more rope out of the bag. She fumbled

315

with it as she rushed back to Jason's side, and leaned over his chest with one end of the rope outstretched. It took some force, but, with a little jabbing and paying close attention to what she was doing, at last Amber managed to thread the thin rope straight through their hands. She secured it in a triple knot, and repeated the process, a little more smoothly this time, through the amateur holes in the soles of their feet.

'There. That'll…have to…do…Urgh!'

With the final restraint secured through the wide wounds, tying the happy couple together, Amber dropped her weight to the floor, strained from the effort. She allowed herself a minute to recuperate, before regaining her energy and stomping across to the area where their heads lay sparsely responsive.

With both hands free, she grabbed onto the duct tape over their mouths, and pulled. The screams that followed were not as enthusiastic as she had liked, but at least the yelping was confirmation enough that they had remained at least partially awake during their punishment.

She hovered above them, and smiled down with a satisfied grin.

'You thought you'd be together forever? Well guess what. Now you will be! I've made sure of that for you. No need to thank me, of course.'

She started for the stairs to head to the shower, but

turned back at the last second before ascending. 'Oh, and don't bother trying to escape again. You clearly can't be trusted on your own, so I'll be staying here all night.'

Then she added with a grin before returning the basement to darkness:

'Sleep tight!'

Remnants of water dripped from the shower head. It plinked against the porcelain on the bottom of the bath; the suite had been only recently installed after Amber's grandfather had been forced to replace the old rusting cast iron tub. His wife had died long before the project had ever been underway, and he had only ever bathed, refusing to use the new-fangled modern technology installed above the bath. For Amber, however, the shower had been exactly what she'd needed.

It had washed away the blood, and swirled it in a diluted milky pink down the plughole. The steam from the hot water had helped to clear her mind. However, as soon as she stepped out onto the mat and dried herself off with a towel, the fog that smothered any chance she had at contentment descended down on her with force.

She slipped into the pyjamas she'd brought with her, buttoned up the front of the shirt, and crawled under the duvet. The bed was positioned directly beneath the window; it would have been a blessing in summer, she was sure, but she would need to remember to push it over to the other side of the room the next day if she didn't want to catch a chill. For now though, she hadn't the energy to do anything except fall straight into a deep sleep.

Unfortunately, such a slumber did not occur for Amber that night. She was uncomfortable on the mattress, despite it being free of lumps or protruding springs, and spent most of the hours that followed tossing and turning.

Occasionally, when the bedroom was overcome with silence, she could hear the faint cries drifting up from the basement. Every now and then, as if Victoria had been mutely building up her agony, a long, loud scream could be heard. It always faltered towards the end as the efforts drained out of her.

Even with the pillow pressed firmly against her ear, there was little Amber could do to block out the distraction. She could only lie there distressed, praying for rest, as she could no longer fight against the irrefutable tears that spilled from her eyes and drenched into the pillow.

Chapter Twenty-Nine

The next morning, as the early hours crept in, Amber had finally managed to summon a light sleep. She remained in her dreamland for a little over four hours, before the rising sun poked through the curtains and cast its rays across the bed. The birds of autumn were perched on the leafy brown branches of a nearby tree in the garden, singing the day into life.

Inside the house, everything was silent. The shower had ceased its dripping. The only clock that emitted a tick was downstairs in the kitchen, and too far away to be heard. The screaming from the basement had stopped.

This wasn't immediately apparent to Amber, who struggled to wipe the sleep away from her bleary eyes as she shuffled upright. She propped the pillow up behind her, and rested for a few more minutes, before finally sliding her legs out from the duvet. The air exploited its bitter chill as it bit into her naked ankles. She slid her feet into a pair of slippers, and sloped over to the window.

As she peered outside, the bright glow of sunlight washed over her face in a sickly paleness, making her exhausted eyes look even puffier as she observed the scene below. Her grandparents' garden looked different in the morning glow. The burnt colours of orange and brown leaves and apple-green grass looked luscious, almost fragrant. It was funny how everything always appeared so much better in the morning, as if humanity had been programmed to not appreciate nature when it flourished in the darkness.

Leaving those thoughts behind, she made her way down the stairs to stick the kettle on. Once she had built her finances back up, she would have to invest in a proper cafetiere, she thought to herself as she spooned out the instant granules into one of her grandfather's old mugs. A splash of milk and a spoonful of sugar followed, before she stirred in the hot water, then wrapped her hands around the mug to steal some of its warmth.

She alternated between sipping at the hot drink to absorb the day's first hit of caffeine and puffing on her first cigarette of the morning. She rested lazily against the kitchen worktop as she scrolled through her phone, checking for any messages. One from Claire, two from Greig. She bashed out quick replies to each, then headed upstairs, coffee and cigarette in tow, to dress.

If anybody had observed Amber over the next forty-five minutes, they'd have fairly assumed that she was lagging for want of rest. However, if she were to admit the truth to herself, her stalling was premeditated.

She washed her face with artistic precision. Each tooth was cleaned almost in turn. She brushed her hair with meticulous effort until it was so smooth and silky that it nearly shone. She wrapped it up in a bun on the top of her head, then pulled on each garment in turn, but only after laying them all out on the bed in front of her first, as if making a flat and lifeless version of herself.

Only then, with no other excuse for procrastination, did she creep down the stairs to the ground floor, heading straight for the basement door.

As she started down the wooden steps to the space underground, she became suddenly aware of the lack of noise. It was as if it had gone completely unnoticed before, the absent sound inaudible and therefore unknown to her. Now though, as she paused midway on the staircase, the basement still in darkness until she had fully descended, did she hear it.

'Jason? Victoria?' Her concern was too prominent for her to worry about masking any of the emotion in her voice.

There came no reply.

Amber opened her mouth to call out to them again, but as she did so her nose wrinkled in protest. A repugnant aroma flew up her nostrils as she inhaled. She couldn't quite place it though as she tried not to breathe in the stench. It was rancid, a little meaty with an odd metallic aftertaste that lingered at the back of her throat.

Brushing her hand down the edge of the wall to guide her, she made her way to the bottom, and flicked on the light. The source of the smell, much more poignant now, became instantly apparent.

The two bodies lay motionless, side by side, still with the ropes bound around their limbs. They had now also been connected by the blend of their own congealed blood, which had seeped heavily form the gaping wounds in their palms and on their soles. Even from where she stood by the stairs, Amber couldn't miss the partly sticky, partly crusted dark brown patches that had settled around about them.

She walked slowly towards them, her eyes fixed in their direction. She stopped just in front of a pool of dark drying blood, and kicked the side of Jason's leg with her foot.

No movement.

Unnerved by his unresponsiveness, she crouched down, and shook him loosely by the shoulders. She moved more frantically now, not taking much care to avoid staining her hands and her clothes and her skin with the sticky sweet fluid.

She leaned across Jason's body, her chest pressing against his, and repeated the actions on Victoria.

Neither stirred. Neither showed any sign of movement or breathing. Neither had held onto any hint of life.

'No! No, no, no, no!'

The penny had dropped. Unable to comprehend how this had happened, Amber leapt up to her feet and rushed around to Victoria's side. She knelt, a congealed pool of blood slippery and sticking beneath her knees, and splayed her palms across Victoria's bare stomach. Leaning over, she pressed her ear against her naval, and listened.

She had expected to hear the beating heart of her unborn child. She had needed to feel some movement, a stirring, any kind of response to her touch.

Instead, she was met only with a vacant stillness.

'No, no, no!'

There was no controlling her sobs as they blubbered out of her. Snot bubbled about her nose as her eyes flooded with tears. She wailed loudly. Even had she not been so alone, she'd still have been inconsolable as she wrapped her arms around Victoria's corpse. She hugged around her stomach in a desperate and futile attempt to hold tightly onto her lifeless baby.

Chapter Thirty

The car hovered to the side of the petrol station forecourt, the engine still running as the low hum and the vibrations offered a distraction akin to white noise. Lifting her head up from where it rested on the steering wheel, Amber killed the engine, then reached into her handbag on the passenger seat for her phone.

She scrolled through her contacts and hit the one she was looking for, then held the phone to her ear. She kept her eyes low, as if unable to face the world outside of her car.

After a few rings, the school receptionist picked up the call.

'Hello? Hi, it's Amber. Amber Quigley. Yeah, literature, that's right. I'm afraid I won't be able to make it in today.' She feigned a cough, pretending to stifle it with a balled fist. 'Yeah. You know what this time of year is like for the flu. Yeah. Well, thank you. I appreciate it. Soon, hopefully. Thanks. You too, thanks. Bye.'

She shoved the phone into her pocket, took a deep breath, and then released it in a slow, shuddering exhale. She closed her eyes for only a brief moment to centre her thoughts, then, not risking any more delay for fear of changing her mind, sprang out of the car, slamming the door behind her.

She crossed the empty forecourt towards the little shop at the top of the row of petrol pumps. She glanced down at herself as a flash of red caught her eye; she'd somehow managed to stain blood onto her t-shirt when she'd changed out of her earlier outfit. It had probably transferred from her skin, she thought, as she'd not wished to hang around for too long to properly shower. However it had happened, it didn't really matter, so long as she could cover it up by fastening up the buttons on her coat. That seemed to be enough for now.

Before she reached the little shop, her coat pocket vibrated. She pulled out the phone, and fought to hide her irritation as she answered it.

'Greig, hi. No, I'm not too bad. You? Good, good. Yeah, I'm free tomorrow night. Look, can I call you back a bit later on? I'm just about to head into work, and the traffic's looking to be a nightmare. Sure! Okay, speak to you then.'

How easy it was for her to feign nonchalance, how freely the lies spilled from her lips. Greig had offered no signs of suspicion during the brief conversation. But then why would he?

The automatic doors slid open and Amber slipped inside the shop. She gathered up a few bits and pieces, throwing in a packet of cigarettes when she reached the till, and paid for her items. She bundled the loose change into her purse, and headed back out of the door, all in little over three minutes.

She returned to her car, dropped the shopping into the passenger seat, buckled up, and whacked the key into the ignition. Her actions flowed like clockwork, her movements almost robotic as she carried them out absently.

She pulled out of the forecourt and joined the throngs of traffic on the main road. Out of the corner of her eye she could see the petrol can, propped up against the seat as it poked out of the top of the carrier bag. As she turned a corner and headed along the road back to Hampstead, she knew there was no looking back now.

For months Amber had moped around her home, complaining to herself about her lack of employment. As her latest novel had stalled, practically unwriting itself as she had neglected it with her latest bout of writer's block, she had felt like her life had no sense of purpose, at least not until she had returned to teaching. Now though, as the midday sun blended with the late-year breeze to cast a mild warmth around the front room, she was glad of her isolation.

Well, partial isolation, she corrected herself as she swirled the liquid in the wine glass. She took a sip, allowing the vinegary hit to take over her senses, before drawing deeply on the moist tip of her cigarette.

Smoke clouded the room as she battled to push all thoughts of Jason and Victoria away from her mind. As long as they remained beneath her in the basement though, discolouring and transforming in rigor mortis from the humans who had ruined her life to the corpses she had created, they were her responsibility.

A second sip of wine was followed by another nicotine-filled puff, before her attention wandered back towards the petrol can. It was propped up on the table, the plastic container an unpleasant, almost nauseating dark shade of green. The garage shop had only the one container size available, but she was sure it would be enough for her needs.

Reluctantly, she stubbed out the cigarette butt, swigged the last of her drink, and lifted up the petrol can from the table. The front room descended into darkness as she flicked off the light and, petrol can swinging in her hand by her side, headed straight for the basement.

Amber was about to confirm to herself that everything was exactly as she had left it that morning. However, that wasn't entirely the case. The rancid stench of rotting flesh was a much more pungent odour now as it overpowered the tangy sweet scent of blood.

Hesitantly she crossed over to the corpses, half holding her breath, not sure whether she should be breathing through her nose or through her mouth. Already the skin of the bodies – for she could only see them as that now, and not her former lover and his bitch who carried her dead child – had started to discolour. With the blood already drained from them, only faint pinky purple blotches of livor mortis appeared at the sides lowest to the ground; most of this, anyway, was still covered by their blood-and-urine-soaked clothing, shielding Amber from the more severe effects of early decomposition.

Despite the aroma and the visual alterations in the two bodies, Amber still felt it necessary to nudge at their sides to check that they were still dead. Of course, nobody moved, nobody flinched. Not so much as a squeak.

Had she been in a clearer state of mind, it might have occurred to Amber that this could have been a golden opportunity for her to conduct some research. She had a fondness for reading thriller novels, but had not yet attempted to cross over into writing such fiction herself. This, with the fermenting death directly in front of her, would be an opportune moment for her to quite easily make very detailed and accurate notes about the rate of physical human deterioration. After all, how many authors could say they'd experienced first-hand the sheer morbidity of decay after death?

She was blessed with no such thoughts though as she could concentrate only on carrying out this unexpected phase in her plan as quickly and as efficiently as possible. Pulling her focus together, she crossed over to the back of the basement to where the furnace stood. It was old and rusted and showed no indication that it would work, but she would have to force it to.

She pulled off her blood-stained shirt, and threw it into the furnace. After some fiddling and bashing about at the sides, she finally managed to force it into ignition. She slammed the door shut, clicking it firmly into place, and turned her back as the evidence burnt out of existence.

As she returned to Victoria's side, she stared forlornly at her naval. She stroked the taut flesh, which had been drained of its natural colour, then leaned over. She pressed her lips lightly against the surface of the decaying flesh, her hands spread out at either side of the gentle slope to cover her baby in one final embrace.

'Bye, baby,' she whispered.

Then, blinking back the round droplets that pooled in her eyes and clung to her lower lashes, she stood, lifted up the petrol can, and unscrewed the lid.

She couldn't bring herself to look directly at the two

corpses as she poured out the petrol, encasing them in a misshapen oval. She worked slowly and with an unnatural calm as she maintained a neutral, almost numbed, expression. With her actions expertly mechanical and meticulous, she made sure to check that some of the fluid had splashed onto the nearby furnishings, then trailed it in a drizzle towards the base of the stairs.

A small pool of petrol was still left in the bottom of the can. She glanced into it, finding herself pulled slightly back to her surroundings as a slither of doubt infiltrated her actions, before she stepped on tiptoe over the path of fluid and made her way back to Victoria.

Tipping the petrol can upside down, the remaining drops dribbled out onto Victoria's bare stomach. It formed in a tiny puddle in her bellybutton, and dripped down the sides of her waist. Once it was empty, Amber threw the can onto the petrol-soaked remains of her grandfather's old wooden dresser, then made her way back to the stairs.

With the light switch flicked off, the room fell into a mute darkness. She could not see her fingers in front of her as she fumbled in her pocket for the small box of matches. Her hands shook as she tried to steady her movements, grasping at the box and scrabbling for a match. Finally, the brisk and coarse sound of the match as it struck against the side of the box penetrated the deathly silence.

The match remained between her fingers for what in reality was little more than two seconds, but to Amber it felt like minutes as everything unfolded before her in slow motion. She was somehow both numbed of all emotion and yet doubtful and disturbed by her own responses; it was as if she was two versions of herself at any one time, her reactions permanently divided between her life before and after Jason.

Her face was illuminated by the narrow glow of the match as she stared deep into the flame. It caused her tears to glisten as her wet eyes looked almost dazzling in the faint light. She thought about none of this though, was not even aware that she was crying, as she flung the swaying flame into the trail of petrol before she changed her mind.

As soon as it hit the ground, the flames whooshed into a flickering dance. The room became cast in a hellish fiery glow as she snapped into her natural mode of survival. The adrenalin took hold as she charged up the stairs, slamming the door behind her, and raced towards the front door.

She leapt into her car, crammed the key into the ignition, and flew forward as she sped away from the house. She didn't look back, didn't check her mirrors, didn't allow herself to think about Jason and Victoria and her dead baby as their rotting corpses burned in the dank basement, filling the air with a putrid aroma of charcoaled flesh as they lay surrounded only by fumes and flames and the tranquil

331

quietude of isolation.

Chapter Thirty-One

The water hissed as it sloshed into the mug, colliding with the dry granules as they blended into a swirly pool of caffeinated liquid. The splashing of milk was followed by the clinking of the spoon as it whirled around both mugs, before it was tossed into the sink alongside that morning's crumb-coated breakfast dishes. Amber lifted both mugs up by their handles, precariously flicked off the kitchen light with the tip of her nose, and carried them through to the living room.

She handed one to Greig then dropped down beside him on the sofa as they both sipped on the warm liquid in a moment of untainted contentment. They had reached that golden stage in their blossoming relationship where they could enjoy each other's company without the need to constantly fill previously awkward silences with equally uncomfortable small talk. Now the gap between them was closing in, with Amber's knee lightly brushing against Greig's thigh, his arm resting behind her head on the back of the sofa, not too far away.

Greig blew on the surface of the coffee, then sipped and swallowed. After a moment of enjoying the hot liquid as it slipped down his throat in a slightly frothy warmth, he broke the silence.

'So what do you fancy doing tonight? We could grab something to eat if you like? Or go and see a film? It might be a bit busy on a Saturday, but I'm pretty sure there's a new Tim Burton picture showing if you're in the mood for something weird…'

It had barely registered with Amber that Greig had spoken to her. Her pale expression remained vacant to an oblivious Greig, and only managed to return her distant eyes to his attention as his sentence tailed off.

'Weird? What? No, I…Not tonight, no. Actually, I don't feel too well.'

Greig raised an eyebrow. 'Do you want me to fetch you a glass of water?' he suggested.

Actually, she did look a little woozy, he noted, as she shuffled forwards to perch on the edge of the sofa, her fists balled and pushed into the seat cushion as she took her breaths slowly and deeply.

He stood up, but, before he had a chance to head into the kitchen, Amber had already sprung to her feet and fled from the room. A few seconds later, he heard the echoing retching as she hunched herself over the toilet bowl.

'Are you okay?' he asked a little sheepishly. It was a stupid question, but he was out of his comfort zone now. What else was he supposed to say?

Amber attempted to heave again, but realised she didn't need to. She wiped the phlegm away from where it had smeared onto her lips and down her chin, and stood up.

'Y-yeah,' she replied weakly as she supported herself with the bathroom sink. She turned on the tap and sipped at the flowing water, then lifted her head up to meet her own reflection.

God, she looked awful.

Her near illuminative skin was now blotchy from the strain of throwing up, and her eyes looked bloodshot and faint. She was unsure whether she looked worse than she felt, or felt worse than she looked.

She would feel right as rain in no time, she was sure. That's what her mother always used to tell her when she was growing up. A nasty tummy bug wouldn't last forever, and with a little medicine and some bed rest everything could be put to right again. Amber couldn't help smiling at the memory as she reached into the medicine cabinet to hunt out something, anything, that would ease the rising taste of bile. Still, she should be counting her blessings; the bitter taste of vomit that coated her tongue battled against the stench of death that lingered in her nostrils and clung to the back of her throat, stoppering any attempt she made to forget about the events of that morning.

Forcing her thoughts back to the bleak image in front of her, she pulled back the mirrored door to reveal the cluttered contents of the cabinet.

Waiting for her at the front of the cabinet nothing that would suppress her nausea; instead, it had the reverse effect, the little bottle reminding her of just one of the many stupid, foolish, and irreversible mistakes she had made in her life. She reached for the empty bottle of antidepressants and turned it around in her hand. She wondered if she would be able to order any more any time soon. Probably not, as the bottle had been almost full when she'd tipped the pills out. Besides, the dizzy sensations that washed over her from time to time were bound to fade eventually. She would just need to ride this one out.

Deciding not to give it any further thought, she tossed the plastic bottle into the little wicker bin in the corner of the room, then returned to the cabinet. She moved around a few boxes of aspirin and unidentified blister packs of unfinished medication that had been in there for longer than she cared to think about. It wasn't until her hand brushed against a small cluster of sanitary products that she halted her search.

As her hand collided with the box of tampons, she found herself wondering when she had last used them. It hadn't been too long ago, certainly not months and months, but she had always been fairly regular, and…

She was late. Very late, in fact. Everything around her lately had been moving so quickly that she'd not had the time to think about her cycle. It was possible that the stress of returning back to work, and the subsequent change in her sleep pattern, had caused her body to shift a little. It certainly wasn't implausible.

But what if there was another explanation?

With haste she shut the cabinet door, and turned her attention to the drawer beneath the sink in which she kept an assortment of fluffy towels and face cloths. She could hear Greig clattering around in the kitchen down the hall, no doubt making himself another drink, but she gave him no thought as she reached to the bottom of the towels to retrieve the cardboard box that had been sitting in there since before she had conceived her first child.

She pulled the pregnancy test out of the box and held it in her hand. She didn't need to read the instructions; she had done this so many times now that, even after so long, it felt like second nature to her. She glanced towards the door, nibbled on her lower lip as she cast a glance down towards the test, then opened the door slightly.

'Greig?'

'Yeah? Are you alright? Want me to fetch you anything?' His voice drifted through the flat.

'No. No, I'm okay. I'll be there in a minute, okay? You just stay there and put the TV on or something.'

That seemed to be to Greig's liking as she heard him return to the living room and switch on one of the sports channels. Closing the door, she made sure it was firmly bolted, then did what she knew she had to do.

After peeing on the little stick, she found herself pacing around the room. Her hands flapped by her sides as she struggled to control her breathing. A few more laps around the small room, circling the bath rug. Then another glance at her watch. It was time.

She dashed over to the sink where she had left the test. Her eyes were clamped shut as she clasped it in her hand, praying for a miracle.

She opened her eyes. Stared down at the test.

Her heart skipped a beat. It couldn't be true, was too good to be believed. Fewer than twenty-four hours had passed since her baby, the one Victoria had been carrying for her, had slipped away from her grasp as its spirit returned to the heavens. But now, without a shadow of a doubt, that baby had been returned to earth where it belonged.

*

There was nothing quite like the post-lunch challenge of trying to quell the enthusiasm of a class of rowdy Year Tens. The rain had battered against the classroom window into the afternoon and showed no signs of stopping any time soon; only the bravest of pupils had stormed through the torrential weather for their soggy sandwiches and wet paper pouches of salty chips, forcing the rest to relinquish their hour of freedom in favour of a dry, dull spell in the canteen.

Still, it could have been worse. Amber could have been faced with the unresponsive Monday morning period with the school's youngest pupils. It was always like pulling teeth from those bleary-eyed little cherubs. She did love her job, but she loved even more the idea of having the first two periods of the week free to catch up with paperwork and marking.

'So what do you think Shakespeare was trying to do with the character of the Ghost?' she asked as she attempted to pull the attention of the class back to the board at the front of the room. She'd taught this lesson countless times over the last few years, and knew the text inside out, but for the children it should be fresh and engaging. *Should*, of course, being the operative word.

One girl, who sat by choice at the front desk, raised her hand, but didn't wait for an indication to speak. 'Was he trying to show that ghosts are real, miss? If Hamlet could see him, then he was encouraging the audience to too?'

Thank God for teacher's pets, Amber thought as she flashed a smile towards Clara. They could always be counted on to shatter the unanimous lack of commitment to what many of the lesser-unenthused pupils unjustly considered to be a dry and stuffy incomprehensible Shakespearean play.

'A good thought, Clara. That's certainly an interesting idea.' Then, back to the rest of the class, she asked, 'What about the character of the Ghost in connection to Hamlet's madness?'

Patrick, the scrawny blonde boy two rows from the back of the room, chimed up with a cocky grin. 'He was a crazy fool!'

The class burst into laughter as they appreciated his faux American accent. Often wondering if she too was still young and juvenile at heart, Amber couldn't help smiling either. There was such admiration to be had for the innocent camaraderie of youth.

Before she had a chance to coax the class back to calm, there was a subtle rap on the classroom door.

She flashed her head in the direction of the closed door, but couldn't see anybody through the frosted glass, over most of which she had stuck a grainy poster of Virginia Woolf anyway so it wouldn't have been much use even if they had stood directly behind it.

'I'm not sure that's the politically correct term, Patrick,' she chuckled as she headed over to the door, 'but thank you for sharing your opinion!'

She opened the door to find the headmistress standing behind it.

'Mrs Rea?'

Doris Rea took a small step over the threshold and glanced at the pupils, before angling her attention towards Amber.

'Miss Quigley, would you mind coming with me for a moment please? There's somebody here who needs to speak to you.' She shifted uncomfortably, and there was a quiver in her voice as she spoke with a hushed tone.

Amber's eyes flitted to her class, then back to Doris as she tried to mask the sudden flare of worry. Nobody ever needed to speak to her at work. Not so out of the blue like this. Had something bad happened? Had they…no, they couldn't have linked her to Jason's disappearance, could they have done? She'd covered her tracks. She was sure of that.

'Can't it wait? We're right in the middle of a discussion and I—'

'I'm afraid it can't, Miss Quigley. Don't worry, Mrs Todd has a probationary in with her, so I'll ask her to cover your class for the rest of the lesson.'

Amber paused, her jaw slack. Finally, she nodded. There was no point in fighting it. Besides, it could very well just end up being about nothing. Doris had been vague, after all, and she wasn't exactly unknown for making mountains out of molehills.

She turned briefly back to her class. 'Right, everybody. Find a partner. I'd like you to go through Act One, Scene Five again. And remember your characters! I won't be long.'

One final glance towards her desk, then she sidled out of the classroom, leaving Doris to shut the door gingerly behind them.

Despite the dreary conditions outdoors, the staffroom felt hot and stuffy, with the heating on full whack. With the other teachers busy in their own classrooms teaching or marking or generally avoiding any kind of social interaction during a free period, only Amber and Doris were in there.

Well, Amber, Doris, and the two police officers.

They had stood up when Amber entered the room, both extending their hands out to greet her. Had she allowed herself to believe that the police had come to take her away, she certainly hadn't expected such an introduction. If PC Barry and PC Larry, as they had offered their names, had come to arrest her, then they'd have twisted her arms behind her back and clamped on the handcuffs quicker than she'd have had the time to deny anything. No, this was not the expected greeting at all.

Doris remained standing beside her as Amber perched on the arm of an old, battered armchair. She kept her head bowed low, fearful of her eyes giving anything away, as the two police officers returned to the long sofa.

PC Barry leaned forward, his hands clasped together in between his parted legs. 'Miss Quigley, I'm afraid that we've got some very bad news. Unfortunately, there's…well, there's been a fire. Quite a bad one.'

What? How did they—?

'I'm sorry to have to break it to you like this. It was lucky that you had changed the house ownership into your name recently, as it meant we could find your name on the database. I'm also, um…I'm really sorry to hear about your grandfather,' he added nervously. 'There's never a good time to hear news like this anyway, but it must be a really difficult time for you at the moment.'

This cop had clearly done his research. But not thoroughly enough, it seemed. He showed no hint of understanding the bigger picture.

'Is there anyone we can call for you?' PC Barry asked after he had explained what had happened – or the accident that they assumed had happened – to the house.

She shook her head, her eyes still to the ground as she nibbled on her fingertips. 'No, thank you. I'll be okay. Honestly, I hardly ever went up there. Certainly not after my grandfather passed away. Too many memories.' She didn't need to add that the memories were more recent than either of the two policemen could imagine. 'I'd sorted out the paperwork, but beyond that...'

'You had no plans to move in there yourself?' PC Larry queried.

'Oh, it was unlikely,' Amber said. At last, she lifted her head to meet his eyes. 'A big old house like that? I wouldn't know what to do with myself.'

Doris, ever one to help others wherever she could, leaned in to take part in the conversation. 'I told her she should rent it out to bring in a bit of money. Didn't I?'

'Yes, yes you did,' Amber confirmed before Doris shuffled back to lean on the chair again.

PC Barry's eyes spoke briefly to Doris, and then back to Amber. 'Well, I'm afraid that's really not going to be possible anymore. We can drive you up there if you'd like. We've secured the area, but it's in a pretty bad state. Because it's in such a remote location, by the time anybody noticed the smoke and called the fire brigade, the flames had taken hold of the entire building.'

'Do they know how it started?'

'Unfortunately not. We were informed that it was likely that there had been a gas leak or some dodgy wiring. Perhaps your grandfather had had some work done recently before he passed, and there had been complications. It's not presently safe enough for further investigation though; the floors are all…' PC Barry hesitated. 'Well, at any rate we can surmise that a house that old could have had any number of faults that could have started the fire.'

'So they didn't find anything?'

'What do you mean?' PC Larry asked with a cocked eyebrow.

'I…I don't know, really.' She rubbed at her forehead. Having not allowed herself to think about the aftermath until she was forced to confront it, it was no struggle for Amber to appear disturbed by the news of the inferno. 'It couldn't have been kids or anyone messing around? There wasn't anything…suspicious?'

Oblivious to his colleague's stern expression as he shifted closer to the edge of his seat, PC Barry replied, 'No, nothing like that. Of course, it's not something that could be completely ruled out. Kids these days are far too clever for their own good. What with all the crime dramas on TV nowadays, they think they know all about covering their tracks and getting away with breaking the rules. Still, while it's possible it wasn't an accident, with no CCTV and no evidence, there's little else we can do at this stage, I'm afraid.'

'No, of course. I understand.'

'It's a blessing at least that nobody else was in the house

at the time. You're certain that's the case?'

Amber could only nod.

PC Barry sighed. 'There's that at least to be thankful for. A house that beautiful though. Such a shame.'

'It's a sad loss!' Doris chimed in.

Having given up on his hope of finding out anything interesting from this woman, a bored PC Larry hauled himself out of the sofa. PC Barry followed his lead, and they both headed towards the door with Doris in tow.

'Well, if you do happen to think of anything else that could have caused the fire, if only so we can completely rule out any suspicious activity, you've got our details.'

PC Larry nodded briefly towards Amber, before turning his back and disappearing from view.

PC Barry offered his hand, which Amber took limply. Her own hand was shaking and her palm clammy as he shook it. 'Feel free to give me a call if you need anything.'

Amber angled away from the door as Doris escorted both officers down the hallway to sign them out. She stood with her arms folded into herself, her expression transfixed, with the ends of her fingers resting on her mouth, her eyes glazed over, and remained that way until Doris returned a few minutes later.

Doris sidled up to her and reached up to place a hand on her shoulder. Amber didn't flinch, and, before Doris could offer any words of comfort, Claire came rushing into the staffroom.

'Amber! Doris just told me what's happened. I'm so sorry! That's such awful news!'

'Are you alright?' Doris asked. 'Do you want to sit down? I can fetch you a cup of tea if you would like—'

'No. No,' Amber rushed. The last thing she needed was people fussing over her, giving her attention that she neither deserved nor craved. 'I'm fine.'

'Are you sure? Because I could—'

'Honestly. At the end of the day, it was just a building, wasn't it? I've not lost my life.' Then, closing her eyes, she wished away the tears, and whispered, more for her own benefit than theirs, 'Just a building.'

Chapter Thirty-Two

Nothing ever seemed to change inside Jo's office. No fresh flowers. No new scatter cushions. No suggestion that any of the books on her shelves had been read or that her desk had rotated any of its clutter. It seemed to be frozen in time, each visit exactly the same as the last, never going anywhere, never moving forward.

Now though, for the first time since she'd dragged herself along to the therapy clinic all those months ago, Amber actually felt like things were starting to change, at least inside of her body and in her mind, if not in her immediate surroundings. She may even have been willing to say that she was finally allowing a little happiness into her life.

Jo poured out two glasses of water from a jug, handed one to her patient on the sofa, then carried her own back behind her desk.

'Honestly, I didn't know what to think when I read

about it in the newspaper,' Jo said once she had made herself comfortable. She wore a genuine expression of sympathy – or was it disappointment? – as she mourned the loss of all that money Amber could have made from the sale of the house.

Amber shrugged. 'It never really felt like mine to lose. I'm just surprised they bothered to report it at all.'

She wasn't lying either. Fires happened every day, didn't they? And once she'd managed to calm herself down that evening after she'd been visited by the two polices officers, she'd been able to count her blessings, just as she had done every night that week. The police knew nothing about how the fire had started. They had no leads, no clues. Not even any real suspicion. For now at least, since they were unable to enter the building, what with its soft and caving floors and unstable ceilings, she had got away with it. She was safe.

'By the looks of things, it was quite a blaze! And they really don't know what caused it?'

'Not a clue.' She had to force herself to hide the relief that tickled at the sides of her lips.

'Well, never mind. If it *is* foul play, I'm sure they'll be caught. As my mother always used to say, evil will always be punished.'

Amber sipped from her glass, concealing her mouth as she turned her eyes away from her therapist.

'I really am happy for you and your baby though. Truly,

that's wonderful news, Amber. But I do hope you're taking it easy. One step at a time and all that. Your emotions are already all over the place. You've had a very fragile year; it's nothing to be ashamed of.'

Who said anything about being ashamed?

'Have you told anybody yet? Besides your new man?'

Amber sniffed. 'No, I haven't told anybody. I don't want to jinx it.'

'I understand. But you might benefit from some moral support outside of whatever relationship you have with this Greig.'

'I've got you,' Amber responded with a smile.

Jo's own upper lip curled. There was nothing that filled her with less delight than the idea of having to listen to the woes of parents.

'I mean a friend,' she explained. Somebody you can go to for a general conversation. A lot of my patients rave about the values of close friendships.' Then, muttering to herself as she shuffled some paperwork, 'Personally I can't see the point in it, but…'

Jo lifted her head back up so that she was looking directly at Amber. 'Anyway, it says here in the medical note that you're still on the same medication. Have you considered requesting an increase in the dosage?'

'What for?'

Learning forward, Jo perched her glasses on the edge of her nose so that she could observe Amber with beady eyes from over the rim.

'To help you feel more like yourself.'

'I feel fine. I doubt it would make a difference anyway.'

'Well, I can't tell you what to do, I suppose.' As much as she'd like to. 'As long as you're feeling happier – and I mean truly happier within yourself – then I suppose it's not too much of an issue if you stay on the same dosage for now.'

Amber just shrugged again, so Jo pressed her:

'Tell me honestly then, Amber. Are you sure you feel more like your old self? You're not just saying that to make me happy?'

Amber couldn't steady her grin. As if she would do anything just to please Jo.

'You know what? I actually think I do. It's just like you're forever telling me: everything always works out alright in the end, even if the road to happiness isn't what we expect it to be'

'I said that? Doesn't sound like me. Well, that's good.' Did Jo look disappointed as she leaned back in her chair? There was no pleasing some people. 'It'll definitely help you enjoy your pregnancy more. I'm sure you've got a lot to look forward to.'

A hand fluttered towards Amber's stomach as Jo's hint

of sarcasm washed over her. 'Yes, I really do, don't I?'

'Of course, you're going to need all the support you can get. Don't worry, we can have as many sessions together as you need – that's both between now and when the baby's born, and afterwards too. I see a lot of new mothers, and they really find my services to be of great help to them'

Jo reached for her appointment book, barely attempting to mask her elated smile. It was impossible to tell which of them was more moved by the pregnancy: Amber, for finally conceiving her child after suffering from so much heartache, or Jo, whose head was filled with sweet thoughts of booking in Amber for another slot of overpriced therapy sessions to help her cope with the new surge of emotions that would soon be coming her way.

She scribbled down some notes for the following week, then looked up from the book to address her patient. 'You're going to be a great mother, Amber.'

Without missing a beat, and with a hand placed across her stomach, Amber replied, 'Oh, don't worry. I know.'

Chapter Thirty-Three

Amber rushed into the living room, sweeping toys off the floor and cramming the odd thing into her handbag as she grabbed it from the back of the sofa where she'd hastily discarded it earlier.

She paused to wipe at her brow, the sticky heat of the early summer prickling against her skin. The room was bright and refreshing with the gentle breeze drifting in through the open window, but she had hardly stopped to sit down all morning, and could have done with a break.

However, there was something she had to do first before she could relax for the rest of the day – or at least for as long as she could steal away during nap time. If the previous afternoon was anything to go by, she didn't count on that being very long at all.

She grabbed her keys from the coffee table, crammed them into the pocket at the front of her jeans, then called up the stairs. 'Greig, where did you put the car seat?'

'It's in the porch,' came the reply. 'Why? Are you going out?'

The sound of heavy feet running down the stairs ceased as Greig entered the living room.

'I just thought I'd go for a drive. It might help him get off to sleep.'

Greig wrapped his arms around Amber's waist, and pulled her close. 'Good idea! And perhaps when you're back we can have some grown-up time?' He spoke with a slightly sultry tone as he swayed her from side to side. He kissed her on the forehead before she pulled away to head to the porch to grab her shoes.

'We'll see,' she replied with a forced smile. It was far too hot and she was far too tired to think about anything remotely physical at the moment. Still, anything to keep him sweet.

'I won't shouldn't be too long,' she added for his benefit as she glanced up from tying her laces. It was true enough; she didn't plan on spending too long outside. Still, she could worry about tending to Greig's desires later. Right now she had something more important with which to concern herself.

By the time Amber drove from the south of London up to

Hampstead, the early afternoon air had cooled. The sky was silent and overcast as she pulled up in front of the remains of her grandfather's house.

She had driven past the house shortly after the fire, only so that she could see just how much damage had been done. It had been worse than she had imagined, having burnt almost into nonexistence, a broken shell of cindered history.

The police officers had been right too: it would have been far too dangerous for the fire fighters to enter the building for any length of time, what with the walls crisp and crumbling, the floors and ceilings turned to mush. She hadn't been near the building since that week though, and by the looks of things now, apart from the odd bit of spray-painted graffiti on the walls and the remnants of police cordoning tape that had been left behind after they'd removed the majority of it at the end of their worthless investigation, there was nothing to suggest that anybody had been back since.

Bracing herself with a deep breath, Amber climbed out of the car, walked around to the side door, and unfastened her gurgling son from his car seat. She held him close to her chest, his cardigan soft against her arms as she hugged onto him, and hooked a carrier bag over her wrist.

She crept her way over to the rubble that lay at the entrance to the house.

'This used to be your great-grandfather's house, you

know?' she said to the child as she tried to keep her balance on the debris.

Her eyes swam over the building, taking in every inch of blackened wood and shattered window. This was not the home her grandfather had left behind, but it was the way she would always think of it now, no matter how hard she tried to fight it.

Clutching her son tightly, she took a few more steps towards the remains of the front door. Somebody had marked it with their initials just above the letter box; no doubt if the house had been in a busier area nearer the centre of a town, it would have succumbed to a lot more interference.

The door had been shut over, but the wood around the frame and beneath it had buckled away from it. As Amber crouched down, balancing the child on her hip, she peered down beneath the narrow gap. It was dark, but in the pale daylight she could just about make out where the old floorboards had given way and fallen into the basement below. If she'd had a torch with her, she would have undoubtedly been able to see straight down into the basement itself.

With one free hand as she balanced the child's head against the inside of her arm, she prised open the carrier bag, and pulled out the teddy bear from inside of it. She placed it in front of the door so that it appeared to be looking down through the hole, the stitching on its paw pressed up against the twisted ledge.

Amber repositioned her son, then scooped up a small handful of the dusty earth from beside the teddy bear. She stood, her fist clenched.

As she stared over the top of the bear's head, her eyes followed his own as they both gazed down towards the basement. Then, in a muttered monotone, she said: 'Ashes to ashes, dust to dust.'

The earth sprinkled down towards the ground, some of it coating the bear's soft fur as the larger, heavier pieces of rock and stone tumbled straight down towards the basement.

She dusted her hand against her thigh. The wind whipped around her as she drew her son closer to her own body. For another minute, completely alone in their surroundings, she stood facing the house, her eyes locked in the direction of the basement. At once she thought of nothing at all and yet also everything at once as she succumbed in an instant to the memories of the events that had happened over the last two years. This was not the life she had expected to be living. The man she had once loved was now dead. She had lost two babies. There was so much sorrow in her life, but she knew, could never deny, that, although this hadn't been her plan, she had so much to be

357

thankful for.

And she did, each and every night and day, make sure that she counted her blessings. After all, she was alive and free.

Something in the distance akin to the snapping of a twig dragged her thoughts back to her surroundings. She turned towards her son, as if suddenly remembering that he was beside her, protected in her arms. She kissed him softly on the forehead, glanced back at the house, and then turned her back.

As she sauntered back to the car, she smiled at the infant. 'Well, Jasey, I guess it really is true what they say. Everything always works out for the best in the end.'

Without once turning back to face the house, she bundled her son into the car, secured herself behind the wheel, and pulled away without further thought. There was no need for Amber to return again. Whatever paperwork remained could be handled remotely. She would not need to sully her mind with guilt after it had been cleansed with her chance at a fresh start in life. For Amber at least, her existence could be enjoyed freely once more; the nightmare was over.

The sound of the engine grew fainter as she drove off, until only silence surrounded what remained of the house. Until further notice, it would stay largely undisturbed, a dirty and damaged former family home, wherein lay alone and forgotten the cremated remains of Jason and Victoria and the foetus that would remain ever loved but forever without a name.

About the Author

To echo the words of Romantic poet Lord Byron, 'If I don't write to empty my mind, I go mad.'

This is the quote by which Amy McLean abides. Although she spent her childhood scribbling out short stories, it wasn't until she began studying English Literature at the University of Sunderland that she realised her dependence on writing. In 2014 she graduated with a first-class degree and a published dissertation about Lord Byron.

Death and mental health are common themes in Amy's writing, both of which she loves to explore in many different approaches. Over the years, her work has frequently called upon parallel timelines between past and present, heaven and earth.

Spending her childhood between her Aberdeen birth town and the North East of England, Amy developed a taste for travel at a young age. She now lives with Medora the cat in Hampstead, London, where she watches too many Tim Burton films, reads too many crime novels, and spends too much time on YouTube.

www.ingramcontent.com/pod-product-compliance
Lightning Source LLC
Chambersburg PA
CBHW051324250626
47155CB00007B/2436